THE BASTARD'S WEAPON

THE BASTARD'S WEAPON

JOSEPH M. ORLANDO

To order additional copies of this book, contact:
Xlibris Corporation
1-888-795-4274
www.Xlibris.com
Orders@Xlibris.com
32431

The Bastard's Weapon, powerful sequel to *The Fisherman's Son*, and the second novel in the Gloucester Trilogy.

Written by Joseph M. Orlando, who has been hailed by the New York Times as "Attorney for the Injured."

Praise for *The Fisherman's Son*:

"Joe Orlando has taken his triplet loves of law, family, and Gloucester and stitched them into a novel, *The Fisherman's Son* . . . Orlando has written about fishing, romance, violence, and devious twists and turns in and outside the courtroom."
—Alan Lupo, *The Boston Globe*

"*The Fisherman's Son*, by Joseph Orlando, is a 'gem.'"
—James Abraham, *The Charlotte Sun*

"Orlando possesses an incredible ability to define and flesh out characters-male and female, rich and poor, good and evil . . . With a plethora of interesting characters, a touch of suspense, a believable love triangle and an inspiring courtroom battle, *The Fisherman's Son* will not allow your attention to wander. Pardon the pun, but I was hooked early on and literally never put the book down, reading it in one sitting late into the night."
—Scott Katz, *Massachusetts Lawyers Weekly*

"Joe Orlando has written a great legal thriller, . . . I can't recommend this book highly enough."
—Kendall Buhl, North Shore 104.9 FM

"*The Fisherman's Son* is as gripping an inside novel as I've encountered in years. Hooked from the start, I couldn't put this cliffhanger down."
—Joseph E. Garland, Author/Historian

"Joe Orlando wrote the book of the fishing people. I was spellbound."
—Vincent Ferrini, Poet/Author

DEDICATION

For my parents, Phyllis and Mike Orlando.
My Dad, who believed in my potential.
My Mom, whose positive outlook helped me to believe in myself.

ACKNOWLEDGMENTS

The writing of my first novel, *The Fisherman's Son*, was an eye-opening experience.

A glance at Amazon.com and BarnesandNoble.com shows the wonderful reception of readers across this great country. While positive reviews in newspapers, magazines, radio and television are critical to commercial success, readers who invest their money and take the time to read my novel and post their impressions offer a great compliment. That there are twenty-one reviews posted and all have rated *The Fisherman's Son* as five stars, is gratifying. Thank you.

A special thanks to Bonnie Waldron, Barbara Morrissey, Edith and Ed Nelson and Elayne Alanis who dedicated time and energy to promote my novel.

Thanks to Professor Donna Marie Pignone, who has honored me by designating *The Fisherman's Son* as required reading in her History Course, "The Many Manifestations of Italian Culture," at Montclair State University. To be on a reading list with "The Odyssey" by Homer and "Twilight in Italy and other Essays" by D.H. Lawrence is thrilling and humbling.

Thanks to my friend and secretary, Ruth Katsikas, for typing every word and not complaining (much) at the countless changes.

Thanks to Jim Perry, Linda Quince, and Sue Morrison, dear friends who read this novel and offered helpful suggestions. Sue, we'll find a project to collaborate on.

Thanks to Ellen and Joe Morrissey, who once again provided insight.

Thanks to the thousands of readers of *The Fisherman's Son*, please keep the e-mails coming.

Thanks to the people of Gloucester, my friends and my clients. It has been an honor to be your advocate.

A special thanks to my children, Amanda, Lisa and Joe. You are everything to me.

Thanks to my sons-in-law, Kevin Kesterson and Wesley Fornero. Wes, a gifted photographer, created the cover of both this novel and that of *The Fisherman's Son*.

You can view and purchase Wes' photographs at *www.Fornero photography.com*.

A special acknowledgment to my grandson, Alexander William Kesterson, born quite fittingly on Thanksgiving day. Papa loves you, Alex.

Above all, thanks to Connie, my wife and my love, it's been a great ride.

AUTHOR'S FOREWORD

The Bastard's Weapon is a novel. The characters are fictional. Any resemblance to actual persons is unintentional.

This novel, the second in the Gloucester Trilogy, is a story of Gloucester, her fishing fleet and the people who inhabit this most beautiful Cape.

The author was born and raised in Gloucester. My father, uncles and grandfathers were fishermen and I am a maritime lawyer, who for twenty-six years have battled powerful, deep pocketed insurance companies on behalf of fishermen and their families. It is not a fair fight. Insurance companies have lobbyists with access to the most powerful people in Washington, and vast advertising budgets to sway the public (future jurors) to their views. In contrast, fishermen have no lobbyist and no advertising budget. They risk their health and their lives daily as they brave the sea to support their families and supply fish markets and restaurants with their tasty and healthy catch. Still, like my clients, I battle on. It has been an honor and a privilege to be their advocate.

I hope you enjoy *The Bastard's Weapon*, second novel in the Gloucester Trilogy.

For more information on the author and his writing please visit his website at *www.JosephmOrlando.com*.

PROLOGUE

In a shrill and terrified voice, the Mayday call went out.

"Help us, please," the panicked voice pleaded, "help us!"

By the time the Coast Guard helicopter arrived at the longitude and latitude bearings given by the vessel's captain, they found a life raft rolling on six foot seas with Captain Joe Amalfi alone, waving his arms.

The fishing vessel *Mio Mondo* was gone. It sank with all hands, save a thoroughly soaked, bloodied, terrified and rapidly aging Captain.

As the basket, which had been lowered from the helicopter, lifted Joe Amalfi to safety from the choppy seas, he stared, ashen faced, at the point where the *Mio Mondo* had disappeared below the waves to its final resting place on the ocean floor. 'It swallowed up my boat,' he thought. The boat which was the eternal tomb of the three man crew.

It was approaching midnight when an exhausted and thoroughly wretched Joe Amalfi left the Coast Guard station, Gloucester, clutching a blanket over sodden clothes to take the passenger seat in the car driven by his wife, Rosalie.

It had been a very long time since anything remotely resembling passion, love or caring had been the basis of their marriage. For Rosalie Amalfi it was duty. Deep down, beneath the layers of hurt, neglect and indifference she still hoped, but it was duty that had her searching his face. She saw the bandage on the side of his head and face, the shadow of terror in his eyes, something she had never seen before. "Are you okay?" she asked.

"Take me home," he demanded, "just take me home." He didn't even look her way.

She hated to admit that his indifference hurt and hurt deeply. But it still did. Yet, this was different. Behind his eyes there was horror. 'What happened out there?' she thought.

She studied him a moment longer, assessing. "I'm sorry about the men."

He turned on her. There was a crazed look, a mask of torment. "Take me home," he demanded, and buried his face in his hands and wept.

Rosalie Amalfi kept concerned eyes on her husband. Then, inexplicably she felt a shiver down her spine. Realizing that she would learn nothing further, they drove home in silence.

CHAPTER ONE

John Palermo stood tall, six foot two inches and ramrod straight, at the window which overlooked Harbour Cove and Gloucester's fishing fleet. His classic good looks, short black hair framing chiseled features on an angular face and cobalt blue eyes clouded with grief as he watched the sunset over the harbor and the boats at dock. He sipped at the amber colored liquor in the cut crystal glass. Somehow, the bourbon seemed to ease the sharp edges of pain.

Sunset was always the most difficult time for John. It meant the distraction that work provided was over for another day and he would have to return home. Home to the children he dearly loved. But home to yet another lonely night without her.

"You okay, John?" The voice came from behind him and he knew it was Phil. Phil grimaced as his eyes lit onto the glass. He worried about John's drinking which had become a regular feature of his day. He suspected that when alone at night, after tucking in Franco and Anna, John drank to allow sleep.

"She loved the sunset." John said softly.

Phil didn't know what to say. What does one say to a young man of thirty-three who has lost his wife? What do you say to your best friend, whose heart was broken and who now faced life alone and the challenge of two young children? So, he didn't say anything, he just walked over to stand beside his law partner, placing a hand on his shoulder.

"We'd sit. She'd lay her head on my shoulder," he choked. "Sometimes I can still feel her, smell her." There was a long pause as the bright orange ball, ever so slowly, but certainly, settled into the purple sea. "We watched the sunset and then made love."

Phil saw John close his eyes, live the scene and with it feel a new stab of pain. With a trembling hand, John raised the glass to drink.

"I didn't think anything could feel worse than that day on the ship in Sicily," John said. "I stood there. My head just cleared the ship's rail. My Papa stood on the dock waving goodbye." John winced in memory. "He just waved and cried and there I was on the ship, leaving him, heading for America."

"You were only ten years old and he was dying. He put you on the ship to give you a chance." Phil paused. "He loved you, John."

John went on, oblivious to Phil's words.

"Phil, I stood at the rail and watched him through a veil of tears. I was terrified and it hurt so bad."

Nodding his head, Phil said, "I know."

A small smile played at John's lips, challenging the tears that ran down his cheeks. "I swore that I would never love again. But Connie changed all that."

Phil nodded. Darkness was settling over the docks in long shadows making shapes unrecognizable. The moon and stars still weren't out. Phil would listen because John needed to pour it out.

"I was ten, almost eleven, and she was seven. Even then she knew how to reach me, to touch me." He paused. "She brought me into the family. Nobody had a better sister."

Phil knew the story. John's mother had died during childbirth, leaving John's father, Franco, to take care of his infant son. With the help of the women in the Sicilian village of Sciacca, Franco raised his son, taught him to fish and how to feel good inside, where it counted. When John was ten his Papa became sick. Seeing no other option, he appealed to his lifelong friend Benny Amico to take John as his son.

Connie fell in love with John very early, always holding that fact inside, close to her core. She grew into a beautiful and graceful young woman, with numerous opportunities. She dated, but never gave her heart. In a strange sort of way, it was Phil entering John's life that made all the difference.

Having completed his second year of law school, after a four year hitch in the Marines, Phil took a summer internship with the then struggling twenty-seven year old lawyer. John was embroiled in the case that would make his reputation and his fortune, while breaking the back of a longstanding insurance scheme to control the New England Fisheries through threats and intimidation. Phil's legal work on the myriad of motions, pleadings and discovery, which were thrown at John by the high powered, high priced, team of Insurance Company lawyers, helped turn the tide.

Phil had proven himself to John. The insurance company had used its vast financial resources as well as lawyers, adjusters, investigators, a team of highly paid expert witnesses and even thugs to beat and disable John's key witness. John had little money to retain expert witnesses. His team had been Phil Harmon and Connie Amico, his secretary and confidante.

John's client, Busty Barna, his wife Carla and their children faced foreclosure and financial ruin. Busty Barna, physically disabled and spiritually broken, needed a warrior. Busty found him in John. John's passion, charisma and integrity won unlikely allies. His determination and courage to risk all for his client and his people proved to be the difference. With Phil at his side and Connie in support, John won for his client and smashed the blacklist.

Phil Harmon did much more than help John win a trial and liberate a community. He fell in love with Connie. And Connie had responded. It was her response which brought John face to face with his fears. Having lost his mother and father by age eleven, he was possessed by a gripping fear. Deep in his gut he believed that to love was to hurt and to lose. Yet each of Phil's advances brought the reality of losing Connie closer. Faced with a choice between his fears and his dreams, John, hesitantly and trepidatiously, but with heartfelt conviction, made his feelings known. And they were one.

Their marriage was four years of bliss followed by twelve months of hell. They were blessed with two children, Franco and Anna. Together, they designed and built a lovely home on the Magnolia shore, while John continued to grow his thriving practice. Then one pretty spring day while the happy couple laid in the comforting afterglow of love, Connie felt a lump on her chest. Two weeks of outwardly declared optimism, and inner dread, found John and Connie sitting, holding hands, at the Dana Farber Cancer Institute in Boston.

The diagnosis was lymphoma, cancer of the lymph nodes. The doctor assured them that the prognosis was good. When a disease has a 70% cure rate, there is reason for hope, but that 30% lurked and hung over them like Democle's sword.

Connie wanted to live. With a quiet dignity she allowed the doctors to poke and prod. Three rounds of chemotherapy, with the resultant weakness, sickness and the indignity of the loss of her beautiful auburn hair.

Temporary victories, prayers answered, as tumors shrank under a barrage of radiation and chemo. Mocking them, it always came back, determined to destroy itself and the body that housed it. On a bitter cold January day, a physically exhausted Connie Palermo, with John at her side, was told that nothing more could be done, the cancer had won.

Maybe they should have seen it coming, but they refused to believe it could happen. Now, with stunning rapidity death came to claim Connie, almost a year to the day of learning of her condition. It was a soft spring day when John buried his wife and again knew that giving his heart lead to loss and pain. Yet, even with the depth of grief he felt, he knew that the time he had with Connie was worth the worst of it.

"Let's go home John," Phil urged. "Mary Kaye has the kids. Will you have dinner with us?"

John nodded as night fell. He took another pull on the bourbon as he watched a fishing dragger move across the ink black harbor to dock, its running lights playing on the rippled sea. "I guess I know how my father felt when he lost my mother and had to raise me alone."

Phil read the pain in John's eyes. Softly he said, "You're not alone John. We'll be here for you."

John forced a smile that didn't reach his eyes. "Thanks, let's not keep Mary Kaye waiting."

"Okay," Phil said. "I have to shoot by to see my parents. I'll be home in about an hour." He paused. "Are you okay to drive?"

John glanced at the glass and then at Phil. "I'm okay," he assured.

"Good," Phil smiled. "I'll see you soon."

CHAPTER TWO

John walked into the Harmon home and was instantly enveloped in the sights, sounds and smells so familiar to family. The peal of laughter, as four-year-olds, Phil Harmon V and Franco Palermo vied for a bouncing ball. The aroma of tomato sauce cooking and the joy of a beaming Mary Kaye Harmon, eight months pregnant and carrying two-year-old Anna Palermo in her arms.

"Nobody heard my knock," John explained, "so, I let myself in."

Mary Kaye just shrugged as she offered a happy grin. "Who could hear anything in this noise factory?" She asked.

John relieved Mary Kaye of her burden and was rewarded with a tight hug and a wet kiss from his baby girl. The joy of the boys at play and little Anna's affection brought a real smile to John's lips. The kind of smile that lightens the load and helps the eyes to dance. Anna laughed uproariously when John nuzzled her neck.

"Who loves daddy the most?" He asked over the laughter.

"Me, me, me, me," came the response, with a giggle.

John held her close. "And, Daddy loves you."

"Will you stay for dinner?" Mary Kaye asked, hopefully. "I made enough lasagna for everyone."

John smiled at the petite brown-haired beauty with the slightly freckled face, luminous green eyes and large belly. "How are you feeling, Mary Kaye?"

She glanced down with an impish grin that made her look sixteen rather than her actual age of thirty-one, patted her belly and said, "Not bad for an old pregnant lady."

"In that case we'd love to stay. And thanks."

John read the concern in Mary Kaye's eyes. He hated the pity. The 'poor John' expression. His attention was diverted as Anna squirmed in his arms to be put down so she could chase after the boys. He smiled as she set off, a bit shakily, but with a big grin.

"Sit down, John. Let me get you a glass of wine." She waved him to the couch. "Loosen your tie, get comfortable. I'll check on the kiddies."

Mary Kaye waddled more than walked to check the children. Seeing they were okay, she moved to the kitchen, stirred the sauce, checked the lasagna and pulled a bottle of wine off of the wine rack. Pouring herself a glass of apple juice, she brought her drink with wine, glass, and corkscrew into the den, placing the tray on the coffee table before John.

As John worked the corkscrew, Mary Kaye telephoned Phil, to let him know when dinner would be served. Hearing Phil's voice brought the kind of pleasure to Mary Kaye that only can be understood by those deeply in love. John saw her eyes light up, and it brought a smile to his lips and a stab of longing to his heart.

With smile fixed, Mary Kaye plopped down opposite John, then realized her apple juice was still on the tray. John saw the chagrin as her eyes passed over the glass. He quickly rose to hand the glass to a grateful Mary Kaye.

"I used to move as quick as that," she said with amusement. "Now rising is an accomplishment."

"Before you know it, you'll be as slim and graceful as ever. You'll see," he said encouragingly. "Besides, you're still as pretty as you were sitting in the gallery at the Barna trial."

Mary Kaye laughed. As a novice lawyer she had been prevailed upon by her father, Chief Administrative Judge James Waldron, to monitor a trial before the aging and infamous Judge Arnold Bailey and to report to him each day with her notes and observations. During the two week trial she dressed casually, posing as a law student observing a federal court trial. It was during the trial that she met Phil. Their first date had been attending the victory party at the Point Restaurant and Inn. The trial victory was aided by Mary Kaye's reports which exposed Judge Bailey's bias and the corrupt practice of the insurance company to Judge Waldron.

"I don't know about pretty." She laughed. "I do know I'm much larger." She paused, "and I am much happier."

John sipped his wine thoughtfully. "Are you? Don't you miss practicing law?"

She shrugged. "You know, John, I wrestled with that. Phil wasn't buying into the idea of strangers raising our children." With a sly smile, she added, "you know I had that two-seater Mazda Miata."

John nodded.

"I was so protective of that car. When we discussed children, Phil asked me how I would refuse to let others drive my car, but I'd be willing to give our children to strangers." Mary Kaye paused as she listened for the children. Returning her attention to John, a fond smile settled on her lips. "He told me that we didn't need the money I would earn. That we were fortunate, we could afford to give our children the gift of their mother."

"What did you say?"

The smile stayed in place as if she was recalling a happy memory. "I asked him why should I be the one to give up my career? Why not him?" She shook her head and smiled. "It was a hot issue."

John scanned the immaculate house, enjoyed the aroma of the lasagna, listened to the joyous sound of the children at play. "I see you resolved it."

Softly massaging her belly, she laughed. "I guess you're right, But it was close. Phil had no intention of marrying me until we came to agreement. Phil was really old world," she laughed, "or at least I thought so. Still, I wasn't about to turn in my N.O.W. card," she paused, studied John and then said softly, "until Connie stepped in."

John's surprised expression gave away his shock. "Connie?"

With a soft smile, she nodded. "In frustration, Phil had opened up to her." She sat back and smiled in happy memory. "He just didn't understand how a job, any job, could be more important than our children." She eyed John. "He knew it wasn't going to work. No way was he going to leave our children to some daycare center or to a Nanny to whom our children would be nothing more than a job."

"What did Connie do?" he said, softly, reverently.

· "Connie invited me to lunch. As soon as we were seated she asked me if I was in love with Phil? Just like that, bang. Boy, she caught me by surprise."

John grinned. "What did you say?"

"I wound up quickly and told her, Phil was a sexist. A man completely out of step with the times." Mary Kaye shook her head and laughed. "I was all righteous indignation and feminist dogma."

John saw the amusement in her eyes, sat back and listened.

"Connie wasn't buying," Mary Kaye continued. "'Are you in love with him,?' Connie repeated, patiently."

Mary Kaye shook her head. "That infuriated me. 'So what if I am?' I shot back. Connie sighed and shook her head. 'So tell me,' Connie asked, 'would you prefer Phil not to care about what's best for your children?'"

· John laughed, "Good question."

"My anger was melting away like an ice candle. You know sometimes logic stinks!" She laughed.

"'Of course not.' I said. Connie fixed on me with such a kind look. 'You know he's right. Children do much better with their mother than with strangers.' I just nodded."

"'So why are you fighting him?' Connie asked me."

Mary Kaye laughed, recalling a moment when she was pulled back from the brink. The laughter lit her face. "It all made so much sense, but I wasn't about to surrender so easily. Not me. I looked back at Connie and demanded, 'What right does Phil have to ask me to give up my career?' Connie sat back patiently. 'If he's to be your husband and you two are going to build a life together, why shouldn't he ask that or anything else? It's a marriage! You two will be a team. There's nothing he or you shouldn't ask.'"

"I remember looking at her in amazement. You know John, I bought into the Feminist agenda with a vengeance." She shook her head. "Money is everything for them. A woman must have a career. The message, sometimes subtle, more often not, is that men are our enemy, children shackles on our independence." Mary Kaye shook her head and sighed. "They never bothered to tell us that a good job never loves you back."

John poured himself a refill on the wine, his eyes on Mary Kaye.

Her eyes misted. In a soft voice, she continued. "Connie reached across the table and took my hands. She told me that the road to happiness for a woman is different than for a man. It passes through home and family. Too many people have forgotten that and look at the results." She raised her eyes to meet John's. He saw they were heavy with tears and clouded with pain. "I was about to throw all this away. Thank God for Connie. She was so special." Now they were both in tears.

"Yes," he gulped, "she was."

Phil came in on the scene. His gaze moved from John to Mary Kaye. He heard the rattle of the children at play, smelled the tomato sauce and caught Mary Kaye's eye. "John," he said tentatively, "please don't cry." He paused for effect.

John glanced his way, flushed with embarrassment.

Mary Kaye shook her head in dismay. 'Why should he be embarrassed to cry? When he has every reason,' she thought, 'Men!'

Before John could speak Phil added, "I know she cooks like a lawyer, but don't cry." He gave his best loving smile to his wife who joined the men in spontaneous laughter.

"How was I to know that torts were some dry legal stuff and not a course in pastry?" She stated in mock indignation.

Phil moved across, pulled Mary Kaye out of her seat and placed a warm, wet kiss on her mouth. "Hi."

Mary Kaye flashed Phil a warm and appreciative smile. With a twinkle in her eye, she said, "Slow down, we have guests. And it's time for dinner."

"Okay, let's do it," Phil said. "I'll grab the kids."

"I'm with you, partner," John said as they headed to the playroom.

Mary Kaye watched them go, with a sadness in her eyes.

* * *

"This is great!" John exclaimed. "Mary Kaye, are you sure you're not Italian?"

"You like it, huh? Actually, you should. It's Ma Amico's recipe. Connie gave it to me." She smiled, "You don't need to be Italian to cook like one."

"Without doubt." He turned to Phil, "you're lucky to have this girl." John winked at Mary Kaye.

"So what's happening at the office?" she asked.

While Mary Kaye loved being home with little Phil, she did miss the pace of handling litigation cases. Knowing this, Phil sought her thoughts on many cases and situations. And, she had been a real help to him in considering various angles. Most recently, he, for the first time, tried a case against a female attorney.

A trial places two combatants in a ring. In the case of trial lawyers, the ropes are the highly polished maple bars enclosing the lawyers area or pit, as John called it. It wasn't always pretty, sometimes it became downright nasty. But could he mix it up with a woman? He worried. Would a jury be put off by his lack of courtesy? Ungentlemanly conduct?

First, Mary Kaye smiled. Then, putting reality before idealism, helped Phil direct the trial as every bit the advocate he was, while exuding a charm that seemed out of character for the setting, at least outside of the south. On the very first day of trial, Phil, preferring to have nothing between him and the jury, had put aside the heavy wood podium and stood before the jury outlining his case. Handsome, five foot ten inches with a gymnast's body, his green eyes sparkled as he began to connect with the jury. Satisfied, he sat at plaintiff's counsel table before realizing he had neglected to place the podium back before the jury box. Moving quickly, he rose and beat the power suited, slightly overweight defense attorney to the podium. "I'll do it," he said gallantly.

His opponent openly bristled, her eyes spat contempt. "I don't need your help," she snapped; the tone curt, her expression nasty.

Chastised, Phil shrugged and, glancing at the jury, mumbled an apology. He saw it, she had lost the jury before she spoke the first word of her Opening Statement. Their eyes read 'bitch.'

"John had an interesting visitor today," Phil said with a grin.

"Really?" Mary Kaye glanced to John. "Do tell me."

John sipped the Chianti, a perfect complement to the lasagna, sat back expressionless, his eyes moving from the seascape by Fitz Hugh Lane to the photograph by Wesley Fornero.

"That's a wonderful photo," John commented. "The way he captured the light," he paused, "truly captivating."

Mary Kaye beamed. "That's his 'Summer's Day Sunset.'"

Appraising the photograph, John nodded, "it reminds me of a Monet landscape."

Phil nodded. "It does," he agreed. "I think it's the way the light plays on the lapping waves. He's a real talent."

"He's local?" John inquired.

Phil half smiled, half smirked. "He's a Mary Kaye discovery." He shook his head, amused. "She even helped him with his brochures. We have five or six other works by him." Phil sipped the Chianti. "He married a Gloucester girl and settled here."

"I'd like to meet him." John stated, eyes still on the photograph. "I'd love to see more of his work."

"Okay," Mary Kaye agreed. "I'll introduce you, but tell me who was this interesting visitor?"

"Deal," John nodded, a sour look settling on his face.

"An old friend," he replied with a touch of sarcasm. "A real blast from the past."

Mary Kaye's interest was spiked. Her eyes moved from John to the grinning Phil, then back to a dour John. "Well?" She said impatiently.

Phil grinned, "Okay, Honey," he teased, then offered. "Captain Joe Amalfi has deigned to retain our services to collect on his hull policy. Seems his buddies at the insurance company question the sinking of his boat."

Mary Kaye remembered back. "That was a few months ago; September wasn't it?" The incident and all the related news stories flooded back. "Didn't three men die?"

John nodded. "Three good men."

"Yes, I remember. He was on a liferaft, alone," she paused. "No sign of the other men."

"That's right," John nodded.

She shivered at the thought. "Did you send that slimeball packing?" Mary Kaye remembered well sitting in that courtroom, a silent observer as the diminutive captain verbally abused and threatened his crew into lying on the stand. Now he had the gall to come to John for help. She seethed in memory of the beating administered to Peter Novello, at the direction of the insurance company, to prevent his testimony.

Phil saw that Mary Kaye was tense. Placing a hand on her arm, he said, "I'm afraid it's not that easy."

Mary Kaye kept interested eyes on Phil.

"See Honey," Phil continued, "we represent the three widows and the estates of the men."

Mary Kaye nodded.

"So," Phil frowned. "The insurance company will essentially be challenging Amalfi on contract grounds."

John sipped his wine and shook his head. A look of distaste on his face. "See, Mary Kaye," he picked up the thread of Phil's explanation. "The insurance company will challenge Amalfi's claim on the basis of contract covenants." He shrugged. "The maritime insurance policy requires the vessel owner to covenant that he will keep the vessel seaworthy. If the vessel sails, leaves the dock, in an unseaworthy condition, and the insurance company is able to convince a judge of that fact, the contract is void."

"A judge?" Mary Kaye queried. "Why not a jury?"

John laughed. His eyes lit and Mary Kaye recalled the John that laughed so easily and so often.

"It's the Maritime law." John explained. "Unlike most civil cases, under Maritime Common Law there is no right to a trial by jury." He sipped the Chianti. "We have juries in Jones Act cases because the Merchant Marine Act of 1920 provided the right to a jury trial."

Mary Kaye nodded.

Phil leaned forward. "In a case based on Maritime Common Law, such as a claim based on Unseaworthiness or Maintenance and Cure, without a Jones Act Count, there is no right to a jury."

"And, the same is true for a claim based on a Maritime Contract." John added.

"I see." Mary Kaye nodded.

"Back to the main point," Phil stated. "See, Mary Kaye, if we don't represent Amalfi and the corporation, we don't know who Amalfi would hire." He glanced at John. Mary Kaye could see from Phil's expression that this topic had been thoroughly discussed.

"And," John waded in, a look of distaste clouding his face, "if Amalfi loses and the contract is voided, it is voided for the widows and children." He paused and gave a resigned shrug.

Mary Kaye nodded in understanding. "If it takes representing Amalfi to help those families, I guess that leaves you no choice."

John sipped his wine, looking past Mary Kaye through the French doors to the lights playing on Ipswich Bay. "It's never easy," he shrugged, "but whoever said life would be easy?"

CHAPTER THREE

He rubbed his fatigued eyes and took a long pull on his drink. The house was quiet, so very still. His thoughts ran to Connie. He could see her in his mind's eye, the beautiful auburn hair, the soft, smiling brown eyes, the lips curved in invitation. John missed her so much. He took a swallow of bourbon. The bourbon was how he found sleep, how he escaped the pain, the longing was so real and so painful.

He forced himself to sit up and then re-focused on the grainy film that was really a collection of light enhanced grays and shadows. He shook his head in resignation. It was useless. He couldn't focus on the film. In fact, he had been progressively having more and more trouble keeping his mind on work. He emptied his glass, felt the ice cubes cold on his lips and tongue. Hitting the pause button he turned attention away from the set, rose, and peeked in on the children. They slept at peace and in angelic beauty. He leaned against the door jamb as the alcohol numbed his brain and made sleep possible. Even in his drunken state he could see shades of Connie in Anna's peaceful profile. God, how he missed Connie. Exhausted, he wanted to drop into bed, but he needed to view the remainder of the film. And, he thought, that he wasn't drunk enough to face that bed alone. The bed that he had shared with Connie. The bed where he had held her, loved her and where they had planned the future together. He half walked and half stumbled back to his den, plopped into his chair and hit play. The video rolled and he was back on the ocean floor.

The loss of the F/V *Mio Mondo* had prompted a large scale Coast Guard search. Three men gone, with no sign, seemingly trapped inside the vessel. The Captain had explained that he had fallen, after the boat struck something, causing him to strike his head. When he came to, he was on the deck, which was awash with the sea. Recognizing the urgency, he placed the distress call. Still groggy, within moments the boat was gone. After hitting his head he hadn't seen the men. He had managed to climb into the life raft which had self-inflated, as it was designed to, and waited for help.

As a result of the death of three men and prodded by the insurance company, the Coast Guard had used a submersible to locate and film the sunken vessel. Six hours of footage of a boat which set on the ocean

---

bottom, listing hard on its keel in peaceful repose in the utter blackness of the ocean depths. Fitting, John thought, for the three men most likely entombed for posterity within or washed over the side to die alone in the churning sea.

At 2 a.m. he sat, drink in hand, and watched the camera's light play off the rigging, gallows frames, pilot house and fo'c's'le. When the light hit brass, steel or iron there was a dull reflection. When it danced off of the asphalt deck tiles or painted hull and rails the glint was different, more subdued. Finally, it was over and he hit stop on the remote and glanced at the nearly empty bottle of bourbon. John had broken the seal after Franco and Anna had found sleep. Groggy, he rose unsteadily and trudged off to bed. Aware that he would need to review it again, when not so tired, but convinced that he was in for a battle in defeating the insurers' claims. Still, John intended to win that battle and to recover for the widows and orphans of the three brave men. And yes, even for Joe Amalfi.

Sleep found John quickly, but it was troubled. Twice he woke, a thought nagging at him, but hidden somewhere in his subconscious, just beyond reach. Agitated, unable to grab hold of the worry, his mind raced, 'did I forget something the children need?' He even thought that maybe Connie was trying to reach him. A tangle of confused emotion, he dropped back into a fitful sleep.

When he woke, bone weary, it still played at him, but more immediate concerns beckoned. Baths and breakfast for Franco and Anna, before dropping them with their grandmother, Maria Amico.

As always, Maria Amico wrapped her grandchildren in love. Since Connie's death, it had been Maria who had picked up the slack, jumping in to give stability to the children and freedom to allow John to run his practice.

"Hi, Ma," John called as he entered Maria's kitchen.

With shrieks of joy the children ran to their Nonna, exchanging hugs, kisses, and laughter.

"We go to the park today," announced Maria to the delight of Franco and Anna. "Now go see Nonno while I talk to your Daddy."

John watched the children bustle off to the den to see their grandfather.

"Isn't Dad joining us for coffee?" John inquired of the gray-haired, clear-eyed woman who had taken him in as a boy and had been the only mother he had ever known.

"No, John, he'll stay with the bambini so you and I can talk."

"Uh, oh!" John exclaimed. "Am I in trouble?" he teased, bringing a warm smile to Maria's lips.

Maria reached up and placed her hands on John's face. She saw the blood shot eyes and the weariness that played at his handsome face. Her heart went out to John. She knew his pain and she worried that he wouldn't or couldn't control his drinking. Taking a deep breath, she forced a smile. "No, my son, with me, you are never in trouble."

John embraced Maria in an enveloping embrace. "How can I ever thank you?"

Maria pulled back to look up into John's eyes. John saw the love that had been his constant since he had arrived in this home at the age of ten. He also saw the grief of a mother who has lost a child.

"There is no need," Maria said softly. "Taking you was the best thing we ever did." She glanced at the den where Benny sat on the floor with the children. "And, it is I who should thank you for letting me help with the children." She choked. "They are all I have left of my Connie."

In a husky, emotion-filled voice, John told Maria, "I know, Ma. Before Connie died she asked me to bring our children here. She wanted you to raise Franco and Anna."

"And you promised her," Maria stated with a knowing eye.

John nodded. "I did."

Maria offered John an understanding smile. "Please sit down."

Maria moved to the stove and removed a basket of freshly baked Italian rolls, which she placed before John. Then, having poured out coffee for John and herself, she sat opposite him.

Quietly sipping her coffee, she watched John butter a roll and take a healthy bite. "Delicious, as always," he mumbled as he chewed the bread. The coffee was bringing him back from a long night.

She forced a smile into the handsome face, again noting the well groomed wavy black hair and those troubled deep blue eyes. "John, I made Connie some promises, too," she began.

"Really?" John said. "She didn't say anything to me."

Maria read surprise in his face.

"Yes, she made me promise to help you with the children."

"Oh," John nodded. "I see." Hungrily, he polished off the roll and began to lather a second with butter.

"John," she continued, "that promise was easy." She paused and dropped her eyes to her hands. Softly, she went on, "Connie also insisted on another promise."

John looked at his mother, eyes narrowed.

"She told me to give you a message from her." Maria's eyes pooled with tears.

"I don't understand," John stated. "Why didn't she just tell me?"

Maria offered a soft smile. "She told me that you weren't ready to hear her, that you needed time."

"I see," he said as he sat back, eyes on Maria. "Okay, Ma," he felt a surge of nervousness, "what's the message?"

Maria's eyes grew serious. "She told me to wait a year before telling you."

John nodded and swallowed hard, fighting emotion. "Okay, tomorrow will be one year."

Maria choked and covered her face with her hands. Struggling to regain her composure, she wiped her cheeks and blew her nose.

John saw that this task weighed heavy on her heart. "Okay, Ma, why don't you tell me," John urged in a soft voice.

Maria took a deep breath. "Connie said to tell you that one year was long enough for grief. She wants you to find a wife for you and . . ." Maria choked as tears flowed. She sipped some coffee and again wiped her eyes. "And she wants you to find a mother for Franco and Anna."

Overwhelmed by this message, John sat speechless.

"John, she wants you to smile again." Maria paused. "And I do, too."

"That would be nice," John said softly. "I just don't feel like smiling again."

Maria studied her son. "John, life is for the living. And you're so young."

John stood and moved around the table. He bent and kissed Maria's cheek. "I should go," he said.

He needed to get away from this kitchen table and this conversation.

"John, are you okay?" Maria asked with alarm.

"Don't worry, Ma, I'm okay."

Maria looked into his eyes. "Promise me you'll think about it," she insisted.

"I'll try, Ma."

Maria stood and gave John a hug. "That's good."

"Say my goodbyes to the kids. I don't want them seeing me like this." He shrugged. "It would upset them."

"I will," Maria assured.

He opened the door to escape, then stopped and turned.

"Ma, I know how hard that was on you." He paused. "Connie would have been proud."

In no frame of mind to go to the office, John drove the granite-curbed streets of Gloucester. His thoughts were of Connie, so it was natural that he ended standing at her grave, with a single red rose in hand.

Oblivious to his surroundings, he crouched and placed the rose on her grave after bringing it to his lips.

"I miss you so much," he said softly, intently.

He could feel her love.

"I'm not ready, Connie." He thought of her message delivered by Maria. "I know the kids need a mother, but . . ."

"John, you okay?"

Startled, he quickly stood to find Peter Novello standing quietly, hands in pockets, studying him.

'Did he hear me?' John thought. 'Was I speaking aloud?' He just didn't know.

"I'm fine, Peter." He paused. "Why are you here?"

Peter flushed. "Ma Amico called me. She told me that you had left her house upset." He shrugged. "She's worried about you, John." He looked down at his shoes. "We're all worried about you."

John studied Peter quietly. Peter was and had been his best friend since childhood. They played ball together, double dated, and treated each other's homes as extensions of their own. Where John was tall and lean, Peter was five-nine and a rock hard two hundred pounds. There was no more body fat on him today than when he was a bruising, all-conference fullback on an undefeated Gloucester High School football team. If anything, he was stronger after eighteen years of fishing. Their friendship went to the bone.

"I'm okay, Peter."

Peter looked back at him from deep brown eyes. His close-cropped, curly brown hair framed a deeply concerned face. "Ma Amico's right, John. You have to go on."

John bristled as he eyed Peter.

Peter read John's anger, narrowed his eyes and set his feet.

John saw the set of Peter's jaw and those eyes and knew that his friend would not be dissuaded by anger. Resigned, he took a deep breath and stated simply, "I'm lost, Peter."

The admission startled Peter, who walked over to John and directed him to a nearby bench.

"Connie wants you to go on, John," Peter said. "Start dating," he urged. "You can't just die with her."

"I think of her constantly, Peter," John responded, with his head in his hands. "I miss her so much."

Peter realized John just wasn't hearing him. So, he took another tack. "Then do it for the kids, John."

Wearily, John shook his head. "I'll think about it, Peter, I'll think about it."

Peter nodded and fixed his eyes on John. "Take care of yourself, Buddy." He shook his head. "You look like shit."

John grinned. "Thanks, I appreciate your concern."

"No problem," Peter responded, concerned eyes on John. "Call me," he paused, seemed ready to speak, but just shrugged.

John watched him walk away.

Deep in troubled thought, John drove to a spot favored by Connie.

Sweet Amanda's Café was a bakery and lunch spot, with gleaming display cases filled with delectable pastries. He sat at the table by the window from which Connie, cappuccino before her, had often sat with John and excitedly talked about the future.

It was here that she had told John that she was pregnant with Franco. John's excitement and the young couple's joy was evident to all the patrons of the busy Café. Smiles bloomed at every table. There was applause from friends and other patrons of the busy café and called out congratulations.

The pastry chef and owner, Kevin Kesterson, grinning, had emerged from the kitchen with a chocolate souffle alive with candles.

Kevin, told that Connie needed 'their table' for a special occasion, took it upon himself to prepare the Palermo's favorite special occasion treat. He was the first to shake John's hand and hug Connie.

John hadn't known Kevin long. Younger than John, Kevin had been a fisherman, who had always dreamed of being a chef. As a boy, he would be in his mother's kitchen, banging pots and attempting new creations. Culinary school was nothing more than a fond hope, a dream shattered when at the age of eighteen, he was left with the burden of supporting his mother and little sister, Lisa, upon his father's untimely death.

Accepting his responsibilities, Kevin packed away his dream and signed on as a deckhand and cook on a Gloucester fishing trawler. Always well fed, the crew of the St. Peter, raved over the culinary talents of this novice fisherman. Over time, Kevin became adept at the art of fishing and was, by the age of 22, a respected deckhand and a source of agitation for more than a few fishermen's wives, who grew tired of hearing about how the St. Peter's cook seasoned his bouillabaisse and, ". . . while I love your apple pie, honey, Kevin's is different, really delicious."

John first met Kevin when the young fisherman came to his office after being badly hurt.

John listened patiently as Kevin explained that the boat was at sea and the net and gear were out. The men were in the galley having dinner, when Kevin made a plate for the captain, who was at the wheel in the pilot house, towing the net.

As Kevin emerged from the fo'c's'le and began to head aft across the deck of the eastern rigged trawler, there was a sudden jolt.

"The gear got hung up," Kevin explained.

John nodded, having grown up in the fishing industry, John knew from experience and could visualize, in a way his competitors could only envy, what had occurred.

As the fishing trawler pulled the net along the ocean's bottom, the rollers, heavy iron and rubber attachments affixed to the net's mouth, which help the net bounce over bottom obstructions, suddenly caught on debris from a sunken vessel or a rock formation.

"The boat jerked to starboard." Kevin explained. "I went flying across the deck and was thrown up against the fishhold." He winced at the memory. "I never saw the plate or food, it must have gone overboard." He grinned. "Do Haddock like veal marsala?" he joked.

"I guess it depends on how talented the cook," John joked back, as he took a liking to the obviously bright, powerfully built young man.

"I guess," Kevin laughed.

"Is that when you were hurt?" John queried.

"No, I was okay." Kevin responded. "Until . . ." he paused, the color drained from his face.

"That's when the main wire snapped."

John's eyes grew large at the horror and danger of the main wire snapping.

"You could have been killed," John said, as he visualized the whip of the steel cable cutting across the deck at the young man sitting before him.

"I would have been," Kevin responded. "The wire slashed across at me."

John swallowed as he envisioned every fisherman's nightmare, a main wire under thousands of pounds of pressure, snapping free and whipping across the deck with the force to cut a man in half.

"I heard the tearing sound and dove over the hatch combing to the port side and lay flat." He blanched at the memory of what might have been.

"The wire whipped above me, inches from my face."

"Wow!" was all John could say, glancing at the crutches.

"How did you hurt your knee?"

"When I dove," Kevin frowned. "I hit my knee on a stanchion."

He glanced down at his left knee. "I hit it hard, but I didn't feel anything until I tried to stand."

John nodded. "Sure, your adrenaline was pumping."

Kevin flushed. "Is that a nice way of saying I was scared to death?"

John smiled. He liked this young fisherman. "So, Kevin, what has the insurance company told you?"

As with most personal injury victims, Kevin had hoped to deal with the insurance company and resolve the matter fairly and quickly. After all, that is what they advertise.

Instead, the multi-national insurance company through their adjusting company met with Kevin, while he was still in the hospital. The investigator smiled in a friendly manner, assured the young fisherman that he needed to get all the facts, so this claim could be wrapped up quickly. He took a tape recorded statement, where the well trained investigator framed the questions to a still medicated, scared and unrepresented young man.

The investigator then went and took statements of the crew, establishing that the other deckhands had not seen the incident, as they were having their dinner in the galley. When he took the captain and vessel owner's statement, he reminded the shaken captain that under the insurance policy, he had a duty to cooperate. Then he added, that he hoped this incident wouldn't cause the insurance company to drop his boat. The message was delivered. Captain John Balbo then told the investigator, on tape, exactly what the insurance company wanted to hear.

After a four hour surgery to re-construct his knee and a five day hospital stay, Kevin returned home. He would spend months in a hip to ankle leg brace and endure a painful physical therapy and rehabilitation regime. He assured his deeply concerned mother and sister, now twenty, who was discussing wedding plans, that everything would be okay.

Months later, after the insurance company had completed an exhaustive investigation, Kevin received a letter from the adjusting company for Lloyds of London informing him they were denying his claim.

"He lied to me," Kevin raged, as he sat in John's office. "He said he was there to help me." He shook his head. "Mr. Palermo, my family needs me." He swallowed. "I don't know what to do." There was a pause as Kevin looked down. "Can you help me?"

John shook his head and smiled. 'It never changes,' he thought. 'The advertising is always centered on how quickly and fairly claims are paid. The truth is so different.'

"Of course, I'll help you," He assured. Then he engaged the young man's eyes.

"Kevin, from this point forward, you do not discuss this with anyone." The young fisherman nodded.

"Kevin," John warned. "The insurance company will do anything to diminish your recovery."

John paused, to be certain his words were understood. "The goal of the insurance company, their adjusters, investigators, lawyers, all of them, is to pay you as little as possible. You need to understand that."

Kevin flushed. "I'm seeing that."

"Good," John smiled. "Let's get to work."

John battled the insurance company for his client. The Kesterson family struggled to survive, while the insurance company, through their lawyers, investigators and adjusters, used every delaying tactic at their disposal to break their will.

Kevin often came to John's office, desperation growing. "Will they pay anything?" He would ask. "They'll pay," John assured him. "But, you have to hang in there."

Frustration growing, Kevin snapped, "Easy for you to say. You're not worried about how to pay the mortgage or even put food on the table." John understood. How often he had bristled at the unfairness of the system that allowed, even seemed to encourage, insurance company lawyers to use discovery delays, motion practice and even violations of court orders to push injured, out of work and desperate plaintiffs into accepting a small percentage of their damages in settlement.

At the end of the day, the court removed another case from its docket and the insurance company wins at the expense of a working family who was forced to surrender. John understood Kevin's anger. He had lived it on a personal level and had spent his working career attempting to balance the scales.

"Kevin," John soothed, "I won't allow those bastards to do this to you," he said, with steel in his eyes. "I won't let them cheat your family." He met Kevin's eyes. "I need you to help me win for you."

And win he did. Kevin's knee would never be the same, but he was able to use his recovery to take care of his mother and sister, attend the Culinary Institute of America and open Sweet Amanda's Café, one of Connie's favorite places.

Alone, John sipped his coffee and looked out on the bustling downtown street. He considered Connie's message, as relayed by Maria. Of course, Maria, Peter, yes, even Connie, were right. He had to move on. He just wasn't sure he wanted to.

At the office, John found the latest response from the insurance company on the loss of the *Mio Mondo*. Initially, they had argued that the boat had left port on its last fateful voyage in an unseaworthy condition. This was a direct violation of the warranty of seaworthiness contained in the policy. John answered each of their charges with ease, advancing documentation of superlative maintenance practices. The records, supplied by Captain Amalfi, demonstrated tender loving care in the maintenance of his boat. With all issues rebutted, the insurer still refused to pay the half million dollar hull coverage or the million dollar per man coverage to the families of the three men.

John pressed hard. The games stopped when John invoked the bad faith provisions of the law, which, if proved, could result in treble (tripled) damages. Finally, after months of evasion, they spoke the truth. The insurer would not pay because they believed Joe Amalfi had intentionally sunk the vessel.

The allegation was strangely disturbing. Phil chalked it up to more of the same. Just another insurance company that collected the high premiums only to balk at paying on a loss.

John wasn't so sure. Something about Amalfi's story gnawed at him.

"What do they have?" Phil asked.

With a shrug, John admitted it wasn't much. "The boat sank in 600 feet of water. Not even near any fishing grounds."

"Didn't he say they were heading home?"

"He did." John sat back, deep in thought. "I don't trust Amalfi. The seas weren't that bad. Why did it sink?"

Taking a seat, Phil studied John. There was concern in his eyes, patience in his tone. "John, Amalfi said that he felt a violent shudder. Everyone felt it. The boat filled up in no time."

John nodded, thoughtfully. "That's what he said." Phil could hear the doubt in his tone.

In a soft voice, Phil went on. "John, think of the three widows, six kids who lost their fathers. Their sole means of support." Now more insistent. "John, they need you."

He focused on Phil and forced a weak smile. "I know. I'm working on it."

* * *

With negotiations having broken down, it was a race to the courthouse. A race that the insurer always won.

Plaintiffs, those bringing the claim, are always highly motivated to settle. In this case, John's clients were even more desperate than normal. Three young families suddenly and tragically having lost their provider and family head. Three grieving widows with mortgages to pay and children to provide for, faced foreclosure while dealing with crushing personal losses.

In this case, as always, the plaintiffs' lawyer argued, reasoned, and cajoled to secure a fair offer. The insurance company executives met in high rises that scraped the sky in every major city in America, denied the claim, but ordered suit to be filed before the plaintiffs were told. Thus, the high priced defense attorneys filed their Declaratory Judgement action, (a lawsuit to declare the insurance policy void) before John could file his more expansive and inclusive suit on behalf of the boat owner and widows.

In fact, they filed their action before John even knew that his final offer of settlement had been refused. For keeping with the inherent unfairness in the battle between desperate plaintiffs and insurance companies with bottomless pits of money, John learned of the insurance company's treachery when he received a frantic call from Rosalie Amalfi, wife of Joe Amalfi, who had been served, by the Sheriff, with the suit papers.

As John cursed the perfidy of the insurance company, he frowned as he reviewed the papers and learned that in the random draw of judges, this case had been assigned to the Honorable Charles S. Adams. John knew Judge Adams well. In fact, he had tried a number of cases before him. Charles Adams was a man without a sense of humor. He was stuffy and self-important, never seeing the humor in the human condition. He had a firm grasp of the law, but had a bias in favor of corporations and insurance companies. He was from 'Old Money.' His ancestors hailed back to colonial America and had made their fortunes in steel, railroads and banking. He had been raised to understand the challenges of operating big business, the difficulties in employing a large work force. He had a distaste for immigrants, which he attempted to conceal, and contempt for those who brought, what he believed were, 'meritless claims.' Charles Adams believed that the litigious nature of the American worker cost corporations millions to defend, many more millions in jury awards with the result that American companies were unable to compete against foreign competitors with their lower overhead.

John knew well that generations of inbred belief was not easily left in chambers when a judge took his place on the bench. John Palermo didn't kid himself. He knew that it was the wealthy who donated to political campaigns and who were rewarded with plum positions such as federal judgeships. The field would never be level for his clients. Charles Adams was just another obstacle to justice for his working class clients.

He shook his head and sat back as he reviewed the papers. He believed that the insurance company had acted in bad faith. A fact he intended to use. John knew the way insurance companies work, their corporate conscience, such as it is.

The insurance industry functions to avoid risk. 'What's the exposure?' is their mantra. A small chance of a large loss weighs heavily. Yet, justice does not enter at all in their calculations. Widows, orphans and disabled persons are of no concern. All that matters is the bottom line. Denying justice to a person proffering a valid claim is ample reason to celebrate 'victory'. Defense lawyers pocket large fees, based on hundreds of hours at $300 to $500 per hour. Insurance companies that advertise their compassion, kind hands and concern for policyholders construct yet another skyscraper. And blue-collar Joe or Joan limp away, bitter and pained at justice denied.

John met the insurance company's Motion for Declaratory Judgement with a motion to dismiss and a lawsuit naming the three widows as plaintiffs along with the boat *Mio Mondo, Inc.*, the owner of the fishing vessel *Mio Mondo*. He added counts for bad faith seeking treble damages and attorney's fees. These claims would be heard by Judge Adams, so, John knew their was little chance of success. Still, he hoped, the allegation would cause a claims supervisor somewhere to take note. Hopefully, it would help to lead to a fair settlement.

CHAPTER FOUR

Judge Charles S. Adams cut an impressive figure on the bench. Tall and lean with a body toned from a rigorous exercise program and a moderate diet, he sat on the bench, looking down on the lawyers before him. Educated at Harvard University and Harvard Law School, he followed in the Adams tradition of attending the prestigious University on the Charles River. While at Harvard he rowed single sculls and was an alternate on a U.S. Olympic Team. He could still be seen on summer mornings slicing down the Charles River in his scull, when he wasn't at his home on Martha's Vineyard. The rest of the year he used his rowing machine in the basement of his Beacon Hill brownstone. Charles S. Adams had lived a life of exclusive luxury. From one of Boston's oldest and most revered families, his view of life was from the heights of Beacon Hill. His family tree included two U.S. Presidents, members of Congress, a governor of Massachusetts and powerful and influential business and corporate leaders. His wealth was staggering, but distributed between corporations, proprietorships and trust funds to keep his name out of the news of the richest men in America. Justifiably proud of his family's legacy, Judge Adams nonetheless had never known the battle to support a family, pay a mortgage or worry from where the money for college tuition would come. His had been a life of exclusive privilege, with the accent on exclusive. During a session in the judge's chambers, in a case tried by John the previous year, Judge Adams had made what John considered a disparaging reference to his clients heavy Sicilian accent. John had smiled and reminded Judge Adams that everybody who lived in the United States was or descended from immigrants. John saw Judge Adams close up as he fixed John with his penetrating gray eyes behind his steel rimmed glasses. He had meant to intimidate John, as he had intimidated many lawyers who had appeared before him over his twenty years on the bench. John simply made his point and won for his client.

Today's hearing was a serious matter. Before him in the otherwise empty courtroom stood two consummate professionals. John Palermo at plaintiff's table and James Bolton at defense table, representing the interests of the insurance company. Years of presiding over complex matters had taught Judge Adams that every case, like the people affected,

---

was unique. The facts and rulings in another case may be close on some points, vastly different on others. Thus, judicial discretion, the well balanced reasoning of how these particular facts fit the applicable law, must temper legal precedent. This was where Charles Adams injected his personal philosophy to shape the outcome of litigation.

"Mr. Palermo," boomed the judge's powerful voice. "You have moved to dismiss the insurance company's Declaratory Judgement Action and seek to substitute your all-encompassing lawsuit."

"Yes, Your Honor."

"Well, Mr. Palermo," the judge continued, "if Mr. Bolton is correct and I rule that the policy is voided by a breach of warranty or by the vessel owner's fraud, are we not all served by limiting the litigation to this core issue?"

"Certainly," John conceded. "However, as there does not exist a reasonable likelihood of success by the insurance company on the Declaratory Judgement Action, to split the case would mean two discovery periods and two trials. That would be a gross waste of the court's time." He paused. "Further, such a delay would cause irreparable harm to three young widows and their six children."

"How so, Mr. Palermo?" inquired the judge as he leaned forward.

"Your Honor, the three widows of the deceased crew are in a desperate financial situation. Their sole provider has suddenly and tragically died. Their mortgages are already in default and the bank is rumbling about foreclosure." He set his eyes on the elevated judge. "My clients do not have the luxury of time. For these ladies, justice delayed will in fact be justice denied," he stated dramatically.

Judge Adams nodded and turned his gaze to Jim Bolton. "Okay, Mr. Bolton, why should I deny Mr. Palermo's motion?"

Bolton rose. He had been aware that John would focus on the widows. Bolton would aim his guns squarely at Captain Amalfi. "Your Honor, this is a contract issue. The simple question posed in my action is, 'Does the policy apply or is it voided by the actions of the corporation?'" He paused, glanced at his papers, then turned his gaze to the court. Through horn-rimmed glasses his eyes were clear and alert. "Your Honor, we believe that Captain Amalfi intentionally sank the vessel."

Judge Adams narrowed his eyes. Having read the briefs submitted, he knew this was the insurer's position.

"I too feel sympathy for the three women and their children." Bolton stated. "My clients take no pleasure in their difficult position. They are innocent victims."

John knew Bolton's statement was true. The insurance company took no pleasure in the widows' predicament. In fact, he knew, the insurance executives were pained by the deaths of the three men. The difference was, the pain the insurance company's decision makers felt was not sympathy for the widows and orphans. Nor was it compassion for the horror of their situation. In fact, it would have been easier to take if they simply didn't care. What enraged John was that their pain stemmed from the complications the death of these three fine men posed for the insurers' chance of success.

Widows and orphans evoke sympathy from juries, thus the Declaratory Judgement Action. The deaths also tended to cast doubt that this loss was a well-planned sinking for the insurance proceeds. And most of all, John knew the deaths raised the ante considerably for the insurance company. So, when Bolton cited his clients' displeasure, John knew he spoke the truth, while misleading those without an understanding of the insurance industry. He knew that Judge Adams knew the insurance company's motivation well. John worried that the judge just didn't care.

"Still," Bolton continued, "this case is about the application of an insurance policy to the sinking of the fishing vessel *Mio Mondo*, not the deaths of the crew. If the policy was breached by Captain Amalfi or if we can prove a fraud, the policy is voided." He paused. "That is the issue. If the court grants Mr. Palermo's motion, discovery will be extended, the trial will be lengthy and likely the jury will be misled by sympathy. "Therefore, it is our position that the court's well-established quest to promote judicial economy will best be served by denying Mr. Palermo's motion and proceeding with the Declaratory Judgement Action." He cleared his throat. "Which, by the way, has priority by date of filing."

Judge Adams pursed his lips in thought. Bolton had not challenged John's statement regarding the likelihood of success of his action. That omission, though honest, was significant.

"Mr. Bolton, would you agree that the events leading to the vessel's sinking are in dispute?"

"Yes, Your Honor."

"If the facts are in dispute, then a jury could deal with all of plaintiffs' claims. A properly worded special verdict form would deal with your concerns."

"Discovery could settle the facts, Your Honor," Bolton stated.

Nodding, the judge added, "If so, you should file a motion for Summary Judgement. That would work as well as a Declaratory Judgement." Judge Adams tapped his finger on his firm chin. 'An interesting case.' He thought. Recognizing he could rule either way, he decided to split the difference, give each party something and limit the matter to one trial. "I'll allow Mr. Palermo's motion," he stated thoughtfully, "And I'll shorten the discovery period to six months." The judge paused and smiled. "That should please both of you, based on your arguments."

John nodded. 'Excellent,' he thought.

"And there will be no extensions granted," Judge Adams warned.

He turned to his clerk. "Mary, do we have an opening in November?"

Mary Allen flipped through her calendar. "Yes, Your Honor. The week of November 10th is available."

"Very well." The judge stated emphatically. "Trial November 10th at 9:00 a.m. Mary will send you the discovery schedule and filing dates for pre-trial motions and jury instructions."

The trial clerk stood and turned to the judge. "Your Honor, shall I schedule the final pre-trial conference for November 3rd at 4:00 p.m.?"

Judge Adams nodded, then turned to the lawyers.

"Gentlemen, if I can be of assistance in helping you settle these claims, please feel free to contact Mary and we'll set up a conference." He paused. "Are there any other matters, Gentlemen?" the judge asked.

"No, Your Honor," John answered.

"Not at this time," Bolton responded, a noticeable edge in his voice.

"Very well." Judge Adams rose and left the bench with his clerk in close pursuit.

"Good work, John," Bolton complimented. "Although I must say, a bit surprising."

John ignored the compliment. He knew that Judge Adams had a reputation for being intrigued by maritime cases. John didn't kid himself into believing that this ruling indicated that Judge Adams was sympathetic to his widows. All that occurred was that the case would be tried before a judge who would favor the insurance company.

"Jim, how about we talk settlement on the widows' claims and fight out Amalfi's?" John proposed.

Bolton shrugged and smiled. "Why would I do that?"

John leaned back on the table and eyed Bolton. "I can think of a few reasons. First, a jury will love them, Jim. And a sympathetic jury would kill you. And second," John paused, "you'd be helping people who've been through enough."

"And Amalfi?" Bolton asked.

John's shoulders sagged. "He's my client, what can I say?"

Jim Bolton picked up his briefcase as John watched him quietly. Ready to leave, he turned to face John. "I'll think about it and let you know." Then he walked out of the courtroom.

John stood alone in the empty courtroom. He thought of Joe Amalfi, shook his head, grabbed his briefcase, and headed out.

*   *   *

Exhausted after a day of arguing, cajoling, and demanding, John drove the granite-curbed streets of the ancient fishing port. He stopped his car on Atlantic Road, deciding to clear his head with a walk along the ocean. He looked out to the twin lighthouses on Thatcher's Island, watched waves crash on the rocky shore below his feet and felt the gentle May winds ruffle his hair and clear his mind.

He was in for a fight, he knew. Jim Bolton was no fool. John closed his eyes and took a deep breath. His thoughts raced to Marc Morrissey, his boyhood friend. With a sigh, he scanned the ocean, the beautiful, powerful ocean that gave this city and his people a living and a life. John thought of the thousands of men who had sailed from this port for three hundred fifty years, never to return.

His mind moved to Joe Picardi, Luke Alves and Marc Morrissey. Three young men cut down in the prime of life. Their wives and children now looked to John for hope. 'So young,' he thought. John stood tall and looked out to the horizon. "Okay Guys," he said aloud, "you can count on me."

CHAPTER FIVE

Dressed in black, her blue eyes still grieved for her lost love, Katarina Morrissey sat primly in her living room as John explained the details of the upcoming deposition. Not yet thirty-years old, mother of two-year-old Kelly and widow of Marc Morrissey, Katie Morrissey was a tall, willowy, strawberry blond.

With an easy grace she poured a cold beer for John into a frosted mug.

John's eyes flashed amusement as he took in the mug. "Thanks, Katie." He couldn't help but grin at the 'UMASS MINUTEMEN' stamped on the glass.

She saw the grin and it broke the somber mood.

"He loved it when you teased him about being a Minute-man." She smiled at the memory.

"As I remember, he gave it to me pretty good as well."

They laughed, then repeated together Marc's favorite line. "Let me know when Boston College acquires University status, will you?"

Her laugh dissolved into misted eyes. "He was so fond of you, John. And he was proud of you."

John nodded. "I know, he was a good friend."

There was an uncomfortable silence. She dabbed at her eyes, then said, "He always told me to call you if anything happened." She paused and reflected. Then she choked, "I just never believed . . ."

John took her hands in his. He noted her fair skin and striking Scandinavian beauty. "I know," he murmured and felt the stab of pain. "I know."

Katie's eyes met his as her thoughts raced to Connie. "I shouldn't be doing this," she apologized. "You've had enough."

He forced a smile that didn't quite reach his eyes. "We can help each other."

Attorney and client used the better part of two hours to prepare her testimony. John was impressed by her quick mind and command of the details of the financial side of her family life. When John played the role of insurance company lawyer and peppered her with a harsh cross-examination, he was amused by the fire he saw in her eyes and her quick and dignified retorts.

Satisfied, John sat back. "You're a good witness." He paused. "I'm sorry this is so difficult."

She shrugged. "Don't apologize. I know you need to be thorough." She managed a smile. "I appreciate your help."

John rose and stretched his arms and shoulders. "It's getting late." He glanced out the window, saw that the sun had set and checked his watch. He took in Katie and pondered.

"Kelly is with your sister and Ma Amico has my kids. Why don't we go out and get some dinner?"

She hesitated, frowned, then looked up at John. "I don't know."

He saw and gauged her inner turmoil. His first reaction was to shrug, suggest some other time and head home. And he considered doing exactly that. Instead, he walked around the coffee table that separated them and sat down beside her.

Her eyes widened slightly in surprise and uncertainty.

He took her left hand and studied the long graceful fingers and the gold band she still wore. Slowly his gaze moved to her eyes. His lips curved in a soft grin. "Katie, I don't mean to scare you, but the thought of going home to that empty house . . ." He sighed. "I just thought that two old friends could have dinner and kill the evening."

Understanding replaced confusion in her eyes. "How are you getting along, John?"

He forced a tired smile. "Between work and taking care of Franco and Anna my days are busy." He sighed and shrugged. "It's the nights." He paused and she saw the loneliness in his eyes. "When the kids are asleep and I'm alone, that's when it gets me." He forced a smile. "I know what you're feeling."

She nodded and put on a kindhearted smile. "I rented 'While You Were Sleeping.' Why don't you pick up some Chinese food, loosen your tie, have some wine and maybe we'll have a few laughs."

"Sounds good," he agreed with a smile.

Katie noticed how the smile lit his face and his deep blue eyes.

"The usual sound okay?" He asked as he readied to leave.

Chinese take out was customary at gatherings of the Palermos, Novellos and Morrisseys, when babysitters were hard to find and Peter and Marc were ashore.

"Sounds fine," Katie agreed. "See you soon."

John waved as he closed the door and headed for his car.

Katie stood, thinking of those gatherings. Peter Novello telling outrageous stories, some of which were probably true, of fishing voyages or from their youth. Marc laughing easily and comfortably with his arm around Katie. Laura Novello sitting quietly, eyes fixed on Peter, broad smile in place. And, John and Connie, so happy together. Good times, she thought and sighed, wonderful memories. With a shrug she moved into the kitchen to ready plates and silverware and check to see if there was a bottle of wine in the refrigerator.

On his knock, Katie opened the door, dressed casually in a gray sweatsuit, designed to be both comfortable and shapeless.

He carried the bag to the coffee table, where Katie had placed plates, utensils and a bottle of chardonnay with two wine glasses.

He appraised her with an easy smile. "Well, you look ready for a movie."

She laughed, "I hope you don't mind. I just thought I'd get comfortable." She busied herself emptying the bag and placing serving spoons into each of the containers. "John, why don't you uncork the wine while I make up plates." She glanced up and grinned. "And please take off that jacket and loosen your tie. I half expect you to start grilling me again at any moment."

The exchange lightened his heart. Since Connie's death, John had missed the easy intimacy and comfort of being with a woman. In Katie's words and movements he saw and felt Connie. And to his surprise, he felt elated rather than sad. With one smooth motion he pulled the cork from the bottle's neck, then poured the wine.

"No more questions," he laughed as he removed jacket and tie and, without a thought, tossed them over the back of the couch. "That's better," he said as he unbuttoned his shirt collar.

With an exasperated shake of the head, Katie watched the casual dismissal of the expensive suit jacket and silk tie, which lay rumpled on the couch. She moved and took the jacket and tie to the closet, fitted them over a wood hanger, then hung them neatly. 'They're all the same,' she thought.

John stood, wine glass in hand and watched Katie move briskly and smoothly to the closet. He observed that the sweatsuit both hid and tantalized. Her long fiery blond hair hung loosely down her back and swung with each graceful step. Above all, he was touched by the kindness and the caring that motivated the act. And he thought of Connie. With a pang he remembered the care she took with his clothes. He recalled it as an extension of her devotion and love.

Katie turned from the closet, wisecrack ready at his typical male behavior, when she saw it in his eyes. The words slid back down her throat. Momentarily at a loss, she flushed, "Did you pour a glass for me?"

He nodded and recovered. "But of course," he said as he handed her the wine glass. Gently he touched his glass to hers. "To lost loves."

She looked into his eyes and saw the sadness that lurked behind the intense blues, set in his strikingly handsome face. Even as he stood at ease, it was easy to see the muscular athletic body that had won him a baseball scholarship to Boston College. And to her surprise she didn't feel guilt at noticing.

"To the future," she responded with thoroughly mixed feelings.

They sipped, each in their own thoughts. The spell was broken by the sharp ring of the phone.

"Start eating while I get that." She went to the kitchen while he speared a peking ravioli, ran it through its sauce and ate it whole.

"Everything okay?" he asked on her return.

"Fine, Kelly wanted to say goodnight." She put the video into the VCR, hit play and sat on the couch. "I'm ready to eat." She patted the couch. "Come sit and eat, I heard this movie was fun."

John plopped down beside her, stretched his legs and sat back with his plate. Then, he turned to Katie, with a contented smile. "This is nice," he offered as he picked up her lingering scent of wildflowers and thought of how he missed the simple pleasure of being with a woman.

"My pleasure," she responded. To her surprise she found that she meant it.

CHAPTER SIX

The last week of June saw Gloucester finally shed the cool and wet spring and move into summer. From John's office, he had watched as the workmen strung the lights and erected the altar that would serve as the focus for the St. Peter's Fiesta.

Over the previous weeks he had witnessed challenges and old rivalries renewed as young and strong men grouped together and registered as crews for the seine boat races. There was an extra spring in the step of the past champions of the Greasy Pole contest as they strutted about the St. Peter's Club. This was a very special time of year for the Italian-American fishing community. Seventy years ago, a small group of fishermen had commissioned a statue of St. Peter, patron saint of fishermen, to be carved and shipped from Sicily to Gloucester. The statue was kept at the St. Peter's Club on a special platform looking out over the fishing fleet. That year on June 28th, the feast day of St. Peter's, a religious procession began in which eight fishermen carried the statue through the streets of Gloucester to be placed on an altar from which a grand outdoor mass was celebrated. The mass was to thank St. Peter for another year of bounty and for the protection of the men who challenged the mighty Atlantic, in small boats, to pull a hard living from the ocean in their nets. On a year such as this, when men had been lost, the community came together to remember, to comfort and to pray.

Of course, the Fiesta had grown beyond the procession and mass. Sporting events, food stands, music, and a carnival had been added over the decades to celebrate the fullness of life in this most beautiful of cities.

For those not tied directly to the fishing industry, Fiesta maintained a prominent place in their lives, as well. Fiesta, celebrated on the weekend around June 28th, the feast day of St. Peter, was Gloucester's welcome to summer. With school closing for the year and the glory of the New England Summer beckoning, the young took center stage on Thursday night. A rock bank played dance music from the altar ablaze with lights, the carnival rides turned, the sweet smells of food stands, crispy fried calamari, sausage with peppers and onions, Sicilian style pizza and the cappuccino and cannoli stands all added flavor and taste to the act of celebration and remembering.

Under a blanket of stars, wrapped in the early summer's warmth, teenagers danced before the altar. Young girls, feeling beautiful and happy, in their pretty dresses twirled to the music with eager young men in the perpetual dance of life. The old sat and watched, many disapproving of the music and dress of the young, but still tapped their feet to the beat of the music and remembered when they were young and danced before the altar.

John arrived at St. Peter's Square, almost in the shadow of the building he had purchased for his law practice, with Franco and Anna in hand. He smiled at the gleam in their eye as the sounds, sights and smells of Fiesta enveloped them. He knew he would see Benny and Maria as well as his sisters, Anna and Filippa with their husbands and children. He smiled at the thought of seeing Laura and Peter Novello and only regretted that Connie and he would not be joining the Novellos, Morrisseys, and the other friends from their youth at the St. Peter's Club for the Saturday night dance.

"Godfather!" John heard called out, as he turned and saw young Peter Novello, now nine and looking more like his father every day, running toward him. Peter leaped up into John's arms and they exchanged a fierce hug.

"How are you, Buddy?" John asked as he set Peter down. "Wow, you're getting strong."

Peter smiled up at him and John saw shades of his boyhood friend in young Peter's eyes.

"I'm great, Godfather," Peter responded. 'Overwhelmed with excitement was more like it,' John thought, as Peter's eyes took in the grand spectacle.

Peter managed to pull his eyes away from the lights, spinning rides and happy confusion long enough to smile at Anna and Franco. Franco was desperately impressed with Peter.

"Hi Guys," Peter said.

"Hi Peter," Franco responded, as he moved fractionally away from John and stood straighter.

"Hi Peter," Anna waved happily.

Laura and Peter Novello arrived momentarily. Peter with three year old Melissa in his arms and Laura pushing their sleeping infant, Christina, in her carriage.

Peter and John exchanged a hearty handshake before John kissed Laura. "Laura, you look beautiful tonight."

With a shake of her head and a genuine smile in place, Laura embraced John. "Thank you, John. I appreciate the kind words." She studied his face. "How have you been?"

"We're doing fine," John assured, noting the concern and caring in Laura's eyes.

"You know Peter," John glanced into Peter's grin. "When I saw you approaching, I wondered who was the lovely young girl with Peter?"

Peter threw a mischievous smile at Laura. "You're right John, my Laura is a babe."

The three old friends laughed heartily, with Laura shaking her head. "You two will never change," she said with approval.

"Why change the best?" Peter asked, running a hand over young Peter's neatly trimmed head.

"Godfather," Peter asked, "can I take Franco on the scrambler with me?"

Franco's eyes grew huge, so impressed was he with the older, bigger Peter.

John smiled at his Godson, then turned to Franco. "What do you say, Big Guy? Do you want to go with Peter on the scrambler?"

"Yes, Dad!" Franco blurted happily.

"Okay," John grinned, handing a twenty to Franco. "Why don't you two go buy a book of tickets." He smiled into Franco's glowing face. "Stay with Peter and have fun. We'll be right here, okay?"

Peter took Franco's hand. "Don't worry, Godfather. I'll stay with Franco."

"Great," John responded. "Have fun, Peter."

The three adults watched the boys disappear into the crowd in the direction of the ticket kiosk. John lifted Anna into his arms.

"Peter will keep an eye on him," Laura assured, noting the concern on John's face.

"I know." He paused, still looking in the direction they had walked, although no longer visible in the crowd. With a shrug, John glanced back at Peter and Laura.

"Thanks, guys. Peter just made Franco's Fiesta."

"I don't know, John." Peter responded with a sly cast to his eyes. Nodding in the direction of the dancing teens, "It won't be long 'till our boys will be charming the young ladies."

John laughed in response.

"You two," Laura shook her head, but grinned, thinking, indeed, how fast the years passed.

"Of course, it won't be but a blink of the eye that your daughters will be twirling in short dresses and smiling at the young boys," Laura teased.

A look of horror struck Peter's face. He kissed Melissa's neck, which produced happy shrieks from the curly haired toddler, and asked. "Who do you love the most?"

Little Melissa threw her arms around Peter's neck and hugged and kissed her Dad. "You, Daddy. I love you the most."

"See," Peter nodded at his wife, "our little girls love their Daddies." Then he touched Anna's cheek. "Right, Anna?"

The auburn-haired beauty hugged John. "That's right, Uncle Peter," she assured.

A huge grin spread across Peter's face. John smiled with him.

"And," Peter stated with certainty, "should it ever change and our girls decide they like boys." He paused. "It's straight into the convent for them."

The three adults laughed heartily.

Laura put a hand on Peter's arm. "I guess you forget, I was someone's daughter, too."

"That's true, Peter." John prodded.

"Yes," Peter agreed, mocking a serious expression. Then his face and eyes lit with a wondrous and loving smile.

"But Laura, you found me." He slanted a grin at his wife. "And what more could a girl want?"

Laura merely laughed. "I can't imagine."

"Hi Laura," waved Katie Morrissey as she approached with her daughter, Kelly.

Laura remembered well the year that she, Katie, and Connie had all been pregnant together. And within a two month span, each delivered a little girl.

"Hi Katie," Laura waved. "And how's Kelly?" she asked.

The little blond haired, blue eyed girl smiled. "I'm good."

The music drew her attention and the lights captured her gaze. Laura smiled as Kelly's swiveling head tried to take it all in. 'To be that young and impressionable.' Laura mused.

"We're going on the merry-go-round," Kelly proclaimed happily.

Anna's eyes went to John, who grinned in response to her hopeful look. "Don't worry Anna, when Franco gets back, I'll take you on the merry-go-round."

"Hey," Peter called, "why don't we take the girls on together and Laura can take a few pictures.

The suggestion was met with smiles and excitement in the eyes of the three little girls.

As the music played and the teens danced, they stood on the edge of the action catching up and laughing at Peter's outrageous stories.

Laura's eyes passed from John to Katie. She felt an overwhelming sadness for the losses each had suffered and a personal loss for two dear friends who had died at far too young an age.

'Last year we lost Connie.' Laura thought. 'Now Marc.' She took a breath and said a silent prayer. She looked at Peter and smiled as his face was alight with the comic telling of one of the escapades of John, Marc and Peter from their youth. The story ended as it seemed all of Peter's stories did, with the listeners convulsed in laughter.

"Of course," Peter added. "It was a good thing I was there to rescue John and Marc."

Still laughing, John glanced at Laura. "Did you ever notice that Peter's stories are always re-told to cast him in the role as hero?"

Katie and Laura nodded, smiling brightly. John noted just how alive and beautiful Katie looked when she laughed.

"What can I say," Peter shrugged, tongue firmly in cheek. "You two always needed me to take care of you."

Out of the corner of his eye, John saw Rosalie and Joe Amalfi approaching. He felt his gut clench at the site of the diminutive Captain. Joe Amalfi was small in every way imaginable. Barely five foot three inches tall and slightly built, his self-image had soured his view of the world. His face formed in a perpetual snarl, because, in his mind, he was one of the little guys the world laughed at. Early in life, he decided to be better, smarter and nastier than all of them. Long acknowledged as one of Gloucester's best fishing captains, he was most comfortable when at sea and in total charge. Subject to the rigorous discipline of the sea, the Captain's words were law. Crewmen who had sailed with him told stories of his vitriolic outbursts. In a community where fishing was a way of life, Joe Amalfi had long been accorded the respect he craved. He was never concerned with the feelings of others. In the years he was owner and captain of the F/V *Mio Mondo*, he saw the role of his crew to work, to obey orders and to keep their mouths shut.

The result of Joe Amalfi's treatment of others was resentment and bitterness. John represented Joe Amalfi, he did not feel the need to socialize with him.

John put on a smile that didn't reach his eyes.

"Hi Captain," his words spoken icily. When he turned to Rosalie the smile was kind, "hi Rosalie, beautiful evening." John's heart went out to Rosalie Amalfi. Instinctively, he realized that being the wife of Captain Amalfi has been difficult. That the Amalfis were childless was a stab at her heart. 'Not even the distraction of children,' John thought. He read the loneliness in her eyes. He knew Rosalie was a kind, caring woman. Her manner and appearance conveyed order and intelligence. When her eyes lit on the three little girls, her lips curved in a smile and her eyes shone.

Joe Amalfi smiled at the group. "Buona Fiesta." He looked at Peter. "Hello Peter."

With no trace of a smile, Peter merely nodded. "Captain," when he glanced at Rosalie, he smiled, "Buona Fiesta."

Amalfi nodded in the direction of John's office building. "I heard you bought the Gilbert Home." The beautiful Federal Style building set in St. Peter's Square and overlooking St. Peter's Park, Harbour Cove and the working waterfront was a local treasure and landmark. Built in 1750 by the Ellery family, the Gilberts owned and occupied the house for a century, before philanthropist Addison Gilbert donated it to be held in trust for the Aged and Infirm.

Unfortunately, hard economic times resulted in the building becoming run down and with the trust dissipated, the building was sold to John, who had been restoring the building to it's historic lustre.

John smiled. "That's right, Captain."

"It's looking good." Amalfi complimented. "I'm pleased you're doing well."

"Thank you, Captain." John responded, smile in place.

Amalfi nodded at Katie, before turning to Peter Novello. "I hear your boat is doing well."

Peter nodded. "It is."

"I guess the Barna case was good for both of you." Amalfi stated defiantly, eyes on Peter.

Peter's eyes raged, his nostrils flared at Amalfi's words. Peter remembered well a Fiesta six years before when Captain Amalfi, then Peter's captain, had attempted to intimidate Peter in the presence of Laura and his friends. Then, Peter had stood alone among the crew of the *MIO MONDO* and spoke the truth about the unseaworthiness of the vessel and the negligence of Captain Joe Amalfi, that had caused career ending injuries to Busty Barna. To prevent him from testifying at the trial of Sebastiano Barna v. The Boat Mio Mondo, Corp. The vessel's insurance company, with Joe Amalfi's help, had hired thugs who surprised Peter, one dark and lonely night on the dock, overpowered him and administered a beating so savage as to hospitalize him for weeks and fracture any number of bones. Still, Peter testified and helped John break the blacklist that had controlled, terrified and limited the fishermen of Gloucester. John's historic victory had changed everything, giving the freedoms all Americans should enjoy, to his people.

John read Peter's rage and placed a calming hand on Peter's arm.

Softly, he said, "not here, Peter." All smiles and light heartedness had dissolved into anger at Amalfi's presence and at his words.

John kissed Anna, still in his arms, comforting her as she felt the tenseness around her. The kiss won a smile from his little girl. "Anna, you stay with Aunt Laura, okay Baby?"

"Okay, Daddy."

"Remember," John reminded the children, "In a few minutes we're going to take a ride on the magic horses on the merry-go-round."

The three girls exchanged happy smiles. John passed Anna to Laura. "I'll just be a minute, Laura."

Laura nodded. "Take your time, John."

Amalfi felt the eyes of every adult on him. John smiled and moved to him, placed an arm on his shoulder and moved the captain away from the group. John spoke softly, the smile never left his face. Katie saw Amalfi's eyes go large as he looked up at the much larger lawyer. Then Amalfi nodded, and John and he shook hands.

Together they casually walked back to the group. Amalfi nodded at Peter, offered a tight smile to the women and took his wife's arm. "Let's go, Rosalie," he said softly.

"Buona Fiesta," Amalfi offered as he and his wife moved away, in the direction of the altar and the music.

"Buona Fiesta, Captain." John responded with a smile. "Buona Fiesta, Rosalie."

Katie and Laura let out a breath that they hadn't realized they were holding.

John looked at the group, who had their eyes on him. He read the smiles of approval from Laura and Katie.

"What's this?" John asked, grin in place. "Peter," he provoked, "you out of stories?"

John saw the anger drain from Peter's eyes, replaced by his typical mirth. John smiled at his dear friend.

Peter's laugh completely dissolved the dark clouds that had formed, bringing a lightness back to the group.

"John, do you remember the Fiesta when we were about eighteen, I guess," Peter's brown eyes danced in a joyous remembrance. "I was dancing with this pretty girl."

John laughed with Peter.

Peter turned to Laura and Katie and with a sly grin offered. "You know, the prettiest girls always wanted to dance with me."

"Of course," Katie smiled, going with the story. Laura just grinned at her husband.

"Well, I'm dancing, thinking about how all these girls were waiting for the great Novello to ask them to dance."

With a conspiratorial wink, he added. "It's a burden being so handsome and sexy."

"I can see that." Katie agreed with a smile that lit her face and caused her blue eyes to sparkle.

"Don't encourage him, Katie," Laura warned with a knowing eye.

"Anyway, here I am, thinking of all these young and eager ladies." He paused and angled a smile at John. "Of course, being a good friend, I had to make sure to encourage the girls to dance with John here and Marc."

Peter glanced at Katie, whose smile held. "You see, Katie, the girls would dance with those two losers just to be near me."

Laughing, Katie nodded agreement. "Absolutely Peter, they were lucky to have you."

Peter pointed a finger at Katie, as he glanced at Laura.

"Now, this is a smart girl."

"Then," he continued. "I looked over to the altar and standing with a group of friends, I saw the most beautiful girl in the world." He smiled at Laura. "And I lost my heart."

The group laughed as Peter grinned at his wife.

Laura shook her head, smile in place and love in her eyes. "And, of course," Laura paused, "I lost my mind."

"Now, that," John said emphatically, "I can agree with."

The happy group continued to tap their feet to the music and listen to Peter's outrageous stories, when Peter, Jr. holding Franco's hand, arrived.

"How was it?" John asked.

Franco's eyes were wide with excitement. "It was great, Dad."

Young Peter reached into his pocket and handed the ticket packet to John. "Here, Godfather."

John smiled at his Godson. "No Peter, you keep them." John responded. "Buona Fiesta."

Young Peter smiled, "Thanks, Godfather."

"Hey Guys," Katie offered, enthused. "We're going to take the girls on the merry-go-round. Do you want to join us?"

Laura just grinned as the two boys exchanged looks of horror.

"Oh no," Laura explained. "These big boys wouldn't be seen on the merry-go-round!" She smiled at reactions from Franco and young Peter. "I'll tell you what, why don't you three take the girls on the merry-go-round. "I'll get the boys some pizza and then we'll watch the ride and I'll take some pictures."

"Sounds good," John agreed, looking at Franco who was nodding enthusiastically in agreement. "Okay, Buddy, I'll see you over there."

John, Peter and Katie joined the line for the merry-go-round as their girls jabbered at each other with excitement in their eyes.

Katie watched as Peter and John placed their daughters on a horse, holding their waist and sharing the excitement of their little girls. As Katie held Kelly the thought struck, at her heart, that Kelly would never know the special love of a father for his little girl.

John saw the glint of joy disappear from Katie's eye. He looked to Kelly. "You ready for the ride?" He asked with excitement in his tone.

Kelly's eyes danced with glee as she nodded eagerly.

John put his hand on Katie's as the ride began to turn and the carousel music played. Katie met his eyes and offered a smile of thanks.

CHAPTER SEVEN

Captain Joe Amalfi stood at the helm of the dragger *Blue Surf* focused on the fishfinder and loran as he guided the net which dragged the ocean bottom on a line consistent with the chart spread before him. Extra attention was required as this was only his second (and last) trip as replacement captain for the vessel's owner, who used Amalfi's availability to take a much deserved vacation. The *Blue Surf* handled differently as compared to the *Mio Mondo* and Amalfi was still adjusting.

On deck the crew worked ripping, gutting and icing the fish from the prior haulback. Consistent with Captain Amalfi's reputation, the net had bulged and the checkerboards barely contained the haddock, sole, cod and halibut. The dragger rolled placidly on four foot seas under a clear blue sky, as the sun warmed the deck. The crew wore a rainbow of oil skin pants over rubber boots. Above the waist they wore tee-shirts or nothing at all against the building heat and diminishing breeze.

"The bastard's good. My God, look at this deck!" exclaimed John Nicastro as he grabbed solid hold of a haddock and ripped its belly before heaving it into the washbox.

Phil Celluci nodded from his position seated on an overturned wire fish basket. "He is good." Then the grizzled and intense fisherman took in Nicastro. "And he is a bastard."

"I've heard some crazy stories," offered Joe Noto working on the portside and behind Nicastro. "Was he as bad as I've heard?"

Phil Celluci, the longtime mate on the *Blue Surf*, glanced up at the young and eager Joe Noto. Pointedly, he said. "Joe Amalfi was and is as mean as they come. I can't even begin to tell you how many guys he has screwed." He paused. "What he did to Benny Amico was unbelievable."

John Nicastro nodded as did deckhand Larry Aiello, who worked forward on the starboard side. Joe Noto, barely twenty-two, looked from deckhand to deckhand before turning to Celluci. "What did he do?"

The men worked, without break, to get the pile ripped, gutted and iced in the hold before the next haulback. Phil Celluci scanned the wires which ran from the winch to deck blocks and out over the starboard side to the steel doors that spread the net on the ocean floor. Satisfied that everything was working he turned back to Noto. "Amalfi owned the *Mio Mondo*."

Noto nodded. "It sank last year, right?"

"Yeah, it did," Celluci agreed. "Last fall, and three good men were lost."

The men worked silently, each in his own thoughts.

"It must have been horrible for those guys," John Nicastro said softly.

For men who challenge the sea from the deck of small fishing draggers, and do so in all seasons and weather conditions, the spectre of a horrible death, cold and alone, in the violent vastness of the ocean, occupies a permanent place in their psyche.

Heads nodded silently.

"Anyway," the mate continued on with his story, "Benny Amico was the mate on the *Mio Mondo*. He was a good fisherman and a better man."

The men worked at the pile. When the wash box was full, its contents were dumped into the hold, where the holdman separated the fish into pens by specie and iced them down.

"I guess it was about twenty years ago," the mate continued. "A rigging block snapped under pressure and crashed down on Benny's shoulder."

"Wow! Really?" proclaimed Joe Noto as he winced.

Phil Celluci ripped a codfish, pulled its innards and then tossed it into the washbox. "Yup," nodded the mate. "If it had hit his head, it would have killed him."

Joe Noto looked up to the tangle of lines and blocks affixed to the mast and spars, shook his head as he felt a shiver of fear and then grabbed a cod. "What happened?"

"His arm and shoulder were badly damaged." The mate stood and scanned the horizon, hand held at his brow to shield his eyes from the sun. He made a complete 360 degree turn, scanning the empty surface of the ocean for as far as the eye could see. Then he passed his eyes over the gear, observing the angle of the wires as they broke the gentle swells down to the fishing gear on the ocean floor. Satisfied, he turned back to the pile. "He was out of work for a long time." The mate angled his head and narrowed his eyes. "I think he had two or three surgeries . . . Yeah, three I think."

"So what did Amalfi do?" asked John Nicastro, suddenly interested.

Celluci kept his eyes on the large codfish in his hand, a look of disgust on his face. "He made up a story that he had told Benny, as mate, to check the blocks for safety. Benny hadn't done it and unfortunately he was injured due to his own negligence."

Joe Noto twisted his face in disbelief. "Who would believe that?"

Phil Celluci eyed the young deckhand. "The rest of the crew told the same story."

Amazed, Noto inquired, "Why would they do that?"

For the first time the mate stopped working and looked into Joe Noto's eyes. "Because if they didn't the insurance company would blackball them." The mate's eyes flashed anger. "They would put them on a list and no boat would take them."

Joe Noto flashed a glance at the pilot house. "He did that?"

Celluci's lips were thin lines, his eyes narrowed. "And now Benny Amico's son, John Palermo, represents that snake!"

"But didn't John break the blackball, Phil?" asked John Nicastro.

The mate smiled. "He did, and beat Amalfi in the process."

"So why help him now?" queried Joe Noto.

The mate shrugged, "I wish I knew." He paused in thought. "I know John, though, he must have a good reason."

The haulback siren pierced the clear salt air.

"Positions everyone," yelled Phil. "Time to haulback."

The crew scrambled into position, Phil Celluci assumed his post behind the winch. The pile was down as the mate released the winch brake and began bringing in the net. Moments later the doors broke the surface, one to port, one to starboard. Each door was hung on a gallows frame. Celluci then re-engaged the winch to pull the net to the surface. Once the mouth of the net emerged by the rail, John Nicastro secured a strap around the belly of the net and hooked a tackle line to the strap.

Having set the winch brake, Phil Celluci moved to the spinning winchhead and grabbed the tackle line which ran to an overhead block and down to the strap.

The mate took two turns on the winchhead and pulled the net slowly to the surface. Free of the buoyancy of the ocean, he needed a third bite on the winchhead and slowly hauled the net out of the water and above the rail until it swung over the deck. The tackle line was so taut that fine beads of salt water flew out of the fibers. The tackle block groaned at the weight.

Once positioned between the checkerboards and over the remaining fish yet to be ripped, Joe Noto pulled on the cod end strap, opening the bottom of the net and allowing the fish to pour onto the deck.

Phil Celluci shook his head and let surface a reluctant smile. 'The bastard is good,' he thought as he saw the deck again heaped with fish.

CHAPTER EIGHT

From the pilot house, Joe Amalfi watched as the crew, under the direction of mate Phil Celluci, reversed the haul back procedure to return the net, fishing doors, rollers, floats and netwings to the ocean floor. The Captain made note of the meticulous nature of the vessel's mate. Each step, from re-tying the cod-end to his careful study of the angle of the wire as the fishing gear was lowered into the ocean, bespoke of decades of experience and a thorough knowledge of his task.

In the manner of an orchestra conductor, the Mate stood behind the winch, eyes sharp and ear tuned. The slightest error on the part of a crewman could lead to a tangled net, fouled gear that would reject fish rather than capture them. Far worse, a lack of attentiveness on his part, improper timing in the attaching of the doors, or release of the winch cable could create an undue strain on blocks or cable resulting in a steel block crashing to the deck or a parted cable whipping across the deck with a force sufficient to cut a man in half.

Grudgingly, Amalfi admitted to himself that the short, powerfully built mate with the obstinate chin and challenging eyes was as good a mate as any he had seen. That he never worked with the Captain before was no surprise. On his boat, Captain Amalfi had demanded a mate and crew that combined competence and a willingness to accept, without argument, all that he demanded. That was the price of a site on the fleet's highest-earning boat. And due to Amalfi's brilliant, some claimed mythical, ability to know where the fish were, there were no shortage of fishermen who sought sites on the *Mio Mondo*.

At sea, all fishermen understand that the captain's orders are law. Maritime journals refer to it as "the rigorous discipline of the sea." Captain Amalfi brought that concept to an unheard of level in the Gloucester fishing community. Ultimately, many found the reality of working under Amalfi to be intolerable. Then, there were men such as Phil Celluci, who refused to sell his self-respect, even for a single voyage.

Replacement Captain Joe Amalfi looked out on a man who had never sought nor would he have accepted a site on the *Mio Mondo*. The diminutive Captain found that he hated Phil Celluci in the way the intolerant have hated the dignified since time began. And he knew that Phil Celluci had told his crew of Amalfi's history.

Then, the Captain's eyes found the large pile of fish, barely contained by the checkerboards, and for the first time in two trips, he smiled. 'Let them hate me,' he thought. 'Let them all be against me.' His eyes shot venom and his lips snarled. 'They know nothing,' he bristled. 'They know nothing.'

On signal from the mate, the crew returned to work the pile of fresh, still flipping, fish. Amalfi's thoughts were broken by the need to study his instruments and charts. His eyes darted from the crew to the fish finder and to his carefully marked chart. His head ached and exhaustion washed over him.

By dusk, the hold was full of well-iced haddock, cod, and sole. Joe Noto and Larry Aiello scrubbed and hosed the deck free of the sand, grit, rock, and debris brought from the ocean floor. Even the effort needed to scrub the fish scales and innards from the deck could not diminish the happiness of the two young fishermen who envisioned being on the town with a pocket full of money.

The vessel's cook, John Nicastro, busied himself in the galley preparing the traditional end of trip celebration meal. The mate sat propped on the rail, captivated by the glistening ripples on the sea as the sun set on the horizon.

Phil Celluci turned to watch Joe Noto stow the hose and satisfied himself that the deck was clean.

"Joe, go take the watch," instructed the mate. He turned to Larry Aiello, "Larry, why don't you help John get dinner ready."

As the two deckhands followed the mate's orders, Phil turned back to enjoy the sunset. 'A full hold, a beautiful night and tomorrow I'll be home,' thought Phil, peacefully.

The sound of footfalls caused the mate to turn to see Joe Amalfi approaching. In a glance Phil saw Amalfi's fatigued face and thinning body.

"You look tired, Captain," Phil offered conversationally.

Amalfi in jeans, tee shirt and workshoes shrugged. "I haven't slept well."

The bags under his eyes and drawn features told the mate the diminutive captain wasn't lying.

"Something troubling you, Captain?" asked Phil evenly.

"Why did you ask that?" snapped Amalfi, as a facial twitch became evident.

Phil turned his eyes on Amalfi. He realized that the agitated captain was more than simply exhausted. He was also thinner than he had ever seen him. In fact, he appeared a nervous wreck.

"No reason," Phil said coolly, "just making conversation." He paused, eyed Amalfi with concern. "You sure you're okay, Captain?"

The question seemed to further agitate Amalfi. "I'm fine, Goddammit." He stalked away to the fo'c's'le as Phil watched closely. The mate noted that Amalfi stopped before descending the companionway to the galley. Instead, he called down, "bring my dinner to the pilot house." He then moved to a large deck block, sat and put his head in his hands.

It occurred to Phil that in the two trips Amalfi had acted as replacement Captain, he had never once descended the fo'c's'le into the galley for a meal, coffee, or conversation. Always, the cook brought the Captain's food and drink to the pilot house. Strange, to the point of bizarre, was the almost complete lack of conversation. 'Ten days,' Phil thought. 'And other than the orders he barked, he spoke to no one. Strange, very strange.'

'Thank God this is his last trip,' thought Phil. Then he shrugged, took a deep cleansing breath and turned back to the horizon, smiling contentedly.

It was four a.m. as the *Blue Surf* steamed steadily for home. Phil Celluci emerged on deck to take the final watch, which would bring the boat into Gloucester harbor.

He stretched off his sleep as he admired the stars and moon. On the ocean, the stars seemed so close that you felt it possible to reach up and stir them about. The utter blackness, but for the light from the heavens, made you feel one with nature. The night was warm, the sky was clear and the air was scented by the gentle sea breeze. The ocean remained calm with no more than a three foot chop.

Phil felt at peace as he scanned the deck on his way to the pilothouse. Satisfied that all was in order, he climbed the steel steps to the helm. As he entered, Larry Aiello shushed the mate by putting a finger to his lips and then pointed his thumb at Amalfi. "He just now fell asleep." Phil glanced at the bunk and the sleeping Captain at the rear of the pilot house.

The mate checked the radar, loran bearings and compass heading. Pleased that the young deckhand had kept the vessel on course, he nodded and whispered, "Get some sleep. I'll take her home."

After Larry had left, Phil settled into the swivel seat behind the helm, sighing contentedly at the beauty of the night and the thought of home. He chuckled at his anticipation of the dawn, checked the compass and leaned back.

Phil's ears perked at the sound of mumbling coming from the Captain. The mumbling became a panicked cry as the prone figure began to thrash on the bunk. Phil swivelled his seat and watched as some horror chased the peace from Joe Amalfi's sleep. Suddenly with a scream he bolted upright in a seated position, lathered with sweat and with terrified eyes.

———

61

Phil read the fear. "Captain, it's okay, you're with me."

"What?" he demanded, his eyes glazed with terror. "Don't," he cried.

In a soothing voice, Phil said, "It's okay, Captain. Relax, you're safe."

Amalfi's breathing steadied, the panic left his eyes to be replaced with desperation. "Dear God," he pleaded.

* * *

Later, on that beautiful summer day, John returned from court where he successfully argued in opposition to a motion filed by the defense attorney in the case of *Salvatore Curcuru v. Our Lady of Fatima, Inc.* to sanction him for taking a sworn affidavit from the vessel's captain. In the affidavit, the captain had acknowledged his error in ordering the men to begin working in ripping, gutting and storing the fish before the net was out and the brakes set on the winch. As the men worked on the fish at a cutting table in the vicinity of the wire, they were forced to work closely together, in fact, too close. With an eye on the wire and an eight inch knife ripping the belly of the fish, a crewman had ripped through a fish, only to have his knife fly out and stab a fellow deck hand. The injury was serious and the nerve damage prevented John's client from ever returning to sea.

The defense attorney argued that the captain was off limits to John as he was a stockholder of the defendant corporation and, by extension, the client of the defense attorney. His claim was that John had violated the ethical rules which proscribed an attorney from communicating with a represented party. Therefore, as John had violated an ethical rule, the plaintiff should be denied the fruits of the inappropriate communication. And John should be seriously sanctioned by the court.

John had responded to the allegation with two arguments. First, as the captain was a witness to the incident, he was free to investigate the facts in zealously representing his client. His second argument was based on the congressional act in a F.E.L.A. or railroad workers case, that recognized the ethical consideration but determined that the power of the railroads was so controlling that to strictly interpret the ethical proscription would deny plaintiffs a fair trial, by shielding witnesses from volunteering the truth. As the Maritime Law incorporates F.E.L.A., the same standard would apply.

John also concluded his argument by observing that once again an insurance company, with unlimited resources, was attempting to stifle the truth to advance a false theory to deny a just claim.

The defense attorney, a lawyer who John liked on a personal level, lashed out that John had violated rules created to protect innocent litigants.

At that, John rose and smiled. "The rules," he stated, "were created for the purpose of aiding the judicial process, which we like to call our system of justice, in ferreting out the truth." He glanced over at his adversary. "My brother likes to argue the systems, while I focus on justice." He looked back at the judge. "My action in thoroughly investigating my client's claim did nothing more or less than reveal the truth." He paused. "That was the very purpose of the Congressional Act I cited in my opposition." He smiled. "Your Honor, let's not exalt form over substance. Let us not allow the truth to be buried by the insurance company's bottom line. I ask you to deny this motion." As John had hoped and expected, the judge ruled in his favor.

John drove back from Boston with the Mio Mondo case on his mind. He smiled in contentment as he crossed the Annisquam River on the A. Piatt Andrew bridge, saw the pleasure craft bob on the gentle swells and felt the joy of the summer air. He drove to Atlantic Road and the open ocean, looking past Thatcher's Island, to the fishing grounds. He stopped, alighted his car and stood above the breakers. The waves crashed on the rocks below his feet in a foamy turmoil. The sky was clear and a perfect blue, dotted with puffy, pillowy clouds. The sun was a bright ball sending glistening rays on the blue ocean.

John looked to the horizon and thought how achingly beautifully it was.

'I better get to the office,' he thought, admitting to himself it was the last place he wanted to be. Still, there was a great deal to do. Back at the office, he buried himself in his work.

A bit restless, John sat at his desk, eyes on Harbour Cove. A lobster boat cruised on the placid harbor, around the ice house and made for dock.

The late afternoon sun reflected off the water. The schooner, Massachusetts, sails set, cruised across his view, headed for a sunset sail, full with happy tourists. 'Gloucester shines in summer,' John thought. 'And, I need to get out of here.'

His sister Filippa had Franco and Anna for a sleep-over. John, at Peter Novello's urging, had agreed to meet him at the St. Peter's Club. And, he had time for a walk on the Boulevard before meeting Peter for dinner and an evening at the Club.

The Boulevard was alive with the full spectrum of life. Groups of teenagers gathering, young married couples with strollers, families with children playing on the grass or riding bicycles, young couples strolling hand in hand, clusters of retired fishermen with their wives sitting and chatting at the water's edge. John smiled at a group of teenagers fishing in the vicinity of the drawbridge. On a balmy summer night, with the air perfumed by the gentle sea breeze and the harbor alive with colorful boats, John chatted with clients and friends and savored the evening. It was dinner night at the St. Peter's Club and members were treated to a wonderful smorgasbord of seafood delights. John entered into a sea of familiar faces.

"Well, look who's here!" bellowed a familiar voice.

The voice brought a smile.

"Hi Peter," John waved as he moved to the table where Peter sat with a group of fishermen.

"Nice suit," Peter began, beaming as he teased his dear friend. Turning to Joe Scola and Sal Nicastro with a sly smile, he cracked, "why didn't you guys tell me this was a formal event?"

The two fishermen, both crew members on Peter's boat, *Good Fortune*, chuckled in the direction of John, who met Peter's question with a grin and shake of the head.

"Would it matter?" John asked dryly, sticking the needle in. "You can put a baboon in tails and it will still look like a baboon."

John's remark drew chuckles from Joe and Sal and an amused grin from Peter.

"Baboon, is it?" With a shake of the head and a wry smile, Peter glanced at the fishermen. "I'm sorry I asked him to join us."

John shook Peter's hand as he sat. "How's Laura and the kids?"

"Great," Peter responded. "How are Franco and Anna doing?"

"They're good." He scanned the room, taking in the bustle. "Filippa has them for a sleep-over."

"So, you're free as a bird," Peter said, thinking how much John needed a few laughs with good friends.

"Wow," John exclaimed. "This place is busy."

"Hey, what do you think?" Peter laughed. "Free food and fishermen go together."

John's grin expanded into a full smile.

It was with a certain sense of comfort that John took in the room that, with the adjoining office and conference room, had long served as the fishermen's club. John exchanged waves and greetings with former school mates, friends and clients who dotted the room.

One wall was dominated by a polished oak bar, today every stool taken by fishermen, drinks in hand, smiles ready and anticipating a good, plentiful meal. On the back wall above the bottles on a raised shelf were scale models of the various eastern and western rigged trawlers that call Gloucester, America's Oldest Seaport, home. John noted the comfortably worn look of the room, the heavy wood tables and well used chairs, the two pool tables against the far wall and in stark contrast a wall mural of a three masted fishing schooner on the fishing grounds and at anchor. Around the schooner were dories, two men to each dory, handlining the depths for cod, haddock and halibut. The painting, as always, caught John's eye, as it did most of the rough dressed and tough men who fought the sea for a living. It told of a rich history of a seagoing people, providing a sense of continuity and tradition.

A loud whistle announced that the buffet was ready. John laughed at the quick scraping of chairs as the men scrambled for the head of the line.

Peter stood and grinned. "Never get in the way of hungry fishermen." He scanned the table, "beers all around?"

Heads nodded as John rose and placed his hand on Peter's shoulder. "Allow me, Peter." He made a quick count. "Eight beers on the way."

"Hey," Peter grinned. "We're thirsty, don't schmooze us into dehydration." The group laughed. "And," Peter added, "don't let your suit get dirty."

Shrimp marinara over linguine, baked haddock and fried grey sole enjoyed with a bottle of chianti had John and Peter relaxed and sipping espresso.

The banter at the table and across the room had John at ease and giving as good as he received.

"Hey, John," called a voice from three tables over, that John recognized as Jim Perry, a former classmate with whom John had played high school baseball. "This dinner is for hard working fishermen." Perry called out, tongue in cheek. "Not for old, broken down ballplayers."

"I see," John nodded, acknowledging the point, meeting Jim's smile with one of his own. "And, nobody would know more about broken down ballplayers than you."

The laughter rippled through the room.

John continued, "as for hard working, Wow! I gave that up years ago."

"You got that right," yelled out Rob Favazza, a fisherman, friend and client of John's.

John stood and in a grand gesture spread his arms. "You just don't stay this handsome with hard work." He paused. "Hell, look at Peter here." John gestured to Peter Novello who was laughing openly. "Nobody works harder than Peter and he looks like crap."

The fishermen burst into laughter as they called out their agreement.

"Nah," yelled Joe Scola, over the noise, "you're wrong about Peter."

"Thank you, Joe." Peter added, a smile playing at his lips and lighting his eyes. "Straighten this guy out will you?"

Joe Scola stood, looked across the table at John, with a thoughtful expression on his face and a shake of the head. "John, let me set you on the true course."

John nodded sagely, failing to stifle a smile. "Okay, Joe."

"I speak with authority on the subject of Peter Novello." Joe Scola began. "As mate of the *Good Fortune* for these past two years, I've had

---

65

the opportunity to know my beloved Captain." Joe smiled at Peter Novello. "And, I can tell you to a certainty, John, it is completely untrue that Peter works hard."

"True, true," Sal Nicastro, a deck hand on the *Good Fortune*, affirmed by pounding the table.

Laughter mixed with shouts of agreement erupted through the room.

"Now, now," Joe Scola held his hands up trying to maintain order. Turning to John, he added, "but, you were right about one thing." He paused and smiled. "He does look like crap!"

General applause broke out as Peter stood and took a bow. John joined his tablemates and numerous others in a deep, heartfelt laugh.

Peter glanced his way, pleased that his good friend was laughing, relaxed and joyful. He thought it was so much like the John he knew before Connie's death and had not seen since.

As the evening wore on, John and Peter found themselves relaxing, away from the group, with an after dinner drink.

"So, Buddy," Peter said nonchalantly, "you going to tell me what's bothering you?"

John sat back and studied his friend. With a resigned shrug, he admitted, "this Mio Mondo case." He paused. "Can you imagine me representing Amalfi?"

Peter's brown eyes became thoughtful. "So, why are you doing it?"

John let out a sigh. He grimaced. "For Marc," he said softly. "I promised Marc that if something ever happened, I would take care of Katie and Kelly."

"Okay," Peter nodded. "Why Amalfi?"

John shook his head. "If the insurance company beats Amalfi, the policy will be voided." He sighed. "And, Katie, Helen, Lorraine and the kids get nothing." John explained.

Peter saw the trap and nodded, his jaw set. "And because of what Amalfi did to Benny and to me, you feel trapped?"

"That's right." John nodded, his exasperation showing.

The two friends sat in silence, sipping at their drinks.

Peter thought of Marc and the years of friendship the three shared.

"John," he said softly. He paused and waited for John's eyes to meet his. "Marc was a good and loyal friend." He took a pull on his drink. "Amalfi doesn't matter." Peter's eyes blazed. "You have to do whatever, even helping Amalfi, to take care of Marc's family." He paused. "You know Marc would do the same."

John nodded. "Yeah, he would. He was a good friend." He exhaled. "Yes, I have to and I will."

Peter smiled and offered an encouraging nod.

"And," John added. "Thanks for tonight."

Peter glanced up at the television above the bar. "It's still early, let's grab a couple of stools at the bar and catch some of the game."

John thought of his empty home. 'Nothing to rush home to,' he thought. "Sure, let's see if the Sox can win one."

They moved to the bar and as dinner was over, a number of stools had opened. They occupied two, ordered beers and sat to cheer the Sox on.

CHAPTER NINE

John seldom brought his children to the cemetery. While he often stopped by to lay a single red rose on Connie's grave, he felt it would be more difficult to keep her memory alive in Franco's and Anna's minds if they related their mother to a gravesite. Still, father and children stopped by the cemetery on the knoll above the harbor, on this beautiful July Saturday. It would have been her thirtieth birthday.

Dressed in shorts and a polo shirt with Docksiders on his feet, he sat on the plush grass beside her stone. Lovingly, he ran his fingers over the photo attached to the stone and laid a rose beside the bouquet of sunflowers, which Franco had placed so carefully on the gravesite.

Noting eyes clouded by grief and the awkward silence of his children, John pulled Franco and Anna onto his lap. Once settled, he told them happy stories of their time with their mother.

"Mommy was pretty," Anna said, studying her picture.

John smiled into Anna's serious face. "She was beautiful, Anna." Then he nuzzled her neck, prompting laughter. "And you look just like Mommy, Anna."

Pleased by the comparison, Anna rose and toddled off to investigate other stones.

"You okay, buddy?" John asked Franco.

Franco nodded, then eyed his Dad. "I'm starting to forget her," he said sullenly.

"I know," John consoled. "You were only four-years-old when she died."

"I don't want to forget her, Dad."

"I know," John comforted, as he took Franco into his arms, reading his son's anxiety. "Mom's always with us, deep in our hearts."

They held onto each other, each in their own thoughts.

"Do you know what Mom used to call you when you were a baby?"

Franco shook his head against John's shoulder. John felt the tears through his shirt.

"My prize," John laughed. "I would call her from the office to say hello and she would tell me, 'my prize and I are going out for a walk.'" Then John turned serious. "Franco, losing Mom was tough on all of us. And it's okay to feel sad sometimes."

Franco nodded into his chest.

"Still, it's better to think about happy things."

"Like baseball?" Franco asked.

"Yeah, like baseball," John agreed as he flipped Franco over onto the soft grass. The sound of his laughter delighted John.

Franco scampered to his feet, sadness forgotten, and raced after his sister. John watched contently as Franco and Anna raced around headstones and scampered over an outcropping of granite. Satisfied that they were okay, he turned back to the photograph on the stone. He remembered the day the picture was taken. They had taken their first trip to the Islands. Connie was beautifully tanned and her eyes were gleaming with love. Wrapped in a white silk scarf, her tanned skin and auburn hair radiated beauty and health. Oh, if only it could have lasted.

Keeping the visit short and upbeat, John stood, placed his hand lovingly on the stone before calling out, "Hey, anybody here want to go for a burger, fries and some ice cream?"

In happy unison they chanted, "me, me, me," as they raced to him. Happily, he scooped them into his arms.

He took a moment to enjoy the view of the harbor. A small lobster boat made its way across his plane of vision drawing a smile. It was then that he saw a little blond head peek around a stone.

"Hi," Anna said waving.

The pig-tailed little girl responded with a smile.

John then heard a familiar voice and saw Katie Morrissey come into view. She wore shorts, a sleeveless top and a sunhat. John noticed her knees were slightly grass stained from where she had knelt. Otherwise, her legs were long, shapely and kissed by the summer sun. Her strawberry blond hair flowed down her back and sunglasses covered her eyes. She smiled as she recognized John.

"You look industrious," he observed.

Her eyes stole to the rose on the grave at his feet. 'Lasting love,' she thought as she removed her glasses. "I was just pulling some weeds. It started to get hot and then I noticed Kelly had run off."

"How long have you been here?

She shrugged, her lips turned in a frown. "I guess a couple of hours."

He noted the redness and a slight puffiness about her eyes, realized she had been crying behind the glasses. She didn't even have a real gravesite and headstone, he thought. Just a memorial to those who had been lost at sea with a chiseled nameplate and photograph to remember them among the many.

It hit John that Monday would have been Marc's birthday. The first since his death. It was approaching a year and a half from when cancer claimed Connie. He knew what Katie felt and his heart went out to her. Then he had a thought.

"Hey, Kelly," he called.

Kelly looked from her mother to John.

"Do you like ice cream?"

Kelly's eyes widened. Shyly, she nodded.

"Well, I was just about to take Franco and Anna to Hungry Harrys for burgers, fries and ice cream." Theatrically, he moved into a stage whisper. "Do you think we could talk your Mom and you into joining us?"

Kelly clapped and looked hopefully at Katie "Can we go, Mom, pleeaasee?" she begged.

Katie looked from Kelly's hopeful face to Franco's and Anna's, whose smiles spread from ear to ear. Then she cast a critical eye at John. "Bully."

"What can I say?" he laughed. "You have to know your audience." He noted that the light had returned to her eyes.

They all piled into John's car. Katie fastened each of the children into seat belts in the backseat, then sat herself in the front passenger seat.

John dropped in behind the wheel, savored a long look at the children and smiled. Seated between his two dark haired, olive-skinned beauties was a blond, blue-eyed, fair-skinned cherub. And they looked great together.

At Katie he flashed his killer smile and bore his eyes into her heart. Now it's time to live, he thought.

Hungry Harrys was an emporium of delight. A soda fountain with stools dominated one wall. Booths lined two walls and a large open area between the booths and counter was kept free of tables and clutter.

John, Katie and the children settled into a corner booth. Music played on an old-fashioned jukebox and the waiters and waitresses moved in time with the beat. The children squirmed and giggled as John ordered cheeseburgers, french fries and root beer floats for everyone.

The reason for the open floor space became evident when the dance song "YMCA" played on the jukebox. The entire waitstaff moved to the space directly in the center of the diner, and danced to the popular number with its distinctive body movements. Franco, Anna and Kelly danced cutely, if somewhat clumsily, on the cushioned seats while John and Katie clapped to the music. John saw Katie's eyes sparkle as she raised her arms to form the letters YMCA. Then she laughed uproariously when Anna, trying to bend her body into the letter C, fell into her lap. When Katie saw that the fall had frightened Anna, she gave the little girl a hug and kissed her back to laughter.

The happy group followed lunch with a long slow stroll down Bearskin Neck which curled into tiny, but picturesque, Rockport Harbor. John gave each of the children in turn a shoulder ride as he bounced them down the pedestrian passageway between the gift shops.

Thoroughly shaken and wildly happy, the children called for ice cream as they passed Bennett's homemade ice cream stand. John and Katie sat on a well shaded granite bench and enjoyed the spectacle of colorful pleasure boats passing before art treasure "Motif #1," as the children sat at their feet, giggling and enjoying ice cream cones.

Katie smiled on the scene of Kelly sitting between Franco and Anna. Kelly's mouth was covered in chocolate, her eyes sparkled, and her face was animated. Katie passed her gaze over John's equally happy children, then looked up at John. "Thank you, it has been a nice day."

John grinned. "You're welcome." He took her hand and pulled her to her feet. "It's still early." He ruffled Franco's hair. "How would you guys like to go to the park?"

The cheering was his answer.

An afternoon spent at Stage Fort Park on slides, swings and see-saws inevitably led to pizza for dinner. So it was an exhausted troop that dropped Katie and Kelly off at their door.

Kelly was asleep on Katie's shoulder when John walked them to the door.

"Thank you for everything," she said with appreciation. "You turned our day around."

John grinned. "It was our pleasure." He gently cleared Kelly's hair off her face. "Now that's a little girl in need of a bath."

Katie laughed. "She sure does. I better get her inside." Katie turned to the door and fumbled with her key.

John eased the key from her hand, unlocked the door and swung it open.

"See you later, Katie."

Katie heard a change in his inflection, looked from the door to John's face. His lips curved in a lazy smile while his eyes sought hers. She read something there that moved her while it made her uneasy.

"John . . ."

He raised his hand to silence her and gently skimmed her lips with his fingers. Her eyes flew open in surprise. The words froze in her throat.

"You don't have to say anything, Katie." He moved his hand to her cheek and stroked softly. "It hasn't even been a year for you. You're confused and maybe a little scared."

She shivered that he read her so well.

"For now we'll go slow." His face grew serious. "Remember, love doesn't die, but Connie and Marc are dead and we can't die with them." He chuckled. "At least that's what everybody keeps telling me." He

71

quickly kissed her cheek and grinned. "I'll see you soon," he said as he dashed back to the car.

Franco and Anna, exhaustion slowing their movements, waved good-bye as John drove off.

Katie put her hand to the spot he had kissed and stood stunned. A wonderful day ended with plenty to think about.

CHAPTER TEN

It was a year since the loss of the *Mio Mondo* with its crew and something was chasing Joe Amalfi. It denied him sleep and stole his appetite.

In the early morning, again the terror found him. The thrashing and cries woke Rosalie, who shook her husband into consciousness.

Her heart went out to him as it would to a wounded animal. While love had long since left their marriage, duty remained and she was his wife.

"It's getting worse, Joe."

"I know," he said, distraught.

"Joe," she soothed. "The loss of the boat and the men was hard. You almost died with your crew."

He nodded agreement as his eyes darted and his facial twitch flared. She read the terror there.

"After the boat sank these nightmares began, but not every night." She took his hand and to her surprise he allowed it. "Then they got worse and more often until it has become every night."

"I know," he despaired.

What terrified Rosalie was that his eyes were haunted night and day. He wasn't eating or communicating.

"Joe, you're not sleeping," she paused. "And your weight," she misted, "you're going to get sick."

He watched her, suspicion lurked in his eyes.

"You need to see a doctor."

Agitated, he snapped at her, "I saw Dr. Moore."

"Joe," she pleaded, "Dr. Moore is an internist. He wants you to see Dr. Salazar."

"No!" he screamed. "I won't see a shrink. I'm not crazy." He pulled his hand away.

She looked down at her hand, then back to his eyes. She saw terror, but also a wildness there.

"Of course you're not," she assured. "But if you talk to Dr. Salazar he might be able to help you deal with the nightmares."

He shook his head as he drew away from her. "You leave me alone. Just leave me alone." He jumped out of bed, grabbed his robe and stalked out of the room.

She watched him go and knew that this couldn't go on.

*   *   *

"Thank you for seeing us, John."

John smiled at Rosalie Amalfi as the Captain eyed him with suspicion. "I'm glad you called."

John took his place behind his desk in his large, well-appointed office. The Amalfis sat across from him. Neither man was comfortable with each other, but John was determined to win for Joe Amalfi. 'I am a professional and personal feelings should not enter into the equation.' He told himself. Also, to win for Amalfi was to win for the three widows and their children.

Amalfi avoided John's eyes. He focused his gaze out the window on Harbour cove, and the boats at dock.

John studied the Captain. He noticed the facial twitch, bags under his eyes, and a profound loss of weight. And, strangely, Amalfi was sweating in the air-conditioned building.

"Captain," John began formally. "Mrs. Amalfi told me that you're not sleeping and I can see how much weight you have lost."

Amalfi shrugged, eyes on the harbor.

"You do know," John continued, "that seeing a psychiatrist or psychologist may well help your case."

Amalfi snapped suspicious eyes on John. "So you had a talk with my wife."

John glanced at Rosalie, saw her distress.

He looked back to Amalfi. "Yes, I spoke to her when she called." Now his voice became friendly. "Joe, I'm your lawyer. I want to help you. What happened out there had to be horrifying. If you see a doctor, his testimony will help your case, but also it will help you deal with these nightmares."

John saw confusion and terror in Amalfi's face. "Please Joe, Dr. Salazar will help you," Rosalie pleaded.

His eyes changed, now they calculated. "What would he do?"

John recognized that something he had said at least had Amalfi considering it. "I don't know exactly. He'll listen to what you say, help you to face whatever haunts you." He shrugged, "maybe he'll use hypnosis."

Amalfi bolted to his feet. "I'm no guinea pig," he exploded. "Forget it." He glared at Rosalie. "We're leaving."

Without another word, Captain Joe Amalfi stormed out of John's office with Rosalie following even as she offered her apologies.

Suddenly the room was quiet. John walked to the bar and poured himself a drink as he replayed the meeting, his impressions, and his client's words over and over again.

He sipped the bourbon and wondered if Joe Amalfi would make it to the trial.

CHAPTER ELEVEN

Phil and Mary Kaye settled their children at Phil's parents for the night. Patiently, Kathleen Harmon listened to Mary Kaye's instructions on the care of little Tara. Phil and his dad exchanged amused smiles at Mary Kaye's anxiety.

"Relax, honey," Phil indulged. "Mom raised me and I turned out all right."

Having caught the glint in Phil's eye, Mary Kaye smirked. "You think so, do you?"

Phil's father burst into laughter. "She got you there, Phil."

"I guess so," Phil chuckled as he put his arm around Mary Kaye. "They'll be fine, honey."

"I know, I know." She turned to her mother-in-law. "I hope I haven't offended you."

Kathleen Harmon smiled warmly as she shook her head. "They have no idea, Mary Kaye. None, whatsoever."

"Thanks, Ma."

"I don't understand why John wants me. I don't know anything about fishing boats," Mary Kaye said as she and Phil drove from Rockport to John's home in the Magnolia section of Gloucester.

Phil drove on Thatcher Road and threw a smile at Mary Kaye. "He said that he needed your eye for detail." He shrugged. "I think he feels a bit guilty about all the meals he has had at our house and all the time you have given to Franco and Anna."

"Maybe," Mary Kaye calculated. "With all he has been through, that's the last thing he should worry about."

"I agree," Phil said. "Still, if it makes him feel better to give us a meal while we put our heads together for this case, what's the harm?"

Mary Kaye studied her husband. "So, what's on your mind?"

Phil glanced at Mary Kaye before turning his eyes back to the winding road which ran along the Magnolia Shore. "This road wasn't designed for cars," he observed. "It's more for oxcarts."

Mary Kaye smiled. "You're right, this road was a foot path that became the main road from Gloucester to Manchester." Her eyes remained on

Phil's thoughtful expression. "A lot more horses and wagons have tread this path over three hundred fifty years than have cars." She added.

"I guess." Phil agreed, absently.

"So, do you want to tell me what's troubling you?" Mary Kaye asked in a soft tone as she placed her hand on Phil's arm.

Phil slowed the car as his eyes met Mary Kaye's.

Phil nodded. "I've been worried about John." He paused. "Since Connie died he's been hitting the bottle hard."

Mary Kaye kept her eyes on Phil.

"He's drinking everyday." He sighed. "And, I think he's drinking heavy at night."

"Really?" Mary Kaye responded, surprise in her tone. "John was always a red wine with dinner kind of guy." She added. "I don't think I've ever seen him drink more than that."

"Losing Connie ripped his heart out." He glanced at Mary Kaye. "I think he drinks so he can fall asleep." He paused. "Sometimes, I think that life has just pounded the crap out of John." He shook his head. "First, his mother dies delivering him. His Papa gets cancer when John's ten and sends him alone on a ship to America to live with strangers."

Mary Kaye felt a chill, but kept her eyes on Phil.

"Then, he finally finds happiness with Connie." He shook his head and sighed. "Wife, children, a good practice." Phil grew quiet. "Then, he loses her." He slowed the car to turn. "Man, nobody should have to deal with what he's been through."

Mary Kaye nodded. "John's strong," she stated. "With our help, he'll be okay."

"Honey," Phil smiled at Mary Kaye. "I hope you're right." He grew serious. "Sometimes, I wonder how I would handle it if," he hesitated and glanced at Mary Kaye. "I don't think I could handle it."

Mary Kaye smiled and leaned over to plant a kiss on his cheek. "Don't you worry, Honey," she assured. "I'll always be with you." She grinned. "And, we'll help John through this."

John answered the door on the second series of knocks.

"Thanks for coming," he smiled. "I appreciate you giving up a Saturday night for this."

"No problem, partner," Phil responded.

"I hope I can be of help," Mary Kaye offered.

"Oh, you will be," John assured.

They walked into the well appointed family room. Mary Kaye could see Connie in the decor and vivid colors. 'He hasn't changed a thing,' she thought. And it hit Mary Kaye just how much she missed Connie.

They sat comfortably before the big screen television as John inserted the video tape into the V.C.R. Taking his seat, he turned to them. "I thought we would view the most relevant segment before we break for dinner."

"What are we looking for?" Mary Kaye asked, sincerely wishing to help.

"The entire six hours are taken on the ocean floor," John explained. "At six hundred feet, no surface light gets to the wreck. So, the only light will be from the submersible. As the light flashed on the boat, where it sets on the bottom, different surfaces reflect the light differently. For example, brass will be brighter than galvanized steel. The painted hull will be different than the black deck tiles." He paused. "Even with the light, the film is gray and murky."

Phil nodded. "Is there anything specifically that we're looking for?"

"Anything and everything," John responded. "The insurance company claims that Amalfi intentionally sank the boat." He paused and read the disbelief in Mary Kaye's eyes. "They believe that the deaths of the men resulted from a miscalculation or terrible accident. And, that Amalfi is covering up. So, we need to study the film to see what, if anything, supports their claim."

"This is insane," Mary Kaye protested. "Not even Amalfi would do such a thing."

Phil looked from Mary Kaye to John. "Maybe not," he stated thoughtfully. "Still, John will need to be ready for everything."

"Okay," Mary Kaye agreed. Then, a thought struck, sending a shiver through her. "We won't see the men, will we?"

"No," John assured. "And that's a problem."

"I don't understand," Mary Kaye stated, eyes wide.

"Where are they?" John asked softly. "Where, in God's name, are they?" Then he grinned. "We won't have to sit through the entire tape. I figure about an hour will give you a full view."

John hit play and the *Mio Mondo* materialized on the screen.

It was with morbid fascination that Mary Kaye watched in the darkened room as the submersible slowly circled the doomed vessel. Her concentration was total as she studied the boat in the inky quiet of total blackness.

The camera recorded what the light allowed. Phil pointed out the stern, then as the submersible cleared the pilot house, the deck came into view. The gallows frame and deck blocks, the hatch and fo'c's'le, the glint off the steel rails of the stairway leading to the pilot house from the deck.

One revolution of the *Mio Mondo* followed another. The submersible's videotaped camera shot from different angles.

"That's the prop," Phil said solemnly. Then, after a long silence, the submersible, directed from the tender at the surface, rose to view the boat from above. The deck came into view, wires and blocks still hung from the mast. When the submersible stopped above and just at the stern, everything forward of the pilot house was delineated.

"Why is it so murky?" Phil said in frustration. "I can't make out . . . damn!" The submersible moved to a new position.

"John, play that back," Phil said with urgency in his tone.

"Which part?" John asked.

"The shot of the deck that we just saw."

Having hit rewind and then play, John watched Phil lean forward to peer through the murk. Nervously, John sipped water to relieve a dry mouth.

Again, the shot from above showed the deck.

"What do you see, Phil?" John asked evenly.

"I don't know," Phil said softly, eyes fixed on the screen. Then the camera moved to a new position and Phil sat back.

John flipped on the lights and hit the stop button. "This is a good spot to break for dinner."

"Good," Mary Kaye said cheerily. "I've had enough of the ocean depths." She eyed Phil, who was deep in thought. "You okay, Phil?" she asked, concern in her voice.

Her question broke the spell. Phil turned to Mary Kaye and offered a sheepish smile. "Sure, I'm fine." He paused and shot John a questioning gaze. "Are you okay, John?"

The partners' eyes met. John offered a curt nod. "I'm fine, let's have dinner." He stood and moved to the kitchen.

Mary Kaye read the exchange, watched John's departure, and turned to Phil. "What did I miss?"

Phil's eyes followed John until he disappeared around the bend. "I can't be sure," he said as he rubbed his hands over his face. "I'll need time to think about it."

"Is there a problem?" Mary Kaye asked, her concern mirroring Phil's.

"Could be, honey, could be." He sighed. "At least, I understand John's concerns."

Instinctively, she knew not to ask. She merely placed her hands on his. "If I can help, please let me know."

"I will," he smiled his thanks. "Now, let's go see what John plans on poisoning us with."

Mary Kaye laughed, an exuberant and loving sound that always delighted Phil. Her green eyes sparkled and anyone in her presence felt lighter, as if a load had been lifted.

"Well, at least we know dessert will be tasty." Phil offered.

Mary Kaye grinned at Phil. "A tiramisu from Sweet Amanda's Café, I'll bet."

Phil's eyes sparkled. "John likes Kevin's tiramisu."

She poked Phil. "Oh, only John likes the tiramisu?" she teased.

"Well," Phil shot back, with a gleam in his eye. "To be polite, I just might have a wee piece."

The petite brunette rose on her toes to kiss Phil. "You're okay, Harmon," she said softly.

"Do you two need a room?" John asked as he came in on the kiss.

They shared a laugh as Mary Kaye hooked John's arm. "Let's have dinner."

CHAPTER TWELVE

To celebrate their wedding anniversary, Phil and Mary Kaye had planned a day, free of children, sailing on Phil's sloop, *Carpe Diem*, and a picnic on Wingaersheek Beach.

To Phil's surprise, Mary Kaye had urged him to invite John. "It will be good for him, honey," Mary Kaye nudged.

Phil shook his head and grinned. "You want a chaperone on our anniversary?"

Mary Kaye placed her arms around Phil and teased. "Just for the day. The evening will be ours. I promise."

Phil's smile met his wife's. "Okay, I'll talk to him. But you know John." He paused, reflecting on his partner. "He spends the weekends with his kids."

Mary Kaye grinned into Phil's concern, then tantalized with a kiss. "I think a great advocate, such as yourself, will be able to carry the argument."

Phil could only laugh. "Okay, Mary Kaye, I'll talk to John." Still embracing, he angled loving eyes and planted another kiss. "Just you remember, the night is ours."

Phil came into John's office late in the afternoon. "Hi, John, what's going on?" He frowned as he noted the glass of bourbon at John's elbow.

John looked up from a file. "Oh, hi Phil." He shook his head and raised his arms to stretch his back. "I need a run."

Phil walked to the bar, hidden behind bi-fold oak doors.

"I'll join you."

Phil laughed. "I'm sure it's 5 PM somewhere."

"Okay," John agreed. He rose and moved to take a seat on an easy chair in the more casual section of his office. The seat provided a nice view of Harbour Cove and the boats at dock. He used the opportunity to stretch his shoulder muscles before sitting. Then he plopped comfortably in an easy chair, studied the activity on Harbour Cove and smiled. He took his drink and lifted it to Phil. "To health," he paused. "And more days like this."

Phil nodded and took a sip. "It is a beautiful day." He agreed. "The harbor is glistening." He paused and smiled at John. "Speaking of beautiful days, Saturday is our wedding anniversary," Phil offered casually.

John smiled. "That's right. What is it, five years now?"

"That's right." Phil agreed.

'Five years, two children, and a great life,' Phil thought appreciatively. "John, Mary Kaye wants to spend Saturday on *Carpe Diem*. A nice sail and picnic at Wingaersheek."

"Sounds great," John agreed. "I'll bet she could use a day away from the kids."

"True," Phil agreed amiably. "She wants you to join us."

John laughed. "On your anniversary? Why?"

"I guess she thinks you could use a day free of responsibility as well," Phil responded. "She really wants you to come."

John shook his head, thinking of Franco and Anna. "I don't know, Phil."

Phil knew not to press. "Give it some thought, John. It will do you a world of good."

"Okay, I promise." John nodded. "I'll give it some thought."

Mary Kaye had left no stone unturned. When John arrived at the Amico's to pick up his children, Maria had embraced him and suggested that they stay for dinner.

"Your father took the kids with him to pick up some dessert at Sweet Amanda's Café," She enticed. "They should be right back and, I made vinegar pepper pork chops," She offered hopefully.

John laughed. "Okay, Ma, we'd love to stay."

"Have some wine and talk to me while I cook."

John sat at the kitchen table, in the seat he had occupied for every meal from the day he arrived to live with the Amicos at age ten. He poured Benny's homemade red wine into a glass, swirled it and took in its aroma. "Smells great." He sipped the wine and his brows shot up. "Hey, this may be his best, ever."

John sipped the wine and recalled the countless hours he had spent with Benny selecting and buying the grapes, pressing the grapes to extract the juice and the musk and babying the sweet grapes into a potent red wine. It had been John's first chore when he had arrived that long ago summer. It seemed only a few days after he had arrived from Sicily that Benny had taken John with him to Boston, to the outdoor produce market at Fanuiel Hall, to select and purchase the crates of grapes Benny would use to make his wine. On the drive, Benny told John stories of his youth in Sciacca and his friendship with John's Papa, Franco. At first, John had cried, but before long the stories of the fun Benny and Franco shared, had ten year old John laughing with Benny.

As they drove back to Gloucester, with their truck bed filled with grapes, over the bridge which spanned the Annisquam River and connected the island to the mainland, Benny pointed out the pleasure boats cruising the river, turning port and starboard, to avoid the ever shifting sand bars.

"This is your home now, John," Benny stated softly. "I loved your Papa. He was my best friend." There was silence as John watched the boats ply the river. "Your Papa wants you here. My family wants you here." He paused. "We want you to be part of our family." Benny grew quiet. He knew this would take time and patience, but they had plenty of both.

As they pulled up at the Amico house, Benny asked John to look at him. John did, eyes brimming with tears.

"Son," Benny began. "I know this has been hard on you. I know that you miss your Papa." He paused. "But we're here for you. Okay?"

John nodded, "Okay," he responded.

Benny grinned. "Let's get these grapes into the basement."

John's reverie was broken by the noisy entrance of Benny with Franco and Anna in tow.

"Daddy!" They yelled in unison and went to John. "Nonno bought a ricotta pie for dessert. Can we stay for dinner?" they pleaded.

"Sure we can," John responded. "But first I need hugs and kisses."

Happily, Maria served her special pork chops with vinegar peppers. After a prayer of thanks, she helped Franco and Anna slice the succulent pork.

"Ma, this is wonderful." John smiled at Maria. "I love your vinegar peppers." He turned to Benny. "And Dad, this wine is excellent." He paused and grinned. "How did you ever do it without me?"

Benny met John's query with a chuckle. "You were always a better baseball player than a wine maker."

"I guess," John agreed with a laugh.

They sat over dinner, conversed about a range of topics, while Nonna Maria fussed over the children.

"Franco has his dad's appetite." Maria noted with approval. She touched her grandson's cheek. "You'll grow up big and strong like your Daddy."

The comment brought a smile from Franco and a wink from Nonno Benny.

Little Anna seemed more interested in the conversation than her plate.

"She eats like a bird." Maria whispered to John.

John smiled into Maria's concern. "The doctor says she's fine, Ma." He reached over and patted her hand. "Don't worry, she's fine."

John sat back, a satisfied smile set on his face. "Ma, I always eat too much when I'm here." He laughed. "But I love it."

"Relax, my son," Maria said with approval. "I'll settle the bambini and make coffee."

"Come on," Maria told the children. "I'll put on the "Little Mermaid" and we'll let your Dad have coffee with Nonno and Nonna."

With Franco and Anna settled, Maria poured three espressos and sat with Benny and John.

"I hear Phil and Mary Kaye asked you to spend Saturday with them on Phil's boat," Maria stated.

John nodded. "Ya, they did, but I don't think so. I promised the kids I'd take them to the park." He paused. "How did you know about the invitation, Ma?"

Rolling over the question Maria responded. "We'll take the bambini to the park on Saturday. You go with Phil and Mary Kaye." She paused, building up a head of steam. "It's not good for you to work, work, work and then take care of the kids." Maria scolded. "You need some time for yourself."

John sat back, a quizzical look on his face. He smiled at Maria, then turned to Benny. "Come on Dad, what's up?"

Benny smiled while he served John a slice of ricotta pie. "It's time to live, John," He said softly. "It's not good for a man to be so alone. Have some fun."

John shook his head and smiled at Maria. "Ma, how did you know that Phil asked me to go sailing on Saturday?"

"Mary Kaye called me," Maria responded. "You're lucky to have friends like Phil and Mary Kaye."

John nodded in agreement. He looked from Benny to Maria. "You're right Ma, they're good friends." Still, John had his suspicions, but just laughed. "Okay, Ma, I'll go sailing on Saturday."

*   *   *

John arrived at the Harmons on a perfect summer day, to find Mary Kaye smiling broadly and dressed for a day under sail. After having little Tara, Mary Kaye had worked hard to regain her figure. Today, she wore a green and white bathing suit with a pale green cover that matched her eyes.

"Mary Kaye, you look great," John declared with a smile.

She laughed and twirled. "Not bad for an old married lady."

John laughed in response.

"Phil's lucky he's my friend or I might just ask you on a date," John teased.

"John, you always say the right thing."

They laughed together.

"Where's Phil?" John asked.

"He's in the cove readying the boat." She grinned. "What a beautiful day."

Kathleen Harmon, Phil's mother, joined John and Mary Kaye on the terrace. With Kathleen was a petite woman of about Mary Kaye's age.

"John, you remember my friend, Barbara?" Mary Kaye queried. John shook his head and smiled at Mary Kaye. His suspicions borne out, he turned to the attractive young woman.

"I'm sorry, have we met, Barbara?"

"Yes, we did meet, at Phil and Mary Kaye's wedding. I was a bridesmaid."

"Of course," John recalled, taking Barbara's hand. "I remember. We talked about Boston College. You were a cheerleader."

"Yes, that's right," Barbara smiled. "And Mary Kaye's roommate."

"I take it you'll be sailing with us today?" John queried.

"Yes," Barbara responded, still holding John's hand. "It's a beautiful day for a sail."

As the ladies settled in, John pulled the anchor from the sandy bottom, neatly coiled the chain and fastened the anchor, before joining Phil, Mary Kaye and Barbara in the cockpit.

"Okay Captain," John grinned. "Anchor's up."

Mary Kaye sat with Phil, leaving the other bench seat for Barbara and John. The day was glorious. A sky so blue, it was difficult to see where the sea ended and the sky began. The sun warmed and glistened on the rippled bay.

John took his place next to Barbara.

"So what do you do now, Barbara?" John asked.

The wind was steady and *Carpe Diem* sliced through Ipswich Bay with a careless grace.

"I'm a high school literature teacher," Barbara responded.

"And the cheerleading coach, I'll bet?" John teased.

"She is!" Mary Kaye proclaimed with a laugh.

Barbara Holden had retained her cheerleader's body. Small and lithe, but shapely, John thought.

Her face was pretty and she smiled easily, naturally. She was comfortable to be with. And, John felt his guard relaxing.

Once anchored at Wingaersheek Beach, John suggested a swim. Barbara agreed, rose and removed her cover. Small indeed, John observed, with an approving smile, but well toned and quite attractive in her white French cut bikini, which set off her well tanned skin. Barbara noted John's smile and decided that the bikini was a worthwhile purchase. Her blue eyes sparkled and the blond hair was attractively styled to frame an oval face.

John dove off the side of the boat with Barbara right behind. First they came to the surface reveling in the cool of the water on their sun warmed skin. John took Barbara's hands as they gently kicked to stay afloat. He smiled. "You look great, Barbara." He complimented. "I'm glad I came."

Barbara met his smile. "Me too." Then she pulled free. "I'll race you to the beach." She challenged.

John laughed. "You're on."

They swam, side by side, to the beach and stretched out on the warm sand.

The conversation turned to books and John discovered that her life work was well chosen.

"Do you focus on the classics or do you throw in a steamy romance novel now and then?" John asked, tongue in cheek.

She laughed. Her laugh came easy and seemed natural.

"Actually, I love the classics, but I'm always on the lookout for new works that will one day be considered classics," She offered.

John nodded. "There's a lot of nothing out there," he suggested.

"Too true," she responded. "But every so often you find a gem."

"Really? Any suggestions?" He asked with a smile. More and more he found Barbara's company a pleasure.

Her eyes narrowed but the smile held. "Are you serious or are you just humoring me?

John rose on an elbow, moving closer. He grinned, "a little bit of both I guess."

She looked into his deep blue eyes and saw his lips curve into an easy smile.

"Actually, my literary club is reading an excellent novel now." She grinned. "I enjoyed it so much I devoured it in one sitting."

"Really? I'm sure it's wonderful," John teased.

She liked it when he teased her. It brightened him and brought a smile to a face that looked like it could use some happiness. And, she had to admit to being very attracted to him.

"Really!" She shot back, giving him a playful punch.

"Violence?" He laughed. "I thought you literary geeks were passivists."

"Geeks!" She proclaimed, surprising John by pushing him onto his back. And then reaching across his chest to pin his shoulders.

John's laugh matched Barbara's. "Okay, okay, I'll read this great novel." He promised.

"Literature through intimidation!" He proclaimed. "What's this, a new teaching method?" he queried, still laughing.

"I'm not letting you up until you take back the geek comment." She stated with a smile, her face inches from John's.

A quick move and John flipped Barbara onto her back, straddling her hips and pinning her shoulders.

Still laughing, John proclaimed himself the champ.

Barbara lay quiet, smiling into John's moment of release, enjoying his sparkling eyes and beaming smile. When he looked into her eyes, saw her smile, felt her quickened breathing, he surprised them both by lowering his lips to hers.

Surprised, but pleased, Barbara savored the kiss. Aware of John's situation, she enjoyed John's spontaneity as she was captured by his good looks and well muscled frame.

As they separated, John saw her accepting smile. Barbara saw conflict, even guilt in his eyes.

"I shouldn't have done that. I'm sorry," he said, all traces of the smile gone.

He lifted off her, rolled onto his back. She turned to him.

"Why?" she teased, "you don't kiss geeks?"

"Barbara," he began, rising to an elbow.

She raised her hand, cutting off his explanation. "I'll accept your apology if you read the novel and we discuss it over dinner."

John's smile returned. "So, I have to read this great novel and buy you dinner? That's a bit much, don't you think?"

Barbara grinned. "You have to accept the consequences of your transgression," She stated decisively.

"It was only a kiss," He countered with a shrug.

"Oh," she smiled. "The kiss was nice. The penalty is for the geek crack."

"Okay, okay, I surrender." John implored. "So, what's the title of this great novel?"

She rose, looking more radiant than ever.

"*The Fisherman's Son*," she said, as she turned and ran for the water, "I'll race you to the boat," She challenged over her shoulder. "And this time, I'll win." She proclaimed.

Laughing, John was right behind her, plunging into the surf.

On *Carpe Diem*, Mary Kaye leaned back against Phil, her head in the curve of his shoulder, eyes on John and Barbara. "They look good together," She observed.

"Good work, Honey. He hasn't smiled like that in a long time."

Mary Kaye watched them swim toward the boat. "It's nice to see him smile," she offered. "Connie would be pleased."

CHAPTER THIRTEEN

John surprised himself by picking up a copy of *"The Fisherman's Son,"* the novel Barbara had described as a brilliant, compelling work. He found that Barbara was right, it was a good read. The author's plot development was gripping and the characters true to life.

'Joseph M. Orlando,' he thought, 'I'll have to remember this author.'

Having read the novel over two evenings, John hesitated to call Barbara so soon after their day with Phil and Mary Kaye.

He examined his feelings. 'Was he attracted to Barbara?' he asked himself. 'She's attractive, no doubt,' he conceded. 'Above all, she was fun. He hadn't felt so happy and relaxed since . . .' He stopped, then grudgingly admitted 'Since before Connie was sick.' He missed the laughing and playfulness he had shared with Connie. And, he missed the passion. Still, Barbara wasn't Connie, nobody could be. If he called her it would seem like a date. He wasn't ready or interested in dating.

As busy as he was with his work on behalf of his clients and taking care of Franco and Anna, days went by. Yet, he found himself thinking of Barbara. When he saw his copy of *The Fisherman's Son*, which was on his night table, their day together came back. It always brought a smile.

The following week he was on trial. With the intense preparation of the trial documents, himself, the witnesses and trying the case for four days, there was precious little time, too little time, to think of dating.

To celebrate John's trial victory, Phil and Mary Kaye invited John to dinner. Having taken the day off to spend with Franco and Anna, he had brought them to their grandparents for the night. Before dressing and driving to Rockport, John took a run along the Magnolia shore, down to Norman's Woe, where the waves crashed and reminded him of Longfellow's 'The Wreck of the Hesperus.'

He ran and grinned as he recited,

'And fast through the midnight dark and dreary,
Through the whistling sleet and snow,
Like a sheeted ghost, the vessel swept,
Towards the reef of Norman's Woe.

Such was the wreck of the Hesperus,
In the midnight and the snow!
Christ save us all from a death like this
On the reef of Norman's Woe!'

He laughed out loud as the verses came to mind. The run on a clear and comfortable September afternoon was exhilarating.

He stopped by Sweet Amanda's Café and picked up a dozen cannoli, as he wasn't sure how many people Mary Kaye had invited.

Arriving at the Harmons, he walked around the house to find Phil on the patio overlooking Harmon's Cove, sipping wine and enjoying the evening air.

Phil rose to greet John.

"How was your day?" Phil asked. "Take a seat, I'll pour you some wine."

"Thanks," John responded. "I had a nice day. The kids and I had a late breakfast, then we went to the park."

"Sounds good," Phil smiled. "The kids must have enjoyed it."

John nodded and felt the tug of guilt that once again Franco and Anna were at their grandparents rather than at home. He smiled and shrugged, chasing away the thought.

"Nice evening," John commented. "I think we'll get a nice sky tonight."

The partners spoke briefly of a business issue then moved to the Red Sox. They sipped their wine and watched the waves lap at the beach.

"So who will be at dinner tonight?" John asked.

"Just the four of us," Phil responded casually, sipping his wine.

'Four?' John thought.

Phil continued, "Mary Kaye and Barbara are in the kitchen."

John shook his head in amusement. "Barbara's here?"

Phil's face showed surprise.

"I thought you knew."

John laughed. "Don't worry about it. I guess Mary Kaye wanted to surprise me." He paused. "It's a nice surprise." He was amused to realize that indeed it was. John glanced over to the patio table where he had left the box of cannoli. "Why don't I bring these into the kitchen."

Phil rose. "I'll do it." He studied his partner and grinned. "I'll ask Barbara to join you."

In a matter of minutes, Barbara came through the doorway onto the patio.

"Hi John," she smiled. "I understand congratulations are in order."

John shrugged, rose and took her hand. Smiling, he responded, "thank you. It's good to see you, Barbara. How have you been?"

"Fine, busy now that classes have started." She grinned. "The challenge of pulling tenth and eleventh graders out of summer and into Shakespeare."

John laughed. "I remember. Although, I never thought about it from the teacher's viewpoint."

The sun was setting and shadows played across the patio. Still, John had no trouble seeing how pretty and alive Barbara looked. Her eyes sparkled, she was dressed fashionably and attractively in a sleeveless, blue dress that fell softly on her curves. The heels she wore did wonderful things to her legs. Her eyes shone as she enjoyed the feminine pleasure of sparking the desire she read in John's eyes.

"You look nice," John commented.

"Thank you," She smiled, enjoying the compliment.

"Please sit, I'll pour you some wine."

She sat, taking the glass from John. Seated, her dress fell across her thighs. John noted, with a glance, that her legs were toned, sleek and attractive. Barbara was pleased that John noticed.

"I guess the trial interfered with your reading assignment," She noted with a mischievous smile.

John flushed. "Actually, I read the novel." He paused. "It was very good."

In the silence that followed, Barbara considered the meaning behind his failing to call. Quietly, she kept her eyes on him and sipped her wine.

John sat back. "Barbara," he began. "I was about to say that after completing the novel, I went into trial preparation and between the trial and my children, I was too busy."

Barbara, sipped her wine, eyes remaining on John. She noted the deep blue eyes had clouded, the uncertainty in his handsome features. She sat quietly, with a hint of a smile playing at her lips.

He shrugged. "But, that wouldn't be true." His gaze grew determined. "I chose not to call you." He hesitated, glancing away, then back, focusing his intense blue eyes on Barbara. "Although, I wanted to."

Her smile grew soft, understanding. "John, why didn't you call?" She asked simply.

In the fading light, he took in her face, the soft smile, bright eyes, understanding expression.

"I was concerned that you would misunderstand." He hesitated. "I thought you might consider having dinner with me as a date."

Surprised by John's statement, Barbara laughed, the laughter lit up her face.

"Would that be a bad thing?" She asked.

John leaned forward. "Barbara, I don't think I'm ready."

She surprised John by taking his hand. In an understanding tone, she stated, "we had a nice day on Phil's boat." She paused, waiting for John to engage her eyes. "We both had a nice day," She stated. She ran a finger over John's hand. "You know, it's okay to be happy, John."

From the doorway Phil observed the scene. "Sorry to interrupt, but dinner's on the table."

John and Barbara rose, eyes fixed on each other. John nodded agreement, before turning to Phil.

"Sounds great," John said. "What treat does Mary Kaye have for us tonight?"

Barbara took John's arm. "I think you'll enjoy the meal." John smiled, feeling comfort in the contact. "Shall we?"

John closed his eyes in appreciation as he savored the lamb. "This is wonderful," he offered. "Mary Kaye, this is really great."

Mary Kaye smiled, with a gleam in her eye she responded, "surprised, are you?"

John and Phil laughed.

"My girl's become quite the gourmet," Phil stated proudly.

"It really is delicious, Mary Kaye," Barbara added. "You've become quite the cook."

"How about that garlic?" Mary Kaye laughed. "This is a dish you better eat as a couple."

Mary Kaye beamed at John, who, with an expression of sheer pleasure, sliced another forkful and sampled the powerful yet delicate flavor.

When John saw all eyes on him, he grinned. "Sorry for ignoring you," he offered. "I'm involved here."

The group burst into laughter.

"John loves food." Mary Kaye directed her comment to Barbara. "Phil appreciates my efforts, but is basically a meat and potatoes guy." She smiled in Phil's direction. "But, John," Mary Kaye shook her head, "he has a real passion for good food."

Barbara glanced John's way. "It doesn't show."

"No," Mary Kaye agreed. "He works out, runs daily, as does Phil." She grinned as she appraised her husband's form.

Barbara caught the look and smiled. She leaned toward Mary Kaye and whispered. "They do look good."

Mary Kaye flashed a glint at Barbara. "Well, only John's available."

The two old friends laughed heartily. Phil tapped his wine glass with his fork. "Attention, please." He glanced at Mary Kaye. "If you two are done whispering, I'd like to propose a toast to our guest of honor."

All eyes were on Phil, who raised his wine glass and offered proudly. "To John, my partner and friend. Congratulations on your most recent victory."

"Here, here," Mary Kaye and Barbara agreed.

With wine glasses aloft, Phil continued. "To John, a good lawyer, a better man. May you always find the justice you seek. Salute!"

"Salute," the group echoed as they tapped glasses.

A touch embarrassed, John moved to change the subject. "Big game tomorrow."

A grin spread on Barbara's face. "Yes," she agreed. "Miami is always a great game."

"You know," John offered. "We should take in a game, tailgate, show the kids what a great university Boston College is." He angled a smile at Mary Kaye. "You know, I still have good friends in the athletic department. If we three alums all vouched for Phil, we might be able to get him on campus."

"You think?" Mary Kaye responded, a look of doubt on her face. "An Ivy Leaguer?"

Phil grinned broadly while shaking his head.

An expression of concerned compassion showed on Barbara's face. Gently, she patted Phil's hand. "Do you think he could handle the excitement?" She paused. "I mean, 45,000 cheering fans, national television, a top ranking hanging in the balance." She smiled at Phil. "Who's Princeton playing this week, Dartmouth?"

With a fixed grin, Phil responded. "No, actually, we're at Brown," He stated proudly.

John smiled at his partner. "I imagine dozens of people will be there for that battle."

The happy group was laughing.

"Remember," Phil added. "At Princeton our focus is academics, not athletics."

"True, true," John agreed, thoughtfully. "You see, ladies," John explained. "Ivy Leaguers are just not Jesuits." He raised his hands to temper the laughter. "They can only handle one challenge at a time."

"Of course," Barbara agreed.

"Now, at Boston College," John continued, "we seek excellence in all that we do. Academics, athletics, scientific development."

"And we succeed," Mary Kaye stated with emphasis.

They moved to cannoli and espresso and the conversation was lively and fun. The four seldom agreed as alliances shifted depending on the topic.

The evening flew by in spirited debate and lighthearted banter. As John rose to leave, Barbara decided it was also a good time to say goodnight.

Goodnights said, John and Barbara walked from the front door of the Harmon house to their cars.

The temperature had dropped and Barbara's dress, while attractive, was no defense against a cool sea breeze.

As they stood in the driveway chatting, John removed his sport coat and placed it around her shoulders.

"I really enjoyed our dinner discussion." Barbara offered, with a sly grin.

John laughed. "Did anyone agree on anything tonight?"

"Not that I remember," She smiled.

"The lamb," John stated. "We all agreed that the lamb was excellent." That drew a laugh from Barbara.

"And the Fornero prints were very good," She added.

John grinned. "But, politics, music, literature, sports, wow!" He shook his head.

Barbara aimed an amused eye at John. "I think you were pushing Mary Kaye's buttons by design."

"Me?" John, protested, his expression, all innocence.

Now they both were laughing.

John checked his watch, before glancing at Barbara. "Can I buy you a drink?"

Barbara smiled as her eyes glinted. "Sure," she nodded.

"But you still owe me dinner."

John shook his head and grinned. "Okay, okay." He took her hands. "Why don't you leave your car. I'll drive and you can continue to try to explain your theory of the novel as the most profound force for change in our society." He grinned. "Did I get that right?"

"Let's go," she agreed, as she settled in John's car, eyes on John and a smile on her lips. "I'm not sure I'll be able to explain such a complex matter to an athlete, but I'll try."

"Why, thank you, M'Lady," John responded with a grin. "I appreciate the effort."

John took Barbara to the Point, a fashionable inn and restaurant which catered to the smart set. Perched on Eastern Point, in the shadow of the lighthouse, there was ocean on three sides. The windward side was lush green lawn descending to a granite breakwater. Opposite, on the lee side, a white sandy beach overlooked the yacht club. At the point, under the lighthouse, was a stone pier.

They settled into a corner table with a breathtaking view of Gloucester Harbor and the town, ablaze with light, rising from the shore. The Eastern Point light threw its yellow beam across the rippled harbor, the sailboats moored at the yacht club and bouncing off of Ten Pound Island.

As Barbara took in the spectacular views, John studied her. She was all gold and rose, a soft full mouth, blue eyes with the tendency to dream that often sparked passion. She smiled easily and as she sat with her drink, she directed a sweet, soft smile at John.

"This is beautiful," She said excitedly. "The ocean crashing on one side and the sailboats bobbing gently in the protected cove." She sighed. "You were lucky to grow up here."

John smiled. "Gloucester is a very special place. I'm glad you like it." He paused, his eyes on Barbara. His smile widened. "The rooms here are beautiful, fireplaces, soft beds and spectacular views."

She shot him a sly and suggestive smile. "Sounds wonderful, I wouldn't mind you taking me here for dinner."

With a shake of the head and a gleam in his eyes, John agreed. "I'll make a reservation. How about tomorrow evening?"

"That would be great," Barbara said with an inviting smile. "And, it'll give you a chance to re-fresh yourself on *The Fisherman's Son.*"

John laughed aloud. "I'll do that."

Then, they clinked glasses and ordered another round . . .

* * *

Sunbeams illuminated the suite as dawn broke on Gloucester harbor.

John stood at the bay window overlooking the breakwater and ocean crashing on Eastern Point. Always an early riser, John glanced at Barbara, asleep beneath the tangled sheets, warmed by the roaring fire, which he had built well before dawn. Her skin was aglow and a satisfied smile curled her lips.

He turned back to watch the sunrise on the horizon and thought of Connie. A touch of guilt crept in as he realized that during the entire night of passion, Connie hadn't once crossed his mind. He knew some would consider that progress. John wasn't so sure.

"Hi, there."

John turned and found Barbara smiling contently. John shook off the thought and grinned. "Sleep well?"

That drew a laugh from Barbara. "Not long, but well."

"How about some breakfast?" John offered. "I thought we'd eat here."

"Sounds good." Barbara responded, stretching. The covers falling from her.

"You order for us," She suggested, "While I shower."

"Okay," he smiled, eyes on Barbara, as she made her way to the bathroom.

Barbara came into the suite's living room with wet hair combed back and wrapped in the white terry cloth robe provided by the Inn.

"Food's here, I see." She smiled as she sat. She removed the warmer covering her plate. "Looks good." She smiled up at John.

"So do you." John offered, with a grin as he moved around the table and planted a kiss on Barbara's lips.

"Let's eat." He urged. "I'm hungry."

"John," Barbara smiled across the table. "I had a nice time."

"Yes," he nodded, thoughtfully. "Me too," He met her eyes. "It's been a long time."

"Well," she teased. "You sure have a good memory."

That drew a laugh. "You're not bad, either," He complimented.

"Thank you, sir," She grinned. "I aim to please."

He glanced at his watch. "I'll arrange with the Inn manager to have you driven to your car." He began. "I need to head out soon and pick up my children. I promised them that I would spend a few days with them." He shrugged and explained. "When I'm on trial, I just don't have time." He offered a sad smile. "It isn't fair."

Barbara studied John. "And you feel guilty about them waking up at their grandparents?"

His eyes narrowed. "No, not really. I mean they knew I was at Phil's and Mary Kaye's and they would spend the night. But . . ." He trailed off.

She smiled softly. "But, you feel guilty?" She paused. "About me."

He leveled his intense blues on her face and nodded. "I guess I do." He sat back and exhaled. "It's crazy, I know."

"It's okay, John." She reached and took his hand. "I enjoy being with you. And, I like children." A smile lit her face. "I admire your dedication to your children." She paused and offered hopefully, "I'd love to meet Franco and Anna."

John stood and moved to the window, breaking contact with Barbara. Arms crossed, he considered Barbara's words, eyes on the outer harbor, yacht club and the awakening town. He shook his head. "Barbara, until I'm sure about my feelings." He paused. "I can't, I won't bring any woman to meet my children."

Barbara, acutely aware of John putting space between them by his sudden move toward the window, managed a smile and kept understanding eyes on him.

He turned back to face her.

"See," he reasoned. "It just wouldn't be fair to allow the children to become attached to a woman who would just end up leaving." He sighed. "I won't put my needs, my life before theirs." He offered a sad smile. "I hope you understand."

She rose and walked to him. She put her head on his chest and wrapped her arms around him. "I understand." She said softly. "It's okay, John." She looked up into his face, rose on her toes to softly kiss his lips. "No pressure, John. When and if you want me to meet Franco and Anna, I'd love to." She looked into his eyes. "I care for you, John. I want to be part of your life." She rested her head on his chest, felt the beating of his heart. "I can take it slow or at whatever pace you need." She smiled. "I'm here for you, John, just call me."

Her words broke through on some level. John lifted her so that she was cradled in his arms. He kissed her deeply. "I've missed this." His eyes grew fierce. "I've missed being close to a woman. I've missed letting go and enjoying a woman."

Their eyes stayed locked on each other as he carried her into the bedroom and gently placed her on the bed.

She read the desperation and the desire in his eyes. "I'm here for you, John. I'm here for you."

CHAPTER FOURTEEN

The weather had turned, October sunlight, harsh and cold, poured through the tidy bay window and on those gathered in the conference room of the law office of Palermo and Harmon. Its glare was softened by tinted plastic shades as it provided background for John who sat at the head of the conference table.

The room's occupants were by contrast heated by tension. To John's right sat the three widows of the men who were lost on the *Mio Mondo*. Immediately to his left, stenopad before her, was John's secretary, Rachel. Beside Rachel were the Amalfis, Joe and Rosalie.

The strain of life was evident on the faces of the widows. To varying degrees, each had aged beyond her years. John saw troubled eyes and the beginning of blind panic.

"I don't know what to do." The speaker was Lorraine Alves seated to John's immediate right. She twisted and tortured the leather handle of her purse. "I went down and spoke with Mr. O'Rourke. He said they wouldn't wait." Tears of frustration welled.

"I know," John acknowledged wearily. "I met with him yesterday." John exhaled, agitated but rigidly holding his emotions in check. "I explained that the trial was only one month away." A sigh, "'Can you guarantee that?' he asked. I told him that was the schedule."

"What did he say?" Helen Picardi, seated to Lorraine Alves' right, asked.

"He said, 'schedules change. Where is my guarantee?'" John bristled at the arrogance. He took a deep breath. "He made it plain, the foreclosures would proceed."

John scanned the table. With the exception of Katie Morrissey each had their home mortgages with the Bank of Gloucester. Amalfi also had a loan on the boat secured by a mortgage on his home. While Amalfi's loan was current, he needed to collect on the hull policy to pay off the bank. At sixty years old, he had used a substantial portion of his savings to make the monthly payments due the bank. To lose this trial meant the loss of his home. For the widows the situation was dire. Each were months behind on their mortgage payments. Their income from Social Security was a fraction of what their husbands had earned. Young families seldom have substantial savings. These young widows were no exception.

The trial loomed and precious time was wasted by this huge distraction. Katie's mortgage was held by the Cape Ann Cooperative Bank, whose directors had agreed to hold off exerting pressure of any kind until after the trial. That decision allowed John the opportunity to win and the bank's customer to bring the mortgage current.

John focused on Lorraine. "What else did O'Rourke say to you?"

She lowered her eyes, flushed and spoke softly. "He said that I should have gone to work rather than . . ." She choked, unable to finish.

'That son of a bitch,' John thought. He swallowed his anger and reached for the young widow's hand. In a compassionate voice, "Lorraine, that's nonsense and O'Rourke knows it." He paused. "You have three small children, Luke was at sea ten days at a time. It was impossible for you to work and take care of your family." His eyes passed over the women and Amalfi, finally settling on Katie who sat as far from John as she could manage.

John's eyes narrowed as she abruptly broke eye contact with him.

John knew that when a lawyer represented people rather than banks, insurance companies, or corporations, he assumed the added burden of managing their emotions. In this case, it was widows grieving for the loss of their young husbands, while raising children alone and attempting to get by on a social security check. The trial was before them, with their future in the balance. If that wasn't enough, a local bank added the terror of taking away their families' home. And John was their only hope.

"Please, let's not lose focus," he began. "Next month we go to trial against the insurance company that has refused to pay the hull policy and for each of your personal losses." He fisted his hands. "That insurance company is the enemy. And that is the battle we must win."

He took a deep breath and sighed at the effort that would have to be expended to outmaneuver the bank's foreclosures. All that effort would necessarily cut into preparation time for the main bout. Still, John knew there was no choice. If these young widows, Helen Picardi and Lorraine Alves, lost their homes, they would be devastated.

He read the panic in their eyes and set his jaw. "Josh O'Rourke is a fool if he thinks he's going to foreclose on your homes." He stated flatly. "I won't let it happen." With that statement John saw the young women visibly relax.

They didn't ask how and John knew they didn't care. The load had been lifted off of their shoulders and placed squarely on his.

"John."

All eyes turned to Katie Morrissey. Katie wore a burgundy sweater over a black skirt. The burgundy seemed to accentuate the fire in her golden hair. The blue eyes sparked with fight. To this point she had not spoken.

John smiled her way. "Yes, Katie."

"Why won't the insurance company pay us?" She looked hard at Amalfi, then back to John. "First, they said that they needed to investigate. Then, they wanted to take everybody's deposition." She exhaled exasperated. "What is it now?"

John hesitated as he studied each face. It was a difficult coalition of these women and the Captain who had survived. It was made worse by the contempt their husbands had felt for Joe Amalfi.

John shrugged. "They don't buy Captain Amalfi's explanation." He spoke in even tones. "As I've said, your cases are tied to his."

"Our husbands are dead. Do they buy that?" The words shot out of Helen Picardi in a rage.

John understood the rage. He had explained the legal realities repeatedly to the women. Still, he knew from personal experience that when your life was crumbling and terror gripped your heart, anger was easier than acceptance. They hadn't heard him anymore than he had heard the doctors who had tried to help Connie.

Katie Morrissey took Helen's hand. Softly she said, "Helen, John has explained this. When he wins Captain Amalfi's case, he'll be winning our case."

Helen melted into tears and fell into Katie's arms. "I can't . . ." she sobbed. "I miss Joe so much. Why did he have to die?"

John sat back and watched as Katie stroked Helen's hair soothingly. Katie's face had also dissolved in tears. Lorraine Alves reflected their pain in her own as she savagely tortured the strap of her pocketbook. Rachel, John's secretary, diverted her eyes as one would from an accident scene, while Rosalie Amalfi looked on the scene with a heartbreaking sadness. 'A good woman,' John thought. Then John saw Joe Amalfi, his eyes darting, the panic gripping him, his facial twitch flaring.

John bit back hard on his anger. He took a deep breath before he rose and managed a smile at the three women. "Why don't we wrap it up." He suggested. "Rachel will get you some water."

His eyes passed over Lorraine and Helen and settled on Katie. He took a deep breath and directed himself to the group. "I'll call you in the next few days."

John was shaken by the raw emotion of the just concluded meeting and by how close he had come to losing control. While presenting an unflappable demeanor to insurance company representatives and the lawyers they hire, John bled with his clients. As a boy, he had been witness and victim to insurance company treachery, personified by their attorney, Charles Dillon and Dillon's client, Joe Amalfi.

John vividly recalled the humiliation of surrender he saw in Benny Amico's eyes, when the insurance company, aided by Captain Amalfi, had used threats and intimidation to force witnesses to commit perjury to save their jobs. He lived in a home without income for two years as the insurance company spun their web of deceit to defeat a legitimate claim.

John always felt his client's anguish. In this case, with the loss of dear friend, Marc Morrissey, and having to represent Joe Amalfi, he battled daily with his emotions. Deep in thought, he stood, glass in hand, at a window of his office looking out over Harbour Cove. A sharp knock and Rachel stuck her head in. "Mrs. Morrissey is here."

Katie came into the office, lit by soft reflected light as dusk fell. John motioned Katie away from his desk to the sitting area. Wearily, she sat on the edge of the couch. John saw the tension on her face, in her eyes.

"You okay, Katie?" He moved to the bar and poured a glass of chardonnay for her, before taking a seat across the coffee table.

"I'm fine, John."

"Thank you for . . ." He shrugged. "Thanks."

She eased back onto the plush couch, crossed her legs at the ankles and sipped her wine. She closed her eyes in a mixture of fatigue and relief.

John took the moment to drink her in. The fiery golden hair which cascaded to her shoulders, the smooth, fair skin and soft inviting lips, the lithe but shapely body and the long graceful legs. Katie Morrissey had long been a friend. Now, she was a client. And, always, she had been Marc's wife. For all of these reasons, he knew, his feelings for her just weren't right. Still, he had to admit, at least to himself, that Katie had awoken feelings in him that he had not felt since Connie's death. He was attracted to her, of course. Yet, it was more than a physical need. He felt a connection with Katie. A bond, that he guessed had to do with Connie and Marc, the friendship they had shared, their common history. Whatever the reasons, John wanted Katie in his life. He knew that he had to tread carefully. And, he knew that Katie may well not be ready or interested. Still, he decided to test the waters.

"I've missed you, Katie."

Her eyes opened and fixed gently on John. She saw the handsome face, those blue eyes that seemed to look into her soul. She also saw that John was opening his heart to her. And, it scared her. The grief she felt was too fresh and too strong. She cared for John, he was her friend and Marc's friend. Her emotions were tangled. Katie decided not to encourage John, not to give him hope that they had a future. She just wasn't ready.

"I was glad to help you with Helen and Lorraine. And I know it's best if we work with Amalfi, so I'll smooth the way." She paused and sipped her wine, battling her conflicting feelings. Her eyes found the photograph of Connie with Franco and Anna set on the credenza and she recalled the loving way John had caressed her stone at the cemetery. Katie sighed and looked back to John. "I can't give you what you need and deserve. Please forget about me." She stood and placed her glass on the coffee table.

John read the uncertainty in her eyes and heard the slight quiver in her voice. He smiled and stood straight and tall to his six feet two inches and moved around the table to stand close to her. Taking her hands, he looked into her eyes. "Has Kelly mentioned us?" He asked softly.

She nodded as she looked up at him. "She spoke of Franco and Anna just this morning."

"Only Franco and Anna?" His lips curved in a grin.

Her eyes clouded and she nodded. "No. She asked for you, too."

He grew serious. "I think of you every day, Katie." He paused. "And I feel guilty, like I'm cheating or something." He took a deep breath, and looked into her eyes. "I miss you, Katie."

"Me too," she acknowledged and edged closer.

He felt her breathing quicken. His body raced as he fought for control. Softly, he asked, "May I kiss you, Katie?"

'Please,' she thought even as she closed her eyes. Then, faced with a choice, she thought of Marc and she couldn't.

"No John, please don't." Her eyes filled as she shook her head. When she looked into his eyes, she saw the hurt. "I'm sorry."

"Me, too." He released her hands and moved away from her.

"I should go," she said without conviction.

John just nodded and moved to his desk. Attempting to mask any hurt, he sat, glanced at his desk and informed Katie. "After the pre-trial conference, I'll call you."

She hesitated, read the hurt in his eyes, sighed and left his office.

He sat down and took his drink. It was too painful to watch her leave.

CHAPTER FIFTEEN

That special aroma of baking, that so much makes a house a home, honeyed the air. Katie's sister Eileen stuck her head in the kitchen door and saw Katie wrist deep in dough. She smiled. "I guess I picked a good time to drop by."

Katie glanced up at her sister and smiled. "Absolutely, I have hot cross buns coming out of the oven in five minutes. Why don't you put on a fresh pot of coffee?" Katie then turned her attention to the pounding of the dough. Her hair was tied up on her head, but wisps escaped to fall about her face.

"So, how did the meeting go?" Eileen asked.

Katie shook her head sadly. "Between the insurance company refusing to pay and now the bank threatening to foreclose on Helen and Lorraine, John's up to his neck with this case."

Eileen's head shot up. There was anger in her voice. "Foreclose? Isn't the trial soon?"

Katie nodded. "Yes, next month, but you know Josh O'Rourke." Her words were laced with contempt.

"That weasel," Eileen spat. "How could he do that?"

"Well, you know he hates John." Katie shook her head. "I think he enjoys scaring Helen and Lorraine."

"Well, don't worry, John will stop him," Eileen offered confidently. "Is everything else going okay?"

"I think so," Katie mused, "but I feel John hates the idea of helping Amalfi."

"Why do you say that?" Eileen queried. "Do you think it goes back to Benny Amico and Peter Novello?"

"I'm not sure what the reason is," Katie responded, "but the looks John directs at Amalfi . . ." She shook her head. "They're actually frightening."

Eileen sat back and considered that. "Well, don't worry. John will do everything possible to help you."

"I know," Katie said thoughtfully. "I just wish our cases weren't tied to Captain Amalfi's. Marc never spoke well of him." She paused. "And there is something in John's eyes . . ." She shrugged. "I just can't explain."

Changing the subject, Eileen watched Katie pound the large bowl of dough. "What are you working on?" Eileen asked as she measured out the coffee.

"I thought to make some fresh Italian bread for the Russos. You know Lucy just had a baby and is feeling a bit under the weather."

"That's awfully nice," Eileen said.

Katie shrugged, "It's not much, but . . ."

Kelly came bouncing into the room. "Auntie Eileen," she threw her arms up as Eileen lifted her onto her lap.

"So how is sweet Kelly, today?"

Kelly giggled. "I'm good." Then captivated by Eileen's earrings she touched the shiny gold loops. "Nice" she cooed.

Katie glanced at Eileen. "She's into jewelry now. Wednesday I found her in my bedroom wearing three bracelets, four necklaces and with a ring on every finger."

The sisters shared a laugh.

"I guess that's normal. Remember when we got into Ma's jewelry and perfume?" Eileen asked.

Katie laughed at the memory. "Ma was furious but Dad came to our rescue. Remember, he took us out and bought us bags of costume jewelry and play makeup." She paused in recollection. "We must have looked like harlots."

Eileen laughed. "But Dad told us we looked beautiful." The thought hit the sisters simultaneously. There would be no father to run interference for Kelly. No Dad to buy jewelry and tell her she was beautiful.

They lapsed into silence. Each in their thoughts. Katie's hands stilled in the dough.

Kelly looked from aunt to mother. "I'm hungry, Mom."

The immediacy of Kelly's need pulled the sisters back.

"Well," Eileen offered. "Your Mom is about to take some hot cross buns out of the oven. How about if I pour you a glass of milk?"

"Okay Auntie," Kelly chirped happily.

Eileen plopped Kelly onto a chair at the table and made for the refrigerator. Milk poured for Kelly, she brought cups and saucers for the coffee as Katie removed the cross buns from the oven and frosted them.

"These are wonderful, Katie," Eileen complimented. "You have become quite the baker."

Mouth full, Kelly nodded agreement.

"You have been baking frequently of late."

"I have," Katie agreed. "Kelly likes fresh baked goods and it's so much less expensive than packaged cookies and cakes." She shrugged. "And since Marc . . . well, it has been tough."

Eileen thought about that, studied Katie and Kelly, then turned the conversation. "Kelly, have you and Mommy been having fun?"

"Sometimes," Kelly offered.

"Only sometimes?"

"Uh, huh."

"Tell me about the last time you had a real fun day."

Kelly looked skyward and brought her finger to her cheek in contemplation. A move that had the two adults smiling for its beauty and innocence. Then her eyes flashed. "We went to Hungry Harrys with Franco and Anna." She laughed, then the story rolled out in a tangled excitement.

"Do you like Franco and Anna?" prompted Eileen.

"Oh yeah! And Uncle John too." With that she crawled off of the chair and ran from the room.

Katie felt Eileen's eyes on her as she checked the bread trays, determined the loaves had risen sufficiently and put the trays into the oven. She turned to find Eileen studying her, arms crossed and smile fixed.

"It's not what you think," Katie stated firmly.

"Really! What do I think?" Responded Eileen with a grin and raised eyebrows. "I just didn't realize how thoroughly Mr. Palermo attended to his clients' needs."

Katie sat, put her head in her hands, and with a thorough exasperation said, "I'm not ready for this."

Eileen's saucy smile was replaced with sisterly concern. With all suggestiveness gone from her voice she asked gently, "Are you okay?"

The dam broke and the tears came. "He wants to see me. He asked if he could kiss me."

"He asked?" Astonished, Eileen laughed.

Katie could not help but laugh through the tears. "Yes, I could have killed him."

Eileen looked into her sister's eyes. "He's a good man, Katie."

Katie nodded. "I know. He was Marc's friend."

"Yes, he was," Eileen agreed. "And Marc was a good judge of people." Eileen took Katie's hands.

"Katie, do you think Marc would want you to be so alone and so unhappy?"

Katie studied her sister. She shook her head, "No."

"Of course he wouldn't." Eileen agreed. Softly, "Katie, it's been over a year. Isn't it time to let Marc rest and to begin living?"

Katie squeezed Eileen's hands. "When I think of John . . ." she stammered, "like that, it's as if I'm betraying Marc."

Eileen pursed her lips in thought. "Think about John, you know he loved Connie."

Katie nodded agreement."

"Now that poor guy is trying to be father and mother to two children. And run his law practice!" She shook her head, sympathy in her eyes.

It was the perfect pitch.

Eileen continued, her voice dripping compassion. "John is a wonderful lawyer and a good guy." She paused for effect. "And he needs you!"

Katie's eyes narrowed in doubt. "John doesn't need me. I'm the last thing he needs. He deserves a woman who isn't racked with guilt, who doesn't cry herself to sleep every night."

Eileen's eyes widened in surprise. 'Still?' She thought.

"It wouldn't be fair to John," Katie added. "He deserves better."

That angered Eileen. Her eyes flashed. "Look Katie, doesn't John have the right to decide what he wants and deserves?"

Katie readied to answer when Eileen rolled over her. "John knows the pain of losing, too, you know. Maybe he, better than anyone, can help you put Marc to rest and bring you and Kelly back to the living." She paused, the saucy smile returned. "And with his body I'll bet coming back to the living would be a treat."

Katie blushed. "I'll think about it."

Eileen grew serious. "Don't think about it too long, Katie. It would be a shame to lose him."

Katie's lips bent in a pout. "Maybe I've lost him already. He hasn't called in a week."

Eileen nodded, her eyes clouded. "Really? I was afraid of that."

"Afraid of what?" Katie asked, perplexed by the sudden change in her sister.

Eileen met Katie's eyes. In a soft, understanding tone, she added, "I've heard John has been seeing someone."

"John?" Katie exclaimed, surprise in her tone.

"Yes, Katie," Eileen confirmed. "I have a friend who works at The Point."

She paused and considered Katie. Her troubled blue eyes looked out of a pretty face. Her long, flame colored, blond hair flowed down her back. Eileen thought of how she had always envied Katie's classic beauty and shapely body. And, Katie was as nice as she was beautiful. She had loved Marc and cherished her marriage and family. Now, that very love was an obstacle in her moving forward. Eileen knew in her heart that John Palermo was right for Katie. And, she realized that Katie needed to face the reality that she may well lose John.

"My friend has seen John with a woman." She paused, then added, "a number of times."

"At the restaurant?" Katie asked hopefully. "Having dinner?"

Eileen shrugged. "At the restaurant." She paused and offered a compassionate smile. "And, at the Inn."

Katie rose and walked to the oven. Her head was spinning as she went through the motions of checking the bread. She turned back to face her sister and took her seat, still trying to decide how she felt about this news. She drummed her nails on the table, deciding she didn't like the news, not one little bit.

Katie sat back, deflated. "Well, you can't blame him." She acknowledged. "He's a man." She sighed. "And, I haven't given him any hope, in that direction, at all."

Eileen stood. "Then call him. Invite him for dinner, without the kids." Her eyes gleamed. "And do more than watch a movie."

Katie sat back. "I'll have to think about this." She raised her hand to cut off Eileen's comeback. "I know you mean well, Eileen, but it's the best I can do."

CHAPTER SIXTEEN

The boat was tossed by the wind and waves and at the mercy of the ocean.

Down on all fours, Captain Joe Amalfi shook himself back to consciousness. He touched his head where blood spurted as he fought his way onto his feet.

"Help me, Captain." He heard above the wail of the wind.

Joe Amalfi looked to the fo'c's'le. The water was thigh high and he fought the swirling sea to the fo'c's'le. Then he heard a call from the engine room.

"Help me, I'm hurt. Help me, Captain."

Frantically he turned and headed aft. The sea rose on the deck, a wave knocked him off of his feet. He was under water, panic rose in his throat. The boat was sinking and he had to send a mayday. 'I've got to get help.' He thought.

He struggled to his feet and heard a desperate call for help. It came from the winch area. A lone hand rose above the churning ocean.

There was no time left. He turned to the pilothouse. He fought the surging sea. He seemed to move in slow motion against the drag of the ocean. He saw the rail dip dangerously below the surf. Exhausted by the effort, he fought his way to the steel stairway which led up to the pilothouse and radio. He reached for the pipe railing at the steps when an explosion rocked the boat from deep inside. Again he fell, striking his head on the steel railing. He fought to remain conscious as the bleeding worsened. Vainly, he used the backs of his hands to clear his eyes.

Back on his feet he pulled himself up the steel steps, balanced himself against the rail as the boat rolled wildly and managed to jerk open the pilothouse door.

The wind howled and the sea thrashed. The three voices became one chorus. "Help us Captain, help us," they pleaded. He saw their eyes. Even when the sea washed over them, he saw their eyes. "Don't leave us," they cried.

Joe Amalfi knew that if he entered the pilothouse to make the distress call they would be gone, washed away.

He looked to the pilothouse and heard their cries. He looked back and saw their hands reaching, clawing for a hold onto something, anything. Their eyes begged, 'don't leave us.'

A tremor rocked the boat. He moved into the relative peace of the pilothouse. Their cries pierced him. He couldn't think, the blood threatened to blind him. He had to make the call. The cries of the three men grew louder, more insistent, more desperate. "Help us. Don't leave us. Don't close that door!"

He couldn't hear, he couldn't think. He covered his ears with his hands and turned away to the radio. Still he heard them. Tears mixed with blood ran down his face. He moved to the pilot house door. To close it would seal their fate. He saw them through the glass. Now they cursed him and swore revenge if he shut them out.

The vessel sank further into the bottomless ocean. He slammed the door shut and placed his mayday call. A piercing scream and his head swung. In each of the pilothouse windows he saw their faces, the eyes of the men. They pounded on the glass. They begged, they cried, and they swore vengeance.

They were all under water. As they sank into the blackness he still saw their faces, their eyes. Their lips curled in anger and spat hate. Their hands reached for his throat.

"No!" He cried. "I had no choice."

Their hands clutched at him as they sank further into the blackness. "No, please." Three sets of hands circled his throat. He thrashed, blood blinded him. He tried to swim free but their grips were like vices. They were killing him, forcing him down into the black depths of the ocean bottom.

He bolted upward with a cry. Hands were on him. And he batted at them, knocked them away. A light flashed.

"Joe, wake up, wake up," she pleaded. "It's just a nightmare, wake up."

His eyes darted as he put a hand to his head. There was no blood. He gasped for breath but didn't need to. Slowly he realized he was in his bed.

"You're safe, Joe," Rosalie cried.

He turned to face her. There was terror in his eyes, but also a kind of madness.

Rosalie saw the fear and recognized that her husband was being driven to the edge of sanity.

* * *

"We gather today to remember." Father Frank Capelli proclaimed, from the pulpit of St. Ann's Church, to his congregation. Every pew was filled in respect for the men and their families who went down to the sea on the *Mio Mondo*.

"These men, our brothers, faced the sea with all its risks. Risks and dangers they knew and accepted. Risks and dangers they faced out of love for their families." He paused and looked on his congregation. His eyes found Katie Morrissey. Solemn, with eyes that grieved, she sat with Kelly, whose blond beauty rivaled her mothers. Katie's sister Eileen sat close with their parents, as well as the extended Morrissey clan, present in support.

The large church was full of family, friends and those who knew that it could as well have been them or a loved one that died that day. It was that personal and immediate.

Father Capelli had been pastor of "the fisherman's church" for fifteen years. In that time he had made it a point to bring the families and especially the children of his congregation into the life of the parish. St. Ann's Elementary School was kept affordable and available for those who wished their children to learn in the timeless Catholic tradition.

His youth center ran a basketball league and a choir. Father Capelli could be seen running the court, whistle at the ready and smile in place, as referee and teacher. He was no less involved with families in need. When counsel, direction, or support was needed, Father Capelli was available. He saw to it that St. Ann's stayed involved in inter-parish and community projects. As he told his youth groups, it was the obligation of the strong to protect the weak and the blessed to care for the needy. To Father Capelli these were more than words, but a code of conduct for a well lived life.

As Father Capelli stood on the pulpit with his eyes on Katie he sighed in frustration at once again being faced with finding words of comfort for those in such pain. His eyes passed to Lorraine Alves. The small, dark haired woman who appeared to have aged ten years in the past twelve months. All three of the women had grown from childhood before his eyes. All were married in this church. All had baptized their children on this altar.

Lorraine's three children huddled about her in the pew. Young Matthew, who so resembled his father Luke, carried despair in his eyes. Mercifully, the younger children were not yet sufficiently aware of the foreclosure or pending trial to share his anxiety. Then he saw Helen Picardi. Pregnant with their second child when the vessel was lost, she held her infant to her chest as her three-year-old played absently on the pew. He recalled Helen as a gangly teenager, always with a crush on one boy or another, alive in the special way unique to the young. Now, her sadness weighed heavily on his heart.

Father Capelli raised his arms. "Marc Morrissey, Luke Alves and Joe Picardi loved their wives and children." He paused. "Gloucestermen all, they grew to manhood among us. As was their tradition they took to the seas, as their fathers before them; as Gloucestermen have for centuries."

His eyes settled on John Palermo, who met his gaze evenly. "Love for the sea and love for their families are their legacies. The legacy of three good men."

He cleared his throat as he searched and found Josh O'Rourke. Reminding himself to be kind but starkly aware that he was the moral voice of his congregation, he held the banker's eyes as he stated, "since that sad day, one year ago, when three good women lost their mates and these six children lost their fathers, their grief has been burdened further by the threat of foreclosure." His voice rose. "Who could throw these families out of their homes, when they are just weeks from trial?"

His eyes blazed with passion. "Where is the compassion? Where is the community? Where is the decency?"

Josh O'Rourke reddened but held the glare of Father Capelli. His eyes shot daggers as he felt the contempt of his neighbors.

"I appeal to the goodness inside each of you. Please do what you can to help those who would help these women."

The parish hall was reserved by John for a post mass gathering. Caterers as well as the families and friends of the widows piled food on buffet tables. Children ran about as the adults chatted softly and reflected on their memories of the deceased men with the widows and their families. Tears mixed with laughter. A smile at a pleasant remembrance with a pang of loss.

John saw Katie as he conversed with Rosalie Amalfi.

"I'm really scared, John," Rosalie confessed. "The dream was so real, he cried and he begged for forgiveness."

John nodded. "This was last night?"

She nodded, wiping a tear, anxiety in her words. "It keeps getting worse."

John looked into Rosalie's eyes. "We're almost there. The trial is in two weeks." He took her hand. "Besides, it was probably today's mass that brought it out." He smiled. "I'm sure he'll be okay." He won a smile back. "That's right," he encouraged, "you're beautiful when you smile."

Rosalie's smile spread to her eyes while her cheeks flushed. "You are a charmer. Thank you."

John began to move in the direction of Father Capelli when he felt a hand on his arm. He turned and saw Josh O'Rourke. The short, heavyset banker seemed agitated. "Can I help you, Josh?"

O'Rourke's eyes narrowed in anger and embarrassment. He gestured toward Father Capelli, "You put him up to that!" the banker raged.

John shook his head and sighed. "No Josh, you did."

The banker flared. "Then how the hell did he know?"

John ignored the glances that flashed at them. "He talks to his congregation." His eyes narrowed. "See Josh, he helps those who need it. While you and your bank . . ." He stopped, took a breath. "I don't want to do this, here. Please excuse me. I need to speak to my clients."

O'Rourke tightened his grip on John's arm. "You embarrassed me, John. I won't forget it."

John's gaze went to his arm and then back to O'Rourke's face. His eyes narrowed in anger. "First, you embarrassed yourself. And second," his voice became a low growl, "if you don't get your paw off of me I will embarrass you."

Josh's hand fell while they eyed each other malevolently. The tension was broken when Father Capelli approached. "Everything okay here?"

John flashed a smile and with a glint in his eye said, "Of course, Father. Josh and I were just discussing the future."

Father Capelli extended his hand to the banker. He smiled warmly. "It was good of you to attend the mass, Josh."

Josh shifted on his feet and his face reddened. "I have to do my job, Father."

Father Capelli placed his hand on the banker's shoulder. Softly and kindly he said, "Look at you, Josh, you're flustered. I've known you since you were a boy. Even then, when you did something you knew was wrong, you would flush with embarrassment." He paused and grew serious. "Josh, it's never too late to do what's right. Think about it, okay?"

Josh nodded but said nothing.

Father Capelli smiled. "You're a good man, Josh. Don't ever lose that."

"Why don't I leave you two?" John offered, aware that if anyone could reach the heart of a banker, it was Father Capelli.

John noticed that plates were piled high with lasagna, sausage and peppers and chicken parmesan. Glasses of red wine complemented the food and there was plenty of food available. Then he moved to see Helen Picardi. Gently he stroked the cheek of six-month-old Joseph Jr. grinning as the baby gurgled from his carrier set upon a table.

"You okay, Helen?"

She sipped a cup of tea and managed a grin. "I thought you were going to punch him." She paused and flushed. "I wish you had."

John bent and put his index finger in the baby's hand. When Joe grabbed it firmly, John laughed. "Nice grip." He flashed a grin at Helen. "I think we have a ballplayer here."

"Changing the subject?" she laughed.

Dead panned, John responded, "I hate to speak of violence in a church hall before an impressionable child."

They laughed together.

John thought how nice it will be when laughter could again come as easily to Helen as it did when she was a giggling teenager.

John next went to speak to Lorraine Alves. He approached with a smile. "How are you, Lorraine?" Before she could answer he began boxing with Matt. The nine-year-old laughed when he landed a punch on John's arm and the lawyer feigned shock and pain. "I give up," John pleaded, raising his hands in surrender.

"He's getting big!" John exclaimed to Lorraine while he ran his hand over Matt's head.

"He sure is," Lorraine responded wryly. "New pants every few months."

"That's good." He turned to Matt. "You look more and more like your Dad."

Matt nodded, eyes large and moist.

John smiled. "Your Dad would be proud of you."

The boy choked.

John crouched before him. "Matt, I know how it feels to lose your Dad."

Matt looked up at him with eyes that reflected a broken heart.

"If you ever need or want to talk or just to have a catch, please call me. Will you do that?"

Matt just nodded.

John grinned. "When you call I'll be expecting a re-match."

Matt's lips curved in a grin. "Okay. I'll call you." Then the youngster raised his fist. "And I'll win again."

John rose to find Lorraine's eyes pooled with tears.

"Thank you, John."

He winked. "Encourage him to call. We'll have a good time."

His last stop was to see Katie Morrissey. Mary Kaye and Phil stood with the family as John approached to the delight of Kelly who ran into his arms.

John picked up Kelly as he reached to shake hands with Katie's father. Then he turned to shake hands with Marc's dad, Mike Morrissey, and Marc's brother, Arthur.

John took a moment with both fathers before exchanging a joke and smile with Arthur. As a boy, Arthur had always looked up to Marc, John and Peter Novello and consequently, in the way of younger brothers, was always underfoot.

Harold Lind, Katie's father, stood as tall as John. His light hair was running to white and his handshake was firm and friendly. He nodded in the direction of Josh O'Rourke. "I'm glad you set him straight."

John nodded and then smiled at Gwen Morrissey. "Hi, Mrs. Morrissey, it's good to see you."

Gwen smiled at John. "It would be nice if you stopped by." She paused, then teased. "I could make a batch of those lemon cookies you used to like so much when you were a boy."

John laughed. "We could eat a bunch of those cookies." John remembered fondly.

"Those were good days." Gwen said with misted eyes. "I loved having Marc, you and Peter running through my kitchen, eating everything in sight."

"Yes, they were, Mrs. Morrissey." John agreed, offering a smile.

John turned his attention back to Kelly, who was still in his arms.

"Where's Franco and Anna?" Kelly chirped.

Both grandfathers lost their frown and smiled at Kelly, as Gwen beamed.

John laughed. "They're at their Nonna's with Phil and Tara."

"John, it was so nice of Ma Amico to take our children." Mary Kaye smiled.

"Are you kidding?" John laughed. "If you hadn't given her a chance with little Tara she would have been insulted."

Mary Kaye laughed. "Still, it was generous and kind."

"It was," Katie interjected, her eyes on John. "Kindness, it seems, runs in the family."

John briefly met her eyes with his own. The setting was awkward so John turned his attention to Kelly. "And how have you been?"

"I'm having a birthday party!" Kelly exclaimed.

"Really?" John joked as he tickled her under the chin. "No wonder that you're getting so heavy."

Kelly shrieked with laughter.

Phil was engrossed in a discussion with Katie's father and father-in-law. Mary Kaye recognized with surprise the spark in the brief eye contact of Katie and John.

"Can Franco and Anna come to my party?" Kelly asked.

"Sure they can." He glanced and grinned at Katie. "Just tell me when."

Katie flushed as John's eyes found hers.

"It's Sunday!" Kelly laughed.

"Okay Kelly, we'll be there."

John lowered Kelly to the floor where she went off after a flock of children running past in the large hall.

Mary Kaye looked from Katie to John. Smiling, she offered. "Kelly seems quite comfortable with you."

John caught the flash of the eye and the curve of the lip. He smiled. "Yes, we're buddies." he paused. "By the way Katie, doesn't Mary Kaye look wonderful after having Tara only six months ago?"

Katie nodded in agreement. "You do look great, Mary Kaye." She laughed. "After I had Kelly it took me forever to get back in shape." She hesitated, the joy reflected in her eyes oozing away into grief. "Marc said I was his Pillsbury dough girl."

John took Katie's hands. "Marc was a good man and a good friend." He paused. "It won't be long before the memories will be pleasant rather than painful."

Her eyes teared. "I know."

Amidst the noise and the food, John and Katie stood holding hands, remembering lost loves.

Mary Kaye saw the pain as her heart broke for them. She also realized that there was something special happening between them.

CHAPTER SEVENTEEN

"How are you going to play it, John?" John met Phil's question with a shrug. He rose and slowly paced the spacious office, head bowed in thought.

Their years together had taught Phil that John thought best when on his feet. The pacing confirmed that John was mentally stretching and exercising the options.

"Amalfi's troubled." John stated flatly. "It'll be tough to prepare him and get the story out clean."

"Troubled? Isn't that a bit of an understatement?" Phil asked somewhat incredulously.

John stopped and considered Phil. "I suppose."

Phil muttered, swallowed his sarcasm, then calmly suggested. "John, you really should settle this. If Amalfi melts down on the stand he takes three widows and six kids down with him."

The pacing resumed. "Settle for what?" He paused, anger flashing. "Bolton's offering twenty-five percent to Amalfi and the same to the women."

"Twenty-five percent is better than nothing!" An urgency permeated Phil's tone.

John stopped. A tiny curve of the lips followed. "You figure I'm going to lose, Phil?"

"Yes, John, I am." Then Phil's voice lowered. "I'm also afraid you're going to win."

"Phil . . ."

"No, John, listen to me, please. This trial is dangerous for you. Bolton's no dummy."

"True," John said thoughtfully, "but he's no fisherman, either."

There was a pregnant pause as they considered each other. Phil broke the silence. "He can hire one, John."

John stopped his pacing and met Phil's eyes. "Don't you think I know that? I worry constantly, but what am I to do?" He exhaled in exasperation. "If I settle for what's offered, how are the women going to take care of their families?" His gaze cut Phil. "Haven't they lost enough?"

Phil had no answer.

"They need me, Phil. I can't turn my back on them."

"You may be risking your career, John. Is it really worth it?"

John considered the question, he couldn't kid Phil, nor did he want to. "Did you meet Matt Alves, Phil?"

Phil nodded, but said nothing.

"I know what that boy is feeling." John paused and dropped his eyes. "There's no right anymore, Phil, only survival." He pounded his right fist into his left palm. Fire came to those intense blues, as he focused on his partner. "I hate the position I'm in, but I'll be damned if I'll let down Matt Alves or any of the other children."

"John, I understand, but . . ."

"Phil," John rode over Phil's objection with passion. "I grew up with Marc Morrissey. I knew Helen Picardi and Lorraine Alves. That bastard has done enough, I won't put myself, my ethics, before them."

Phil nodded in understanding. "That's why you wanted Mary Kaye to view the tape, isn't it?"

John nodded. "Mary Kaye is one of the brightest people I know."

"And she saw nothing," Phil completed the thought.

"That's right, Phil," John stated. Then, he sighed. "I'll understand if you want to end our partnership."

Phil considered John, waved off the statement with a flip of the hand, then headed on a new tack. "John, Amalfi was all over the place in his statement to the Coast Guard."

John acknowledged the point with a nod. "Sure he was. But remember, he had just lost his boat and his crew. That would rattle anyone." He paused. "And remember the head injury."

Phil sat back. "Does the head injury explain why he's gone off the deep end? My God, John, Rosalie Amalfi is convinced he's unstable."

John frowned.

Phil plowed ahead. "He didn't even show up for the memorial mass. 'He couldn't face it,' Rosalie said." Phil exhaled in frustration and studied his partner. "And don't believe for a moment that Jim Bolton isn't aware of Amalfi's disintegration. My God, he's become a damn skeleton."

"I know." John spoke in undertones. "I'm counting on Bolton focusing on what has happened to Amalfi and on Amalfi's past."

The partners sat in silence as they processed and re-processed their options. Finally Phil added, "and you have Judge Adams." Phil warned as he set a hard glare on his partner and friend. "Be careful there." He paused. Phil rose and walked to John. Placing a hand on his shoulder, he engaged John's eyes. "You have to settle."

* * *

John entered the courtroom of Judge Charles Adams. It was late afternoon and the room was already shadowed. With the lights out, John missed the presence of Jim Bolton seated in the gallery.

"Hi, John. How are you?"

With his eyes adjusted to the dimness of the room, John saw Bolton. The confident smile flashed. "So Jim, are you about ready to pay?"

Jim Bolton frowned and shifted uncomfortably. "It's a tough case, especially with the lost men" He conceded. "But John, the insurance company doesn't think Amalfi has given us the straight story."

'How ironic,' John thought. 'Amalfi lied, cheated and terrorized fishermen to guarantee victory for the insurance companies. Now when he has a claim they won't pay.'

"Come on, Jim," John protested, "three guys died." He filled his voice with contempt. "And of course there's that little thing called evidence."

James Bolton was a rarity in the world of insurance defense attorneys. Bolton was a tough, but fair, man. And unlike so many who represented insurance companies, Jim Bolton was a skilled litigator who would acknowledge the strengths of a plaintiff's case. When convinced of the merits of a claim, he would also recommend that the insurers offer that which he believed represented a fair settlement. Often, Bolton's assessment was significantly less than that of the plaintiff and his attorney, which forced the claim to trial. And more often, even his modest recommendations were ignored and overruled by insurance company representatives who cared little about justice.

"I know," he paused. "And that troubles me. Still, Amalfi has yet to give us a rational explanation of what happened."

John was concerned. Amalfi had told a story to the Coast Guard of feeling the boat rock and shudder, as if they hit something. Then very quickly it sank.

"He struck a submerged object," John responded casually. "Which would make it a covered loss."

"It would." Bolton agreed as he pondered. "He also said the boat sank so quickly he never saw the other men." He paused and eyed John. "John, we dove on the boat."

John nodded, troubled, but said nothing.

"For that boat to sink so fast the bottom would had to have been ripped out. You've seen the plans; you know how solidly it was built. And you've seen the film. We can't even see a hole or rip in the hull."

John sat back. He knew all of this. Intuitively, he had felt that something was indeed wrong. Then he thought of the women and he rallied.

"You know Jim," He began. "Amalfi had a head injury. God only knows how long he was out."

Jim Bolton acquiesced with a nod.

"And for the boat," John continued, "it settled on its keel, listing hard to port. If a plate opened and the fishhold filled, that boat would have sunk like a rock."

"Sure, but the film doesn't show any such opening."

John smiled and spread his hands. "The opening could be what the boat settled on."

Bolton smirked. "You're good, John. But let's be honest, Amalfi's a fiend. A man like that," He shrugged. "well, anything's possible."

"So what's your plan?" John asked, dead panned.

Bolton studied John. "I'm going after Amalfi. I'm going to let the jury see the real Joe Amalfi." He sat back and smiled. "I have the transcript of United States versus Dillon."

John's eyes enlarged slightly, showing surprise. In reality, John expected, even hoped this would be Bolton's direction.

For the first time, Bolton smiled. "It's pretty clear that the good Captain Amalfi fingered Peter Novello for the beating Dillon's flunkies administered."

John's eyes darkened, his face glowered in memory.

Bolton read John's face. "So, after the jury knows just what Amalfi is, maybe they won't buy all the coincidences necessary to sell your case."

"Judge Adams won't let all that crap in," John shot back. "Amalfi wasn't convicted of anything."

"Because he cooperated with the United States Attorney." Bolton said evenly.

"Maybe," John conceded.

"Come on, John," Jim Bolton challenged, "if it weren't for the three widows, you wouldn't even represent that slime bucket."

Saving John from having to respond, Mary Allen, trial court clerk to Judge Adams, emerged from a door set behind the judge's raised bench.

"Are counsel present?" she asked.

John rose. "Hi Mary. We're both here."

"Hello John." She nodded at Bolton. "Hello Mr. Bolton. The judge will see you now."

In chambers, John sat across the conference table from Bolton. At the table's head was Judge Charles Adams. Judge Adams, appeared younger than his fifty-six years. He eyed the lawyers with his usual detached demeanor.

"Gentlemen, are we ready for trial?"

Both attorneys nodded.

The Judge studied the two attorneys. "What is the status of settlement discussions?"

John spoke first. "Your Honor, the vessel was valued at $600,000.00 at the time it was lost. My client is prepared to accept the policy of $500,000.00 plus interest from the date of the loss." He took a deep breath. "And as for the families of the three men, I demand the full million dollars for each." He paused. "For an immediate settlement, they are prepared to waive the interest that is owed."

The judge nodded and turned to Bolton. "Have you made an offer?"

"I have," Jim Bolton stated. "We have offered $125,000.00 on the hull loss, as well as $250,000.00 to each of the three widows on the Protection and Indemnity policy."

Judge Adams straightened. His eyes showed surprise as he took in the attorneys. "Gentlemen, this is a troubling case. Three men dead and you are so very far apart." He paused. "Can I be of help in closing the gap?"

John felt his stomach muscles relax ever so slightly. He hadn't been aware just how stressed he was. For a moment he wished he wasn't involved in this case, with so many trap-doors. Then he thought of Matt Alves and he knew he would see it through.

Jim Bolton leaned forward in his seat. He removed his glasses and rubbed at the bridge of his nose, before replacing them. John read weariness in his eyes.

"Your Honor," Bolton began, "the insurer believes that it hasn't received the truth from Captain Amalfi."

"In what way?" The judge asked, eyes fixed on Bolton.

The defense attorney took a deep breath. A sheen of perspiration showed on his brow. "Our investigation, coupled with Captain Amalfi's reputation, convince my client that the vessel was intentionally sunk for the insurance proceeds."

The judge's eyes narrowed. "Sunk?" He paused, considering Bolton's words. "Three men died."

Bolton shrugged. "We assume that some tragic accident happened after the boat was scuttled." He exhaled. "We don't believe Captain Amalfi."

A silence settled on the conference as each man retreated into his own thoughts.

Judge Adams settled back in his chair. He eyed the attorneys. He noticed John's intensity with a note of surprise. In his previous encounters with John, in both motions and trials, Judge Adams had seen the passion and the empathy of John Palermo, but never in a pre-trial setting. 'Widows and children,' he thought. 'A heavy responsibility.' Still, something seemed amiss to the experienced jurist. "Very well, are there any issues to deal with prior to trial?"

"Yes, Your Honor," John offered.

"Mr. Bolton intends to offer evidence of testimony in the trial of United States versus Dillon to impeach Mr. Amalfi's credibility."

Judge Adams looked to Bolton.

Bolton nodded. "That's correct, Your Honor. Mr. Amalfi testified that he used his position of vessel owner and captain to bully his crew into committing perjury on the orders of the attorneys for the insurance company. Further, he identified a Gloucester fisherman for two men to assault and savagely beat." He paused. "As he participated in Federal obstruction of Justice, as well as felonious assault and battery, I believe that such activities are relevant on the character issues of credibility."

The Judge nodded as he recalled the trial that shook the defense bar of Boston to its core. He looked to Bolton. "Was Amalfi convicted of a felony?"

"He wasn't charged with any crime," John interjected. "In fact he cooperated with the United States Attorney in convicting Dillon."

"He was given immunity?" The Judge asked.

John nodded. "He was."

Judge Adams took in John. With a wizened nod and an appraising eye, he commented. "So now you, Mr. Palermo, are the advocate for the same Mr. Amalfi that you previously skewered. What was it five, six years ago?"

John eyed Judge Adams, then he shrugged. "One battle at a time." He grew serious. "Now I have three young widows, all about to lose their homes to foreclosure, and six children to attempt to guarantee a future for, as well as Mr. Amalfi."

"Indeed," the judge acknowledged. "Life is seldom tied in a simple package."

John leaned forward. "Your Honor, I would appreciate a ruling on this issue prior to trial."

"I agree." Jim Bolton chimed in.

The Judge nodded. "I'll take briefs by Thursday and we'll meet Friday afternoon at 4:30, for argument. I will rule from the bench." He paused and glanced at his clerk. "Is Monday still good for trial, Mary?"

The trial clerk nodded. "It is, Your Honor."

"Very well. We empanel and go forward on Monday, 9:00 a.m."

The lawyers scribbled on pads. When they looked up they saw the judge considering them. Then he leaned forward, elbows on the table. "Mr. Palermo, Mr. Bolton, it would seem that my ruling on Friday is of some importance."

John nodded in agreement as he glanced across at Bolton who also nodded.

"Mr. Bolton, you have the burden of proof here." He paused. "Mr. Palermo, your client has a very questionable past."

John readied to speak, but was shut down by the judge. "I don't want argument now. And as I have not as yet seen the law on the issue, I have no present opinion. Still, these next days would seem an appropriate time for both of you to consider a compromise settlement." He watched the lawyers eye each other and sighed. "Think about it, Gentlemen. See you Friday."

Once back in the courtroom, John turned to Bolton. "Will you increase your offer?"

Jim Bolton grew thoughtful. "John, the insurance company knows that Amalfi is breaking down. The big guys think we can win." He paused and reflected. "Quite honestly, so do I." He shrugged. "They won't increase the offer."

"Then I'll make them pay every penny," John responded testily.

Jim Bolton offered his hand. As they shook he suggested softly, "John, take what's on the table. You can't win this with Amalfi."

John watched Bolton leave. Bluster aside and forced to face the hard facts, he knew that his case was troubled.

CHAPTER EIGHTEEN

Friday night meetings were rare at the law office of Palermo & Harmon. John and Phil agreed that creativity was enhanced by exposure to the varied panoply of life. There is a maxim that law school sharpens, but narrows, the mind. Lawyers lost in their work and whose reading consisted only of legal publications and case reports constrict their ability to relate to others. Exposure to life, literature, theatre and the flow of society broaden an advocate. A side benefit of which was to make it easier to relate to juries. In fact, John believed that defense lawyers by the very nature of their work and billing demands had all creativity knocked out of them. It was one of the few advantages enjoyed by plaintiff attorneys. Nonetheless, on this Friday night there was an attorney's meeting at Palermo & Harmon.

John returned from court with a ruling, as promised, by Judge Adams. The judge ruled that Amalfi's testimony in the case of United States vs. Dillon would be admissible in the trial to begin on Monday next. It was a ruling that John expected. Another arrow in Bolton's quiver, but, perhaps an opportunity for John.

A pall hung over the conference room at Palermo & Harmon as John outlined the ever-narrowing options to the assembled attorneys and law clerks.

"The bottom line is that we start trial on Monday," John concluded.

Phil sat back, frustration in his eyes. "What about settlement?"

John shook his head. "Bolton told me that the insurance company won't increase the offers." He shrugged. "Actually, with this ruling, they've talked about withdrawing the offers on the table."

"Really?" Phil muttered as he gently drummed the conference table with his fingers. John recognized the habit and the faraway look in Phil's green eyes. Phil was sifting the options, so the room grew quiet.

Finally, Phil's gaze stiffened and fixed on John. "Perhaps it's time to recommend that our clients accept the offer."

The partners' eyes met as the Associate Attorneys watched in silence.

"Will they accept the offer?" Phil asked softly, "If you recommend it?"

John considered the question and his partner.

"If I recommend it," John replied thoughtfully. "I believe the widows would follow my recommendation." He paused. "Amalfi is another question. I don't think he would. And the insurance company is not interested in a partial settlement. If they have to pay for a defense, they want the opportunity to win."

Phil sighed. "So, we get ready."

"Absolutely," John agreed and turned to Larry Smith, his young associate attorney. "Larry, you'll try this with me."

"Okay, John, what's the plan?"

John smiled into the face of the eager young lawyer.

"I'll need a trial brief for the court and proposed jury instructions." He paused, thoughtful. "Also, call Peter Novello and check out his fishing schedule." He moved his eyes over the assembled group. "David, please work with Larry on the legal issues."

David Jordan, a second year law student who worked part-time as a law clerk, nodded. "I will."

John stood. "Okay, Larry and David, I'll see you at nine tomorrow."

*   *   *

Rosalie Amalfi opened the door on John's knock.

"How are you, John?" she said, surprised.

"I'm fine. Is the Captain in?"

"Yes, he's in the den."

John noticed dark shadows under Rosalie's eyes and a general haggard appearance.

"Are you okay, Rosalie?"

She smiled. "I'm tired, but otherwise fine."

"Aren't you sleeping?"

She shrugged. "It's tough. Joe wakes up screaming every night now. Sleep is impossible."

John nodded, concern showing in his eyes. "You need to take care of yourself."

She smiled, warmed by his concern. "Maybe when the trial is over." She stated hopefully. "Come on," Rosalie said. "I'll take you to him."

They walked across the marble foyer, past the circular stairway to the den with the commanding view of Gloucester Harbor.

Joe Amalfi stood at the bay window, binoculars in place, studying the harbor.

"Good evening, Captain."

Amalfi turned to face John. His face was drawn and blotched by lack of sleep. His body was rail thin and his skin looked unhealthy. But it was his eyes that drew John's attention. They were black, desperate, but cunning.

"Please sit down, John," Rosalie offered. "Can I pour you a drink?"

John smiled at Captain Amalfi. "Will you join me?"

Amalfi nodded and grunted, then sat opposite John.

Rosalie Amalfi poured each a glass of Amaretto and then quietly withdrew, closing the den door behind her.

John took in the fine wood paneling, the granite fireplace, and ten foot ceilings as he sipped his drink, rose and walked to the bay window. The harbor was ink black but alive with the light that reflected from vessels, fish plants and the Eastern Point lighthouse. "This is a beautiful view."

"Thank you."

He returned to his seat across from Amalfi. "It would be a shame to lose this."

Amalfi peered at him. "What do you mean?"

"Captain," John started. "If we lose your case the bank will take your house to satisfy the boat mortgage." He paused to let that statement sink in. Then added, "The widows will lose their homes as well."

Amalfi swallowed the rest of his drink, went to the bar and poured himself another, then turned to face John. "Why should we lose?"

John sat back, eyes on the diminutive Captain. "The insurance company challenges your version of the sinking. They think you sank the boat and something went wrong which lead to the men's death."

"That's crazy!" Amalfi exploded.

John nodded, as he watched the Captain intently. "I agree, but they feel you won't make a very good witness."

The Captain sipped his drink as he studied John over the glass.

John saw his eyes calculating a response and the facial twitch that appeared whenever he was stressed.

"I don't understand."

John watched Amalfi carefully. He wondered if the Captain could be patched up well enough to present effectively to the jury. Uncertain, he shrugged. "They have a copy of your testimony in the Dillon case."

Amalfi didn't react.

John continued, "It shows that you lied on the stand under oath and were part of the beating of Peter Novello."

Amalfi nodded, recognizing the danger. He looked down and frowned. "I see."

"Also," John went on. "They have been watching you and asking questions." He paused and waited for the Captain to raise his head and meet his eyes. "They know the problems you are having and how much weight you have lost." Softly, he said. "They're convinced that you will fall apart on the stand."

Amalfi swallowed the rest of his drink in a gulp. Then, studied John. "What do you think?"

"I'm not sure, Captain, maybe they're right. Maybe you will fall apart and beat yourself." He paused and studied Amalfi. "Maybe we should settle the case."

"No way," he snapped. "They owe me $500,000.00 not $125,000.00." Slowly he walked to the couch and sat facing John. John saw that Amalfi was calculating and appraising the risks. "Just tell me what to do," the Captain demanded.

John put his glass on the coffee table. "First of all you need to sleep. Do you have those pills the doctor prescribed for you?"

Amalfi nodded as he reached and opened a drawer set into the coffee table. He removed a prescription container and handed it to John.

John opened the cap and looked up at Amalfi, surprise registering on his face. "They're all here. You haven't taken any."

"I'm afraid of pills," Amalfi stated simply, as he returned the pills to the drawer.

John took him in. "Joe, the doctor prescribed them and you have to sleep."

"I know, but . . ."

"Second, you need to eat. At least two good meals a day. Trust me, you will need the energy."

Again Amalfi nodded.

"And be in my office Sunday morning at nine so we can begin preparation."

"I'll be there."

"Good," John said. He shook Amalfi's hand. "We have a tough fight ahead. Those women and children need you." Still holding his hand, his glare became hard. "Don't let them down."

*   *   *

Katie felt the absence of Marc poignantly on the holidays and special occasions. To compensate, she made an event of the important moments of Kelly's life. For her third birthday she invited Kelly's four grandparents, Marc's sister and brother with spouses and children. Also, Katie's sister Eileen, family friends and the children, with their parents, from Kelly's playgroup. The crowd of partiers overflowed her tidy house. John, with Franco and Anna, arrived to celebrate Kelly's big day on a blustery autumn Sunday.

Anna, dressed by her grandmother, wore a party dress, knit stockings, and patent leather shoes. Franco wore tan docker pants, a red polo shirt under a white cardigan sweater, and docksiders on his feet.

Katie greeted the Palermo children with an enthusiastic hug.

"You sure look pretty, Anna," she complimented as she held Anna's hands. "And your hair!" She gushed. "Did your Dad do your hair so pretty?"

"No," Anna beamed. "My Nonna fixed my hair." The little girl ran happy fingers over her auburn curls.

During the exchange, Franco raced off to join the fun as John watched the exuberant crowd of children, somewhat restrained by their party clothes, but bouncing about nonetheless.

Katie rose as Anna happily moved towards Kelly.

"Quite a crowd," John commented.

"You only turn three once," Katie responded with a laugh.

John saw the gleam in her eyes and smile on her face. His mind moved momentarily to the impending trial. He forced his thoughts back. "You look lovely, Katie," he offered. She wore her hair down on the shoulders of her party dress.

"Why thank you, sir," she replied. "Are you ready to go to work?" She teased. "Kelly said you should lead the games."

For a long moment they thought of Marc. "I'd love to," he acknowledged.

Dressed casually in jeans and a cream colored fisherman's knit sweater, John helped coordinate the games and cheered wildly when a blindfolded Franco smashed open the pinata with one wild swing of a baseball bat.

The party proceeded happily through pin-the-tail-on-the-donkey to John challenging all the children to a wrestling match. Katie's laugh came from the heart as ten children crawled over John like frisky puppies, before finally pinning his shoulders and declaring victory. In the spirit of the occasion, John rose and lifted Kelly to the ceiling, where beaming, she raised her arms in triumph.

Katie stayed busy filling the buffet table and tending to her adult guests while John rollicked with the children.

"He's having fun," Eileen commented to Katie as they heard John's laughter as the children worked as a team to win the wrestling match.

"As much fun as the kids, it appears," Katie said approvingly.

The sound of laughter was contagious and Katie and Eileen were swept up in the joy of the moment.

'Sweet music,' Katie thought of the children's full-hearted laughter. She noticed John's smile split his face from ear to ear as he lofted a victorious Kelly to the ceiling.

Katie grabbed the opportunity to cut the cake, calling all the children to the table.

John stood on the periphery of the crowd of adults as Katie and Eileen placed the children at the table. The two grandmothers gave out party hats and scooped ice cream into bowls for each of the children. John noted that the sadness in Mrs. Morrissey's eyes was in contrast to the smile on her lips. Again, he thought of Marc, glanced toward Katie and Kelly, and once more, vowed to win for them.

Eileen had the camera to photograph the cutting of the 'Minnie Mouse' cake. Happily, she posed photos of Kelly, and the children around the table.

John watched as Katie stood beside a delighted Kelly guiding her hand in the cutting of the cake. Franco and Anna had been placed on either side of Kelly. Just as Kelly, with Katie's help, was about to cut into the cake, Eileen urged Kelly to make a special wish. Kelly held the knife poised, her tiny hand inside Katie's, pressed her eyes closed and made her silent wish.

With every child and adult focused on the scene, Eileen slowly lowered the camera, turned to John and directed him to stand beside Katie. The room grew quiet as every eye rested on John. Caught by surprise, he glanced at Katie who flushed as the onlookers' eyes sought her.

Eileen broke the silence. "Kelly, do you want John in the picture with you?"

"Yes, yes," exclaimed an excited Kelly.

With a shrug, shake of the head and grin, John joined Katie behind Kelly. "You okay?" He asked Katie, softly.

"I'll kill her," Katie whispered, her cheeks still pink with embarrassment.

Eileen read Katie's eyes. While the awkwardness of the moment was lost on the children, it was very real to Katie and shocking to Marc's parents.

There was little else for John and Katie to do but smile for the camera and bear the eyes and smiles of the adults. Eileen focused the shot of Kelly cutting her Minnie Mouse birthday cake, eyes alight with wonder and joy, framed by John's children, John, and Katie.

John quickly moved away from the focus of the camera, returning to chat with guests and downplaying the meaning of the photograph by simply ignoring the suggestive smiles and quick glances.

A series of photographs were taken. Kelly with her grandparents, as a group, coupled and individually. Katie and Kelly alone, then numerous shots of Kelly with her friends.

Finally, Eileen stood with Katie behind Kelly as their mother snapped the photograph.

As they lined up for the shot, Eileen noted Katie's still red cheeks.

"Relax, Katie," she offered in a soft voice. "It was only a photograph."

"We'll discuss it later," whispered Katie, with an edge, as she fought the urge to pound her sister.

John had met with Joe Amalfi that morning, to prepare the Captain to testify. He and his team had worked all day Saturday and he wanted to sit with Katie and explain the plan of action for the days to come.

John waited for the last of the guests to leave. Marc's parents had moved from shock, at the suggestion behind the theatrically posed photograph, to dismay at the thought that Katie was moving on. There was no moving on for parents who have lost a child in the prime of life. Gwen Morrissey had spilled tears as she kissed her granddaughter goodbye. Mike Morrissey eyed John with suspicion and resignation.

When the last of the guests, save John and his children, had said their good-byes, smiled coyly at John and Katie and left the party ravaged house, John told Katie he needed to speak to her.

"Come on, we'll talk while we pick up," John said as he began to pick-up the living room.

Katie hesitated. It seemed too much like a husband helping his wife after a successful party. She didn't know how she felt about the silent announcement Eileen had made and was wary of John's motive for staying.

He saw the concern and smiled warmly. "I have to talk to you about the trial."

"Really!" she charged. "You could have called me later." She eyed John with suspicion. "Do you know what they all think between Eileen's little show and you staying behind?"

John saw that she was about to blow. And, as it was inevitable, he glanced at the three children playing on the living room floor amongst wrapping paper and gifts, picked up some plates. "Let's take this into the kitchen," he suggested in a calm voice.

Katie followed him with anger building. In the kitchen with the door closed behind them she snapped. "I won't be manipulated like this." Her eyes spat fury into John's innocent expression.

"Katie," he said softly.

"Save it for the jury," She raged. "Because I'm not buying."

"Would you please listen?" He asked, soothingly.

"Did you see my mother-in-law?" She demanded. "She deserved better."

John nodded with a troubled look in his eyes. "Yes, I did." He recalled Gwen's tears. "Do you really think I put Eileen up to that?"

"No, I don't," she conceded. "Eileen is more than capable of causing trouble on her own."

"So," he shrugged.

"Oh, no." She shot back. "You staying behind like this confirms what they believe." She fixed him with a glare. "You took advantage!" She declared, pointing an accusing finger. "And now you're playing Mr. Innocence."

John put on a weak smile. "I see your point. I guess I could have used better judgment."

Katie stood stock still, holding firmly to her anger.

Her gaze, hard and penetrating, bore into him.

"And, why pretend something's happening between us?" She paused, temper flaring. "When you've been seeing that woman."

John rocked back on his heels, understanding dawning. With an easy smile and a shake of the head, John studied Katie. "Is this about us, Katie?"

Katie hadn't cooled. His smile further inflamed her. "There is no us." She spat the words.

"I see," John responded with an edge to his voice. Fighting for calm, he stated. "Now that I am here, please allow me to lay out the plan for you." He paused and fixed her with his intense blue eyes. "You know, whether you hate me or not I'm still your lawyer and we start trial tomorrow."

The hardness disappeared from her eyes and was replaced with concern. "John," she said quietly. "I don't hate you. If I gave . . ."

He cut her off. "Sometimes, things just can't work." He paused. "Katie, you're still carrying Marc inside your heart. And maybe I'm not past all the pain of the last year with Connie and everything since. So let's leave it alone and concentrate on tomorrow. Is that okay with you?"

She nodded uncertainly.

John then laid out the plan for the trial ahead.

CHAPTER NINETEEN

Trial: Day One

There is a majesty to the law. For John, that majesty resides in the trial courts, in the pit before a jury, rather than the lofty plateau of the Courts of Appeal and Supreme Courts.

Judges aspire to sit on State Supreme Courts and Federal Circuit Courts of Appeal, where they can shape social policy, unsoiled by the press of human beings seeking justice. He believed that only in the trial courts, where disputes were settled by a jury of one's peers, did any hope of justice reside.

His years of practice had convinced him that the judicial system was as imperfect as the people who preside over it. John had witnessed judges who had ignored their constitutional limitations and responsibilities to create personal legacies, for no reason beyond feeding their already inflated egos. John recognized these actions as a threat to the democratic process. He placed his faith in juries, recognizing that the adversarial format of a jury trial was the best guarantor of justice for his clients.

On this cold and windy November day, fourteen months since the date of the loss of the *F/V Mio Mondo*, three widows and six orphans, along with a boat owner, brought their claims for justice to a jury of their peers.

John, as was his habit, was the first one in the courtroom. As Larry Smith quietly laid out the file on the plaintiff's table for easy access, John paced before the empty jury box, alone with his thoughts, readying himself for the battle ahead.

By 8:30 a.m., all counsel were present. In the gallery, Joe Amalfi sat with Rosalie. He wore a double-breasted blue suit over a white shirt and striped tie. John saw that the suit hung on him and that his face was blotched with fatigue, with dark bags below the eyes. As always, Rosalie Amalfi, who sat with Joe, presented herself with dignity in her gray suit, simple gold earrings and a small gold crucifix at her throat. John read the distress in her eyes.

Moments later, Katie entered with Lorraine Alves and Helen Picardi. The strain showed on their faces as they took their places side by side in the gallery. John took a long look as he felt the burden of responsibility. So often, he thought, his trials were about money. This trial was so much more, this trial was about the survival of the three women and their children.

For a brief second, Katie's eyes met John's. In those warm blue eyes, he saw her hope and her fear. He also saw trust. At the moment, that trust weighed heavily on his heart.

Jury selection went quickly. The attorneys accepted that sympathy for the families of the dead crew would be a given. They also knew that contempt for Captain Amalfi was just as certain.

John decided that he liked the looks of the jury panel. In Federal Court, civil juries consist of six jurors and two alternates. Throughout the trial and arguments, the eight stand equal. At the conclusion of all evidence and after final arguments and the court's instructions, two of the eight, selected at random, would be deemed as alternates.

The jury was a mix of blue and white collar workers and evenly split with four men and four women. While predominantly white, a black man and a Hispanic woman sat on the panel.

In juror seat number four sat Linda Noble. Linda, a buxom blond with soft brown eyes, had done everything she could to avoid being trapped on a jury. The twenty-five year old aerobics instructor had taken her business degree and some family seed money to buy a small percentage of a growing health club. Her income depended on maximizing the club's profits. Having to pay a substitute overtime wages to fill her twelve weekly hours of group lessons as well as her six hours of private body sculpting lessened that profit. The sharp, young entrepreneur was more than a bit frustrated with anything or anybody that slowed her rise to the top. This trial was a considerable annoyance.

Yet, she had to admit, she was still woman enough to appreciate the striking athletic form of the raven-haired, blue eyed plaintiff's attorney. His fitted suit and tasteful tie complimented a body used to rigorous conditioning. 'Baseball or tennis,' she thought. The lean, hard body and graceful movements bespoke the agility and athleticism of the two sports that required the rare combination of superior hand-eye coordination and sharp reflexes. Linda smiled to herself at the thought of what other body movements John had mastered. Perhaps, a few days of performing her civic duty wouldn't be so difficult to swallow.

Len Harris, seated in the second row of jurors in seat seven, was the sole black person in the room. That was hardly unusual for the driven, talented, forty-year old architect. Leonard Archibald Harris had defied stereotypes all his life. In doing so, he had entered many a room after prying open many a door thought closed to those of his color and background. Len had grown up on the mean streets of Roxbury, where gang membership or superior athletic skills were the ticket to the kind of respect that allowed a young man to walk the streets safely. Len Harris was no athlete, nor did he need or accept the substitute family of a street gang. Len was blessed with a keen mind and a mother that imbued in him a belief that he could be and do anything he was willing to work for.

When he had lamented as a young teen that 'whitey would always stand in his way,' he was shocked by the sharp slap across his face, the finger pointing at him from his diminutive, but fired-up, mother. "Don't you dare whine to me and make excuses for failing." He remembered her voice rose. "A man doesn't let anybody deny him his rightful place." Her eyes were beads of intensity. "You be better than the others," she demanded. "You work harder and longer than those pampered boys. Demand what you've earned." She paused and with fire in her eyes, she warned, "But make sure you've earned what you demand."

Her words and her belief in him had always been his beacon. And today, the slight, wiry, and energetic architect, with specks of silver in his thinning black hair, was the senior associate at Boston's most prestigious and fastest growing architectural firm.

When he completed the latest project, a sixty story, superbly elegant office and posh apartment building, in the historical district, on time and below budget, he was slated to be the youngest and the only black partner in the firm's history. Len Harris knew life wasn't about excuses. Mama Harris had taught him that lesson. Still, he wished he was on the jobsite urging the workers on, coordinating the sub-contractors, and dealing with the daily crises that went with the job. As there was nothing else he could do, he decided to lead this jury.

He studied the faces and body language of the lawyers and those in the gallery. Len read the tenseness along with the plaintiff lawyers' intensity. The defense attorney displayed a cool detachment. The pressure was on the plaintiff, Len concluded. By the hopeful way in which the three women seated together in the gallery watched his every move, Len guessed that this trial was crucial to them.

Once the jury was seated and the balance of the jury pool excused, Judge Adams turned his tall and lean frame to face the nervous jurors. He began by welcoming them to his courtroom.

"Today, and for the days to come, you sit as judges of the facts, just as I sit as judge of the law." Without taking his eyes from the jury, he raised his right hand and arm and indicated the lawyers and claimants seated before him. "These people, with their lawyers, will present evidence in the way of documents and testimony to persuade you to accept their views of the evidence." He threw a glance at the lawyers. "I can tell you from experience that both sides are well represented. I suggest that you come to no conclusions until you have heard all the evidence, received all the exhibits, heard final arguments from the attorneys and been instructed on the law by me."

Judge Adams sat back and took in the overwhelmed expressions on the faces of the jurors. He offered a thin smile. "Don't worry, it's not all that bad." He won relieved smiles from the jurors.

"Just sit back and let your common sense help you determine who to believe and disbelieve. I will help with rulings on evidence and my instructions will serve as a guide through which to view the evidence."

The judge shifted his seat to face the courtroom and lawyers. "Mr. Palermo, are you ready to make your opening statement?"

"I am, Your Honor."

John rose and walked to the jury box. Technically, he, as the plaintiff, had the burden of proof. But in this case his burden was to prove the date of the vessel's loss and that a policy of insurance was in place. These issues had been stipulated to. What was left was to prove the cause of the sinking was a named peril in the policy. Once that was established, the burden of proving that the sinking was not a loss covered by the insurance policy fell to the insurance company.

John still had the burden of proving the damages that his clients had suffered. This meant that each of the widows would take the stand and tell her story. It was sad, John thought, that these three women would, again, relive the horror of their loss. Yet, it would capture the jury's sympathy and give John the possibility of winning large awards, verdicts well above the policy limits. John Palermo was not above using every device in his arsenal and at his disposal to win. An added bonus was that excess judgments would pressure the insurer to pay at least the policy limits, rather than appeal with the resulting delays, allowing his clients to keep their homes. He took a deep breath and felt the tremor in his gut that went with the responsibility he carried.

John waited as each juror fidgeted in their seats. As they settled comfortably re-directing their attention from Judge Adams to the tall, handsome lawyer standing before them, he studied each face.

Two rows of four people, each with eyes riveted on John.

In the gallery sat Rosalie and Joe Amalfi. In the row behind them and seated together were the three widows. John saw the tension in their eyes. Lorraine Alves twisted the handle of her purse. Helen Picardi stared straight ahead and Katie managed a small smile of encouragement.

"Good morning," John began in a relaxed, easy manner. He used no podium or notes, nothing to get between him and the jury. He focused only on the jurors, looking them directly in the eyes. His smile was different for each. Suggestive, even playful for the two young women; confident and assured for the men.

He began by thanking the jurors on behalf of his clients, his associate and himself. Then he grew serious. "Last September fourth, the fishing vessel *Mio Mondo*, while cruising home to Gloucester, struck a submerged object, rapidly filled with water and sank to the ocean bottom." He paused. "The captain of the vessel and representative of the Boat Mio Mondo, Inc., fell and struck his head and was rendered unconscious." His lips became a hard line as his eyes reflected pain. "In the gallery seated in the second row are the three widows of the men who died that day."

The jurors looked to the gallery; shock, horror and sympathy for the three young women showed on their faces and in their eyes. "Three young men with young wives and between them five children." He dropped his eyes, shook his head. "A sixth child was born six months after his father's death."

Jim Bolton squirmed in his chair. He managed to keep his face neutral while his eyes raged.

Lorraine Alves began to sob quietly. Helen Picardi and Katie sat still with pooled eyes.

"Captain Amalfi recovered consciousness when a wave washed over the deck where he laid. Recognizing the danger, he ran to the pilothouse to send an emergency Mayday."

John stilled in the hushed courtroom. Softly, he continued. "He barely had time to climb into the self-inflatable life raft as the boat and the three man crew disappeared below the waves."

The jurors glanced to the gallery as the full impact of John's words hit them. "He has lived with the horror of that day since. The three young widows face life without their husbands and without the fathers of their children."

John scanned their eyes, pounded his right fist into his left hand and exclaimed. "And the American Marine Insurance Company has refused to pay the captain for the loss of his boat nor the widows for the loss of their mates."

"Objection!" shouted Jim Bolton. "May we approach, Your Honor?"

John's eyes flashed anger at the interruption.

"You may," Judge Adams said.

At side bar Jim Bolton cut to the chase. "I move for a mistrial." His words rolled out. "This trial is not about sympathy, but truth. Mr. Palermo has prejudiced the jury with this blatant and improper play for sympathy."

Judge Adams studied Bolton. He turned to John. "Mr. Palermo?"

John didn't hold back. "This is a trial to determine coverage and damages for the vessel owner and three widows." He paused. "When an insurance company refuses to live up to its obligations, it may be a legal game or posturing for them and their lawyers, but real people are affected."

He grew angry. "This objection is out of order and it has interrupted my opening. I expect the court to tell that to the jury."

"Calm down Mr. Palermo," the judge responded, a small smile played at his lips.

"Mr. Bolton, your motion is denied." He glanced at John. "I don't think an instruction to the jury is needed at this time. Please continue."

Bolton wasn't surprised that John had placed the full scope of the hardship wrought by the insurer before the jury. This was not a dry technical issue of whether a word in a contract meant this or that. This was the future of eleven people. Nine of whom have lost a husband or a father. Still, he would fight John's play for sympathy at every turn. He too, intended to win.

Katie saw the anger that flashed in John's eyes, just as she had seen the charm when he wooed the jury. She wondered how the jurors could possibly resist his passion mixed with his striking good looks. As John moved from side bar to the jury box to resume his opening statement their eyes sought and momentarily found each other.

Back before the jury, John poured it on. He pointed in the direction of the gallery. "Seated in the gallery are five people, Captain Amalfi and his wife Rosalie who have lived with the horror of that day, the loss of his boat and his crew, every day and night for these fourteen months. And also seated in the gallery are Helen Picardi, Lorraine Alves and Katarina Morrissey, three young widows and mothers who are forced to face life without their husbands and the fathers of their children." He paused. "Those five people and the six children involved also share another reality. That reality is foreclosure on their homes." With that John glanced back at Bolton. The defense attorney met his glare evenly. John's eyes dripped contempt. "That's right, ladies and gentlemen, when Mr. Bolton stands before you he will tell you of the hesitance of the American Marine Insurance Company to pay a loss to the undeserving." John nodded his head briskly. "And believe me, James Bolton is a good, highly paid lawyer who helps insurance companies cheat decent people every day."

Bolton slowly rose. "Objection Your Honor, this personal attack on me is unfair and irrelevant."

Judge Adams flared. "I agree." He faced John. In a stern tone he ordered. "Mr. Palermo, you will stick to the expected evidence." He paused, set hard eyes on John.

John stood tall and met the judge's eyes evenly.

The jurors watched the non-verbal exchange with fascination.

Finally, the judge nodded. "Continue with your openning, Mr. Palermo."

"Very well, Your Honor," John said with a shrug. Again facing the jury John stated drolly, "I expect Mr. Bolton to suggest that something was

---

amiss in the sinking of the *Mio Mondo*." He shook his head as he continued. "He will argue that the boat sank too fast. That the clouded, grainy and unclear video of the *Mio Mondo* on the ocean floor doesn't show missing steel plates from its hull." He paused for effect. "But, he won't be able to explain how he or his experts could possibly see the portion of the hull that settled into the soft ocean bottom."

He smiled sadly and shook his head. "Mr. Bolton will then attack Captain Amalfi. He'll claim that the Captain has been inconsistent in his account of what happened." John smirked and shook his head. "Mr. Bolton is unlikely to remind you of Captain Amalfi's head injury that rendered him unconscious on the deck of the sinking boat." His voice was powerful. "Or of Joe Amalfi's horror and panic at the loss of his crew as his boat disappeared while his head poured blood and he sat weakened, in terror and utterly alone in the raft."

Katie watched John closely. His argument was inspired and persuasive. Above all of that, it was delivered with passion and from the heart. He seemed in his element connecting with the jurors, animated and totally believable.

"What Mr. Bolton will not show you is evidence." John paused. "Make no mistake, he will attempt to impugn Captain Amalfi's character." He emitted a sarcastic laugh. "Heck, if he could get away with it, he would attempt to blemish the memories of the three fine men who died that day." He paused and looked to the gallery, engaged the eyes of the three widows. "And they were fine men."

He turned back to the jury.

"Mr. Bolton's client, the American Marine Insurance Company has the burden to prove that the loss of the *Mio Mondo* was not a covered loss under the policy. I ask you to remember three things." He paused and scanned the faces before him. "First, the insurance company took Captain Amalfi's money for years. Second, three good men died on that awful day. And third, evidence, not speculation, is required to carry the burden of proof." He smiled. "Thank you." With a glance back at the gallery he sat.

Judge Adams looked to Bolton. "Mr. Bolton will you be making an opening statement?"

"Yes, Your Honor," he responded as he rose to his feet. "But as it is approaching one o'clock, I request that I be permitted to present my opening statement in the morning."

John rose to object but before he spoke the Judge shook his head at John and agreed to Bolton's request.

When the jury departed John walked past Bolton to the gallery and his clients. "So it begins." He smiled. He focused on Amalfi. "Are you ready?"

The Captain nodded.

"Good, tomorrow he will make his opening statement and then I put you on the stand."

Amalfi shifted nervously. John saw the twitch in his cheek and the fear in his eyes.

Helen Picardi dabbed at her eyes with a tissue. "Thank you, John. You were wonderful."

Lorraine Alves nodded agreement. She glanced over at Bolton who was packing his briefcase and conversing with his associate. "I think you make him nervous."

John shrugged. "He's a pro. Now that the judge gave him all day to dream up a response to my opening, you can expect fireworks tomorrow." John's eyes found Amalfi's. "But we'll be ready, won't we Captain?"

Amalfi nodded nervously.

John turned his attention back to the ladies. "Shall we head home?" He turned and moved back to the plaintiff's table.

As he passed Bolton, the older and experienced attorney put his hand on John's sleeve.

John turned and looked down at the seated defense attorney.

"Good opening, John." He paused and peered at John through his glasses. "I plan on speaking to my client about increasing our offer."

"Okay," John responded evenly.

Bolton studied him closely. "What will it take, John?"

"Jim, my demand hasn't changed. I want the policy limits." He paused. "I may be willing to waive interest."

Bolton shook his head. "You'll have to do better than that."

"No can do, Jim," John said simply. "If you make an offer, I'll convey it to my clients. If not," John shrugged, "I'll see you tomorrow."

Katie stayed behind as Helen and Lorraine left the courtroom. She watched the exchange between the lawyers from the gallery. Then, when John moved to plaintiff's table and Bolton had risen and left defense table with his associate, she nervously walked through the polished maple bar that enclosed the lawyer's area and walked past the now deserted defense table to where John and Larry Smith stood collecting the file. She noted that plaintiff's table butted up against the raised platform where the trial clerk sat. Raised a full three steps was the judge's bench which loomed over the trial area, or pit, as John called it.

She tapped John on the shoulder. John turned and smiled. "Katie, aren't you going with Lorraine and Helen?"

"Yes, I am," she flushed. "I was wondering if I could speak to you."

The bags packed, Larry Smith hefted both, leaving only John's briefcase on the table. "I'll wait by the elevator bank."

John nodded. "Thanks, Larry." When the doors swung closed John and Katie stood alone in the still courtroom, John sat back on the table and smiled encouragingly at Katie. "I'm all yours."

"I wanted to tell you that I think you were wonderful this morning." She hesitated, dropping her eyes from his.

He moved his hand to her chin and gently raised her face so he could see her eyes. "Thank you," he responded. And he waited.

She fumbled for words, as her cheeks blushed pink. "I also wanted to apologize about yesterday." Her eyes filled. "I didn't want it to end like that." She took a deep breath. "I don't hate you John. I . . . I'm so confused about you. I don't know what to think."

He smiled softly. "How you feel is the real issue, I believe."

She looked beseechingly into his eyes. "I have to go, Lorraine and Helen are waiting for me."

"Of course," he agreed.

She cleared her throat. "Would you like to come to dinner tonight, just you and me? We could talk then."

"Absolutely," he said, eyes gleaming. "Should I bring red or white?"

She saw the look in his eyes and felt a quiver of anticipation, excitement and nerves.

CHAPTER TWENTY

John spent the afternoon preparing Joe Amalfi for his testimony to begin the next trial day. First, he walked him through the direct examination, question by question, that John would ask. Then, he became Jim Bolton and grilled him on the events of that fateful day. The assault on the Captain's character was thorough. Few people knew Joe Amalfi as well as John. When he moved into the areas of the criminal prosecution of Charles Dillon and Amalfi's role in the felony assault on Peter Novello, he found an old anger bubbling to the surface.

Amalfi, initially, didn't react well to the cross-examination. With work and direction from John, he improved. Still, when he left, John was unsure if he would be believable to the jury. John knew that if the jury found Amalfi not credible, the entire case would be in trouble.

John watched Amalfi leave with distaste.

"He didn't do very well," commented Larry Smith.

"No, he didn't," John agreed. "Tomorrow, hopefully, he'll be better."

The young lawyer eyed John. "Are you okay?"

John sat back. "I detest that man," he stated with emphasis. "When I think of what he has done," he shook his head, not completing the thought.

"What he did to Peter Novello was awful," Larry agreed.

John rose. "Larry, I need to run this anger out of me. I'll see you tomorrow at six."

"Okay, John, I'll be here."

John ran the Magnolia shore, burning with anger. His eyes teared at the cutting wind as he watched the angry surf pounding the rocky shore.

Cold spray chilled him, but the run had the desired effect. When he returned home and stood under the hot shower he could feel the anger draining out of his system. Now, he was ready to see Franco and Anna.

* * *

Katie was happy that John had agreed to come to dinner. She was embarrassed by her outburst following Kelly's party. On cooler reflection she recognized that John had done nothing to warrant her reaction. And, mentioning the woman he was seeing was way out of line. Where had that come from? John was a young, handsome and lonely man. Why shouldn't he date?

While she had mixed emotions about John, she valued his friendship. And, she had to admit, was flattered by his interest. But, was she ready for this?

She shrugged and smiled as she looked at herself in the mirror.

It had been a long time since Katie dressed for a man. The effort to pick the right dress and jewelry was somehow joyous. The anticipation and nervousness had butterflies flittering in her stomach at the evening ahead. She felt invigorated and wary as she carefully and sparingly applied her make-up.

When she opened the door on John's knock, he saw she had spent her time well. She wore a soft blue dress, which matched the color of her eyes. The material fell on her curves and to the shape of her body. It revealed her long, graceful legs but was modestly cut, to cover and tantalize. At her neck and ears she wore gold, colored with the flame of the ruby, which glistened in a sea of her red-fired, lustrous blond hair. She looked back at him with amused eyes, pleased that she still could draw that hunger in the eyes of the male animal and aware of its danger.

"Hi John, you're right on time." 'And he is,' she thought, although she had given him no specific time.

Her words broke the trance and he returned her smile. "Katie, you look wonderful."

"Thank you," she said, enjoying the compliment that had been expressed by his eyes and his words. "Please come in."

He entered, wine bottle in hand. "I brought a Chianti, I hope it's okay."

She grinned. "It's perfect. Please sit down."

John crossed to the couch in the tidy living room. He wore a blue blazer and gray pants with a scroll tie over a pinstriped shirt. With tasseled loafers, he exuded a casual elegance. His sharp blue eyes sparkled and a ready smile played at his lips. He felt and looked totally comfortable.

"Something smells good," he offered.

"Thank you. I took a shot at Italian. I hope you like it." She paused. "Would you like a drink?"

"A beer would be great," he responded. "And I have no doubt the meal will be wonderful."

John watched her as she walked to the kitchen. She returned with his beer in a frosted mug. For herself, she had a glass of Chardonnay. He knew she was beautiful, but tonight every movement seemed to highlight a different curve or slope of her exquisite body.

"I hope this was a good night for you." She hesitated, uncertainty played at her eyes. "I know with the trial you're so busy and with Franco and Anna. Still . . ." Her lip trembled and she looked so vulnerable and so desirable. "I felt awful about yesterday. I over-reacted." She paused. "I'm sorry, John."

He took her wineglass from her hand and placed it on the coffee table. Gently he guided her onto the couch and moved beside her, taking her hands in his. Seated side by side, their knees touched and their hearts raced. "Katie, this is a great night for dinner." He smiled. "The best night." He grew silent and studied her face as his thumbs softly caressed her hands. When their eyes met he continued. "I'm all prepared for the trial, and as for Franco and Anna, they had dinner while we chatted and they're tucked in at Ma Amico's and asleep." He explained. "That's the reason I arrived when I did. Now they're settled with Ma Amico."

She nodded and dropped her eyes.

John studied her and then raised her hands to his lips. When he brushed his lips over her knuckles she felt a quiver of desire and raised her startled eyes to his. She saw his eyes spark and she flushed.

"By the way," he offered, "Anna mentioned you at dinner tonight."

"Really!" she tried to keep her voice steady. It was anything but steady that she felt.

"Uh, huh." He again gently brushed her skin with his lips. "She wondered why you were mad at me."

Her eyes narrowed. "Where did she get that idea?"

He smiled. "Fascinating, that's the same question I asked." He drew it out, again kissing her hands and then he rose to his feet pulling her with him.

She stood facing him, head tilted back to look into his eyes, lips slightly parted and inches away from his.

Katie had lost the focus of the conversation in the moment, regained it and asked unsteadily, "what did she say?"

He grinned. "She told me that yesterday when she was playing with Kelly and Franco she heard you yelling at me."

"Oh." Embarrassed, she closed her eyes. "Was I that loud?"

He moved fractionally and put his lips on hers.

Her eyes flew open in surprise, then closed in pleasure as a sigh escaped her throat.

John pulled back and their eyes met. "I've wondered how you would taste."

"Have you?" she smiled.

"Yes," he paused. "You did say something about dinner, didn't you?"

"I did," she laughed as she put her hands on his face. "Well?"

He pretended not to understand. "Well, what?"

Her cheeks flushed. "Was it okay?"

He laughed. "It was wonderful and you were that loud."

They laughed and separated. She took his hand and led him to the kitchen.

"Would you uncork the wine?" she asked.

The kitchen table was set with a red checkered tablecloth. Candles had been placed in two stout basket covered Chianti bottles. Katie dimmed the lights and lit the candles while John uncorked and poured wine for Katie and himself.

He sat and watched her move by candlelight. From the stove she filled a bowl with plump ricotta-filled ravioli. Then she piled a platter with meatballs, pork sausage, and brascioli.

As she worked, he watched her in profile. He smiled when the steam from the boiling water, in which she had cooked the ravioli, caused her to flinch back. Her movements were efficient, but so feminine. And, he thought of how much he had missed being with a woman who could generate both desire and affection.

She moved to the table, placing the bowl of ravioli and platter of meat down gently. Then, she moved to the oven and removed a freshly baked Italian bread. It all smelled and looked delicious. Still, nothing looked as good as Katie, nor could anything taste better.

John thought of all the effort Katie had expended on the meal and in making herself so desirable. All for him, he thought. Somehow, it was humbling.

"It smells wonderful," he assured her.

"I hope it's okay," she said as she filled his plate. He heard the anxiety of a dedicated cook in her voice.

He waited for her to fill her plate and settle across from him.

He raised his glass in toast and looked into her eyes. "May we know justice to equal our pain and love beyond all boundaries."

She smiled softly. "Amen," was all she said.

Over dinner they shared stories of their youth. It was the first time since Marc's death that Katie could reminisce on their life together. There were tears, but there was laughter. John told her stories of some of the trouble Peter Novello, Marc and he had found and some they avoided. They drank the wine, with dinner, then had coffee with Katie's homemade strawberry shortcake.

"Did Marc ever tell you about the time the three of us went up to the pits in Lanesville to swim?" John asked with a gleam in his eye.

"No," Katie said, sensing that this would be an amusing tale and smiling in anticipation.

"Remember now, we're city kids. We grew up on the docks, swimming in the harbor."

She nodded, smile fixed.

"Well," John continued. "Peter told us about these old granite quarries in Lanesville with clear, cool, fresh water."

"Peter, huh?" Katie asked, her sparkling blue eyes alight.

John sat back and laughed. "Nobody could get us into trouble or a fight faster than Peter." The memory was sweet.

"Anyway, we were fifteen, so we hitched a ride and arrived at the quarry in the heat of the afternoon. Everywhere we looked there were clothes on bushes and rocks. When we looked around," he chuckled, "we were three surprised city kids to find out that everyone swam naked."

Katie shrugged, puzzled, she said, "You guys were in high school, you were used to showering with . . ." Then it hit her and her smile bloomed. "Was some of that clothing," she laughed, "shall we say, ladies' wear?"

"You bet," he grinned across the table. "The sight before us was," he laughed, "a revelation."

Katie shook her head, thinking about how shy Marc had been.

"How did Marc react?" she asked, grinning.

John raised his brow. "About what you'd expect."

They laughed together.

"Let's just say we didn't have the control of some of the older guys."

The laughing turned riotous as Katie imagined the scene.

Then John added, "Peter said it best." John paused. "Yes, Peter said, 'Now I know what heaven is.'"

Katie laughed until tears ran down her cheeks.

When they moved back into the living room, John lit a fire and they settled on the couch. The conversation turned to more serious matters. In a move that seemed natural, John pulled Katie close. Katie nestled under his arm as she fought guilt and the sense that she was betraying Marc. John had vowed to himself that he would not rush her. Far from certain that the spark they felt would grow into love, he would not bring added pain to a dear friend's wife.

It was almost midnight when the fire flickered down and John rose to leave. Katie walked him to the door, her hand inside his.

They stood facing each other. John smiled softly as he read Katie's eyes. He saw confusion and perhaps fear. His body raced but it was with a gentle hand that he touched her face.

"Thank you," she said.

"For what?" John asked, eyes fixed on her.

"For being a good friend." She began thoughtfully. "For fighting for us." She paused. "And, for being patient with me." She took his hands.

He smiled on her. "Don't be afraid to call me and talk about Marc, your feelings, anything, okay?"

She nodded.

"Before I leave," he added, "I want you to know that seeing you tonight and holding back may have been one of the most difficult things I ever did."

She laughed and kissed his cheek. "Poor baby."

"Will you think about me tonight?" he asked.

She grinned. "Maybe."

"Well, I'll think about you" he assured her.

"I hope so," she whispered. And was surprised that she meant it.

John hesitated as his breathing thickened. He could feel his heart pound as he battled his needs, his wants. Her lips were but inches away, but, he knew a kiss wouldn't sate him. He took a deep breath as he squeezed her hands. "I'll see you tomorrow," he offered with a smile. Then, he released her hands, again touched her face and walked out the door to his car.

Katie smiled and hummed happily as she cleaned up.

CHAPTER TWENTY-ONE

Trial: Day Two

James Bolton used reason as John had used passion.

As he stood before the jury, he saw the distrust in their eyes and knew that John's play at sympathy had struck a chord. Still, the experienced fifty-two year old litigator realized that jurors can be reached on multiple levels. The widows and orphans were John's best card. Passion and empathy for their plight, his best thrust. So, just as John played on their hearts, Jim Bolton would appeal to their minds and sense of fairness.

With an understanding smile, the defense attorney approached the jury box. His thinning hair was running to white and his clear compelling eyes were softened by the glasses he wore. He opened his presentation by thanking the jurors for their time and efforts on behalf of justice.

He grew serious. "Yesterday, Mr. Palermo told you of the unfortunate plight of three women and six children. And, I realize it is difficult to remove their pain from your thoughts." He nodded with his eyes showing compassion. "So I won't ask you to separate their pain from your consideration." He paused. "Rather, I'll ask you to consider the evidence." He smiled. "Yes, the evidence we will offer to show that the vessel did not sink as Captain Amalfi claims." He scanned their faces. The jury appeared, on the whole, more neutral, open to the facts. A jury that was open, even and objective was the best he could hope for. He adjusted his eye glasses, offered a smile and continued.

"The judge will explain that both parties have burdens in this case. Captain Amalfi must show that the sinking was caused by a peril named in the policy of insurance." The jurors' eyes told him that they understood. "And if you believe his story that the vessel struck a submerged object that caused a steel plate to open and the boat to flood and sink, that would indeed be a covered loss." He paused and fixed his gaze on them. "But that is not what we believe the evidence will show." Bolton dropped his eyes, then re-focused them on the jury. "You will see a video-tape of the boat *Mio Mondo* on the ocean floor. You will see the video-tape due to the use of a submersible as the boat is far too deep for a diver." He paused and pointed his index finger at the jury. "That alone is suspicious," he paused. "As the area is not a fishing ground nor is it in direct line to port from any known fishing area."

Bolton watched as a juror flashed a glance at Amalfi. Then he added, "However, it is a good spot to sink a boat to prevent anyone from ever seeing it again." He paused. "Unless, of course, men die and a need arises to determine what really happened!"

He let the meaning of that settle. Then he continued, "We will demonstrate for you that Captain Amalfi has in the past participated in criminal acts to prevent the truth from being spoken." His voice rose. "We will show you that Joseph Amalfi has committed perjury . . . that is, he has lied under oath!" He pounded his right fist into his left palm. "He has ordered crewmembers working on his boat to lie under oath at the threat of their careers." His voice lowered and pierced the jury. "He has even fingered a Gloucester fisherman for a serious, even life threatening, beating to prevent him from testifying against his boat." He paused, made a dramatic turn and faced Amalfi and the gallery. "And he has admitted to all of these crimes!"

Each juror's eyes followed his to settle on the outwardly nervous captain.

It was a long moment before Jim Bolton turned back to face the jury.

"I don't believe his version of events. The naval architect that will testify in this trial does not believe Mr. Amalfi's version and I don't believe you will either." He glanced at Amalfi, then back to the jury. "Thank you for listening."

Judge Adams called a ten-minute recess.

Once the jury had departed, John stood and faced the gallery. Amalfi looked back through tortured eyes. The twitch was visible from his place across the courtroom. So, it would be visible to the jury. He studied Amalfi. Would he hold up? It was time to find out. His gaze passed to the three widows. Their eyes betrayed an otherwise outward calm. The eyes, the windows of the soul, showed fear and a desperate trust. John knew they had placed their trust in him. For these women everything rode on winning this case. They had already lost enough. When he locked eyes with Katie she managed a grin. John saw more than trust there. Katie, the wife of his dear friend, was falling for him, even if she didn't know it.

The thought was shattered by the entrance of Josh O'Rourke. He took a seat in the gallery and signaled for John to meet him. John walked through the bar and to the rear of the gallery. Without preliminaries, John asked. "What is it Josh?"

A small smile crept across the banker's lips. "I'm here to check on the bank's investment."

John glared at O'Rourke. "Are you enjoying yourself, Josh?"

The banker's smile dissolved into a snarl. "I don't think you're so hot, Palermo." He stood, moved closer and hissed. "Personally, I hope you lose this case. We'll see how great you seem to these ladies when they're on the street."

John leaned into the shorter banker. "So what's new Josh? You've spent a lifetime wishing me to fail." He shook his head, sighed and continued. "Sorry, but I don't plan on losing so that you can get your jollies at the expense of widows and orphans."

"Go to hell, Palermo," O'Rourke snapped.

John shook his head. "Good comeback, Josh. You always had a way with words." He grinned into the hatred that was Josh's eyes. "I have to go help some people now. Why don't you go see if some poor guy who has lost his job is an hour late with a payment. Maybe you'll be able to foreclose on his kid's leg braces."

John made his way back to plaintiff's table as the jury was brought in.

"Call your witness, Mr. Palermo," instructed the judge.

John took a deep breath and called Captain Joe Amalfi to the stand. Amalfi looked like walking death as he rose to pass through the bar area to the witness box. His eyes darted from the judge to Jim Bolton and then to John. John saw the fear, bordering on panic, in the eyes set in the sunken sockets of his emaciated face. His body swam in the suit he wore.

John had placed the podium at the far end of the jury box. In effect, John's questions passed over the jury to be heard by the witness. More importantly, when Amalfi faced John to respond, he was looking at the jurors.

The testimony began where his life had, in Terasini, Sicily. He had been born the fifth of nine children to Loretta and Dimitri Amalfi. Dimitri, a fisherman by trade, struggled to feed and keep a roof over his family. Joe, by age eight, had been employed on fishing boats to help support the family.

Short and frail, he was never paid more than a half share, no matter how hard he worked. At age eighteen, frustrated by the taunts and humiliations heaped upon him due to his physical stature, he left for America.

Settled in Gloucester, America's oldest fishing port, Joe Amalfi found opportunity. He worked hard, kept his eyes and his mind open, and his mouth shut.

"Why did you keep your mouth shut?" John asked.

Haltingly, Captain Amalfi responded, "on the boats the captain was the boss. We did what he said, always."

"You developed a plan, didn't you, Captain Amalfi?"

"Yes, sir," Joe Amalfi agreed. "I worked extra watches at the helm."

"Why did you do that?" John asked.

"If I was in the wheelhouse, I could ask the captain questions when he was relaxed, so I could learn to be a captain."

"And did you learn?"

For the first time, Joe Amalfi sat straight in the witness box. "I did learn," he said with pride. "And I became a captain."

"How did that happen?"

"I took a site on the *St. Theresa*," he explained. "The Captain got sick when we were fishing, so he told me to take over."

"And what happened?" John asked.

"We had a big trip," Amalfi remembered with a smile. "When we got home, he asked me to be his substitute captain while he recovered."

"How did you feel about that, Captain?"

Amalfi looked directly into John's eyes. "It was the first time in my life that anyone showed me respect," he reflected. "I was the Captain and nobody laughed anymore."

"What happened to the man who made you a captain?"

Joe Amalfi looked at the jury. "He never got better." He sighed. "After every trip I went to see him." He glanced into the gallery. "That's when I met my Rosalie."

"Your wife, Captain?"

"Yes, she was the Captain's daughter."

"Go on," John urged.

"We married and I stayed the Captain on the *St. Theresa* and then I built the *Mio Mondo*. It was the best boat in the fleet."

"And you were its Captain," John stated.

"Yes, I was the Captain and for twenty years we were highliners." The pride re-surfaced.

"Highliners, Captain?" John asked.

"It meant that we made the most money for the crew, the Captain, and the owner."

"And you were in charge?" John queried.

"Yes."

"And the crew always did what you told them, didn't they?"

Amalfi nodded. "Yes, they did."

"And the crews feared you, correct?"

The Captain looked up at John. "Yes."

"Why was that important, Captain?"

Amalfi bowed his head.

"Captain," John pushed.

"They all wanted to fish on my boat, because I was the best."

"And what else, Captain?"

Lawyer and client locked eyes for a long moment.

Softly, he answered, "when they were afraid they didn't laugh at me."

A poignant silence followed as Amalfi dropped his eyes in shame.

John went to the plaintiff's table to confer with Larry Smith. He sipped his water and re-organized his notes. In reality, he gave Amalfi time to recover before the next phase of soul-wrenching testimony. Then John moved back to the podium at the end of the jury box, looked up at Amalfi and directed his questions to the day, fourteen months before, when Amalfi's vessel and crew had been lost. And with it the hunted look returned.

"In your own words, Captain Amalfi, would you tell us what occurred September 4th of last year?"

The question and answer had been well rehearsed. Still, recalling the day Amalfi gulped as his eyes pooled with tears. Haltingly, he began. "Marc Morrissey was at the wheel." He stole a glance at Bolton. "I had been there, but it was Marc's turn on watch."

Katie sat stonefaced as the pain went directly to her heart.

Amalfi continued. "I was crossing the deck, heading to the fo'c's'le when we hit something." He paused as a tear trickled down his face. "The boat shook and I fell and hit my head."

Amalfi's hands shook and tears ran down his cheeks. John walked to the witness box, poured a glass of water and gave it to Amalfi. "Are you okay, Captain?"

Amalfi nodded as he gulped the water.

"What is the next thing that you remember, Captain Amalfi?" John asked as he returned to the podium.

Panic gripped Amalfi as he recalled the events. John noticed the jurors' expressions of sympathy for the wreck of a man that sat in the witness box.

Amalfi started and stopped before emitting a sound. He took a deep breath. "When I woke up the boat was sinking and everybody . . ." His body heaved with sobs. "They were all gone!"

A long moment passed while the jurors imagined the horror.

Quietly, John asked, "Were you unconscious?"

Amalfi nodded. "When I woke up the seas were washing over me." He paused. "The deck was under water."

"Was it the seas washing over you that woke you up?"

"Yeah, yeah." His terrified eyes sought John. "They were all gone!" He sobbed, placing his hands over his face. "They were all gone!"

John knew he had to get the story out. He pushed on. "Were you hurt Captain?"

He nodded. "My head was bleeding. A lot of blood in with the sea water." He looked up at the gallery and the women. "The blood was in my eyes, all over my face."

Katie's heart went out to the wasted and desperate man. 'How horrible,' she thought.

Lorraine Alves worked at the handle of her pocketbook, as she thought of Luke and cried openly.

"What did you do next, Captain?"

Amalfi looked to the jury. "I was on my knees. I felt so weak and confused." He paused, reliving the horror. "There was nobody there."

"How long were you unconscious?"

Puzzled, Amalfi looked at John. "I don't know, long enough for the boat to be practically under water."

"What did you do then, Captain?"

He sipped his water. His gaze was a long way from the courtroom. It was back on the deck of the sinking fishing boat.

"Captain?" John cut through the fog. "What did you do then?"

"Oh," he choked. "I knew the boat wouldn't last long, so I ran through the water to the pilot house and sent a May Day."

"Is that a distress signal?"

Amalfi nodded. His facial twitch flaring.

"What did you do then, Captain?"

"I yelled for the men." He looked to the women in the gallery. "I called their names. I went on deck." He paused. "They didn't answer." His tears flowed to match that of the three young widows. "The water was up to here." He placed his hand at chest level.

He looked to John. "The entire deck to the rails was under water." He shivered at the memory. "There was no more time."

"What did you do then, Captain?"

The juror's eyes were riveted on Amalfi. His twitch flared, his hands trembled.

"I called for the men, but there was nobody there." He wiped his tears with the back of his hand. "I climbed into the liferaft that had inflated." He paused and dropped his eyes. "The line was connected to the pilot house rail." Pleadingly, he looked up at the widows. "I waited as long as I could. I yelled for the men," he sobbed. "They just weren't there."

The courtroom was hushed silent as each person visualized the horror, the terror, of the scene. Tears flowed from the gallery and the witness box. Rosalie Amalfi had not heard the full breadth of the story. Her heart went out to her husband. At that moment, she understood the horror his life had been since that day.

Finally John asked, "what did you do then, Captain?"

His chest heaved with sobs. The twitch flared.

"I'm sorry," he wailed. ". . . I cut the line and floated away." He paused. "I watched my boat sink."

"And the crew?" John inquired. Amalfi spread his hands, tears ran down his cheeks. "I just don't know. I never saw them."

John let the force of the testimony settle on the jury. He watched the jurors study Amalfi as they reflected his anguish. John stole a look at Katie. It was heartbreaking. The pain was laid bare on the surface. In her eyes the grief was plain. In her soul the agony was bottomless.

"Captain," John asked. "You said that while you were crossing the deck to the fo'c's'le the boat hit something."

Joe Amalfi drank some water, emptying his glass. He nodded. "That's right."

"Are you sure you hit something?"

Joe Amalfi looked directly at John, his twitch fired.

"There is no question, we hit something and the boat sank."

"Thank you Captain." John sat.

Judge Adams called for the morning break.

CHAPTER TWENTY-TWO

Jim Bolton was average in all that didn't matter. Average height and weight belied the clear eyes and keen mind. In truth, he relished shocking the unwary. Those who assumed the average package contained average contents were easy to defeat. As he stood to begin his cross-examination of Captain Amalfi, he knew this would be tricky.

His gut told him something was wrong with Joe Amalfi's story. But, to his credit, John had packaged Amalfi and his testimony as convincingly as possible. John Palermo had his respect. Still, Jim Bolton intended to win.

Joe Amalfi stared at the defense attorney with fear in his eyes. John noted Amalfi's facial twitch. At this point, John hoped that the captain would remember his preparation.

"Are you okay, Captain?" Bolton began kindly as he refilled the witness's water glass.

With a slight nod Amalfi indicated he was fine.

"Captain, do you remember speaking to the Coast Guard when you were brought ashore after your boat had been lost?"

Amalfi nodded. "Yes."

Bolton walked over to defense table and picked up a sheaf of paper. He thumbed through it until he found what he sought. He then glanced up at the witness. "Didn't you tell the Coast Guard officer who questioned you that you had been in the pilot house when the boat struck a submerged object?"

Amalfi's eyes sought John. The facial twitch fired. Amalfi looked back at Bolton. "I was weak from loss of blood, dizzy and confused." He paused, twitched three times so that a dimple appeared under his eye on each twitch. "I meant to say that I had just left the pilot house."

With an understanding nod, the defense attorney settled his gaze on Amalfi. In the moment of quiet, a sheen of perspiration appeared on the Captain's upper lip, his twitch fired again.

'He's lying,' thought Bolton.

Bolton again looked at the Coast Guard report, which was a typed transcript of a recorded statement.

"Let me refresh your memory Captain." Bolton suggested, as he read from the statement. "Coast Guard Lieutenant, Jeffrey Clark asked: Captain Amalfi, where were you when the boat struck the submerged object?"

Bolton looked up from the statement. "You do remember Lieutenant Clark asking you that question, right Captain?"

"Yes," Amalfi stated softly as he shifted on his seat.

In a bold tone, Bolton then read.

"I was in the pilot house, at the wheel."

He paused, the jurors studied the diminutive Captain.

Notwithstanding John's coaching, Amalfi's eyes darted from Bolton to John. The sweat on his upper lip thickened and the twitch dimpled.

In a soft voice, "so, you were really in the pilot house, at the wheel, when the boat struck the submerged object. Right?" Bolton suggested, with an easy smile.

"No," Amalfi demanded belligerently, I told you, that was a mistake. I was on deck." He glared at Bolton. "Why is this so important?"

Jim Bolton smiled. "Captain, the truth is always important." He paused, as the jurors studied Amalfi closely. "And, I don't think you're telling us the truth."

John bolted to his feet. "Objection, Your Honor."

Judge Adams nodded. "Sustained." The judge turned to Bolton. "Mr. Bolton, save your argument for the appropriate time."

Smiling, Jim Bolton responded, "of course, Your Honor."

Judge Adams then turned to the jury. With a smile, he stated. "I've sustained the plaintiff's objection and struck Mr. Bolton's comment." Then the judge turned to Amalfi. "Mr. Amalfi, why don't you let the lawyers ask the questions, okay?"

Joe Amalfi caught John's glare.

"Yes, Your Honor." He deferentially responded.

"Good." The Judge nodded.

"Mr. Bolton, please continue."

Juror Len Harris, sat back. Having supervised and dealt with contractors, sub-contractors, suppliers and the scores of workers required to build the structures that make up the skyline of major cities, he knew bullshit when he heard it. The skeptical set of his eyes on Amalfi, told a story. 'This guy's lying,' he thought.

"Okay, Captain Amalfi," He flipped the pages still in his hand.

"How long were you unconscious?"

The twitch flashed. "I don't know."

"Really, Captain! In the statement you said it was a short time." He paused and smiled. "Shall I read Lieutenant Clark's question and your answer?"

Amalfi stared at him silently.

"Well, Captain, which is it?" Bolton demanded.

Amalfi shrugged and shifted nervously in his seat. "I don't know."

"Is that so?" Bolton remarked as he adjusted his eye glasses thoughtfully. Amalfi swallowed and averted his eyes.

"Captain, the *Mio Mondo* was a well built boat, wasn't it?"

"It was the best," he proclaimed it as a matter of fact.

Bolton nodded agreement. "So, wouldn't you also agree that unless a steel plate fell off the hull, causing a mass rush of water, that the boat's pumps would keep it afloat for a long time?"

John looked hard at Amalfi. The Captain's eyes flickered to John and then back to Bolton. Amalfi straightened and looked Bolton in the eye. "Whether it was a slash in the hull or a plate falling off, if water entered at a more rapid rate than the pumps could handle, the boat would sink."

"How fast, Captain Amalfi?"

He twitched while he shrugged. "I don't know. I was knocked out."

"Were you?" James Bolton queried.

Amalfi's eyes narrowed as he watched Bolton. The twitch flashed as he shifted in his seat.

John noticed certain jurors studying Amalfi closely.

"So when you came to, there was no sign of the crew?" Bolton's eyes enlarged in doubt.

Rapidly, Amalfi nodded. "That's right."

Bolton left defense table and walked to the jury box. As he walked he tapped an index finger to his chin. "Marc Morrissey, Luke Alves and Joe Picardi were experienced fishermen, weren't they?"

The Captain reached with a trembling hand for his water glass. "Yes, they were." He sipped his water.

Bolton turned and faced Amalfi. "How do you explain their total absence when you came to?"

As prepared, the witness shrugged. "I can't."

"What did the boat hit Captain?"

"I don't know."

Rapidly he asked, "What damage was done to the boat?"

"I don't know."

"How long were you unconscious?"

"I don't know."

Bolton paused and fixed a glare on Amalfi. "What happened to your crew, Captain?" He pointed at the three women who sat huddled together. "What happened to the husbands of these women?"

The twitch fired rapidly. "I don't know."

The room silenced in the wake of the insurance attorney's rapid-fire questions and Amalfi's complete disclaimer of knowledge as to what occurred. The jurors read Bolton's contempt for the responses and for the man.

There was a stony silence as Jim Bolton contemplated Joe Amalfi.

"Captain Amalfi, today you testified that Marc Morrissey was at the wheel when the boat hit a submerged object, correct?"

"Yes sir," Amalfi responded.

"The wheel is in the pilot house, isn't it?"

Joe Amalfi nodded, the twitch flared. "Yes sir, it is."

Bolton stood straight, eyes on the witness.

"So when you went to the pilot house to send the distress signal Marc Morrissey had disappeared?" A pause. "Is that what you expect this jury to believe?'

The twitch fired. "Yes, sir."

"So nobody was in the pilot house? Nobody was in control of the vessel?" Bolton asked, a look of disbelief on his face.

Amalfi nodded. "That's right."

Bolton paced back to the defense table, shaking his head.

The lawyer turned to face the witness. "Isn't it required that someone be on watch at all times, Captain?"

"Yes, it is." Amalfi replied in a small voice.

"And, you testified that Marc Morrissey was a good experienced fisherman, didn't you?"

Katie's eyes grew hard. John remained expressionless.

"Yes sir, he was," Amalfi stated.

Bolton contemplated Joe Amalfi as the Captain's twitch flared. "Yet, he abandoned the wheel, which controls the vessel at a time of great danger?" He moved forward. Is that what you want us to believe, Captain?"

Amalfi shrugged. "I don't know where he went."

"Okay, Captain," Bolton queried. "Where might he have gone?" He paused and smirked. "For coffee?"

Amalfi's only response was the twitch in his cheek.

Feigning exasperation. "You're not making any sense, Captain," Bolton stated.

John rose, but before he could object, Judge Adams interjected.

"Mr. Bolton," the Judge spoke in a stern tone. "This is your second warning, ask questions. Do not blurt out statements. You'll have your opportunity to comment on the evidence in your argument."

Bolton nodded. "I'm sorry, Your Honor. It won't happen again."

Jim Bolton paused. He accepted the judge's reprimand, but the point was made. And, a glance at the jurors told the experienced litigator that he had hit the mark.

"I'll ask you again, Captain. It was you who was in the pilot house when the boat began to sink, just as you told the Coast Guard, wasn't it?'

Barely audibly, Amalfi responded. "No sir, I had left the pilot house." The twitch flared.

With irony dripping from every word, Bolton asked, "Well Captain, I'm sure you can answer just why the boat sank here?" He pointed at a chart of the Atlantic fishing ground spread on a tripod facing the jury. He placed a red sticker at the spot. "It was at this point the vessel sank, wasn't it?"

In a soft voice Amalfi said, "Yes."

"Please speak up," Bolton demanded. He jabbed at the red dot on the chart. "It was here, correct?"

"Yes," Amalfi responded.

"And you told the Coast Guard that you had been fishing on George's Bank, correct?"

Amalfi cleared his throat and twitched nervously. "Yes, I did."

With a black marker Bolton circled the area on the chart known as George's Bank.

"We can agree that I've circled George's Bank, correct?"

Amalfi nodded while he swallowed. "Yes, sir."

"By the way, Captain, why do you fish on George's Bank?" Bolton asked.

The question caught Amalfi by surprise. He looked to John, who only smiled.

"That's where the fish are."

"I see," Bolton responded.

With the same black marker Bolton circled the mouth or entrance to Gloucester Harbor.

"That's Gloucester Harbor, isn't it Captain?"

"Yes, it is." Amalfi's eyes shifted to John who remained expressionless.

With the marker Bolton drew a straight line from George's Bank to Gloucester Harbor.

The red sticker stood apart and out a great distance from the black line that represented the direct route home from the fishing grounds.

Bolton stared down Amalfi who looked away from the lawyer's eyes. Finally, the lawyer asked, "why would the renowned Captain Guiseppe Amalfi have his boat so far off course?" He paused, then added sarcastically. "Or don't you know?"

Amalfi's eyes filled, his hands shook and the twitch flashed. "I don't know," he choked out.

"Take a sip of water, Captain," Bolton snapped. "We've a ways to go yet."

Juror Linda Noble, watched the exchange, closely. The shrewd twenty-five year old, who belied the blond stereotype, with her quick mind and good looks, pursed her lips, as she studied Captain Amalfi. Her facial expression showed distaste. The look was not missed by John.

Joe Amalfi followed instructions and gulped at the water. He took out his handkerchief and blew his nose.

"Is it just a coincidence, Captain, that the boat sank at that spot?"

Amalfi peered at Bolton. The facial twitch fired. The Captain shook his head. "I don't know." He stated, eyes lowered.

"You do realize Captain," Bolton stated, "that the spot where the *Mio Mondo* sank is the deepest bottom on this entire chart?"

"Is it?" Joe Amalfi responded weakly.

Bolton sarcastically laughed.

"You mean you don't know this either?"

Amalfi was silent.

Bolton turned to the judge. "With the court's permission I would like Captain Amalfi to approach the chart."

"Very well," Judge Adams responded.

Bolton turned back to Amalfi. "Captain, please come to the chart and take a good look. Then tell us the deepest bottom shown on the chart."

Joe Amalfi left the witness box and walked to the tri-pod. He studied the chart closely, then turned to Bolton.

"Excellent Captain, please show the jury the area with the deepest bottom anywhere on this large chart."

Amalfi, with twitch flaring, put his finger on the red sticker.

"My, my," Bolton said. "Please return to the witness box, Captain."

When Amalfi had settled back into the witness seat, Jim Bolton began a new tack.

"Captain Amalfi, did you testify in the trial of United States of America vs. Charles Dillon?"

"Yes, I did."

Bolton bore in on the witness with eyes that blazed.

"And you admitted while on the witness stand that you had committed perjury on two separate occasions in federal court trials. Isn't that correct?"

Amalfi nodded. "Yes, I did."

"Perjury, Captain. Do you know what that is?" Bolton asked.

"Yes," Captain Amalfi nodded.

The defense attorney stood facing the jury.

"Captain, why don't you tell us what perjury is?" Bolton suggested.

Joe Amalfi cleared his throat.

"It's lying," the Captain responded.

Jim Bolton frowned.

"Actually, Captain, it's lying under oath, isn't it?"

Amalfi nodded. "Yes."

"Under oath, Captain," Bolton's voice boomed. "Perjury is lying after having raised your hand and swearing to tell the truth."

Amalfi nodded, "Yes, that's right."

With a sad shake of the head, the defense attorney added, "Just like today, Captain." He paused. "Again today you raised your right hand, swore to tell the truth, just like the previous times when you swore to the truth and lied to the jury."

Amalfi shrugged, John itched to rise and object, but saw no purpose. 'Let's get through this,' he thought.

Bolton didn't push for a reply. He simply allowed Captain Amalfi to sit, squirm and sweat.

After a long moment, Judge Adams asked, "Mr. Bolton, have you completed your cross-examination?"

Bolton looked up at the Judge.

"No, Your Honor. I'll move on."

The crafty defense attorney had painted Amalfi as a liar. Everything he said, all his testimony would be scrutinized closely by the jury through the prism of his past.

"Okay Captain. Let's move on," Bolton smiled.

"Besides committing perjury yourself, you also were forced to admit to other criminal behavior. Isn't that correct, Captain?"

A slight nod, "Yes."

"For example, Captain, you admitted to ordering members of various crews on the *Mio Mondo* to commit perjury or they would lose their jobs. Isn't that correct?"

Amalfi took a deep breath. "Yes, I did."

Bolton was somewhat surprised that Amalfi was more at ease during this segment of testimony. Absent were the twitch and other nervous gestures. The insurance attorney glanced at John, certain that something was afoot, but not sure just what it was. Still, there was nothing to do but push on.

"Captain Amalfi, you even admitted to pointing out a young man, with a wife and children, for hired thugs to beat and hospitalize to prevent him from testifying in a personal injury case for a man who was injured on your boat. Isn't that so?"

"Yes, that's true." Amalfi acknowledged with downcast eyes.

Bolton paused, allowing the jury to drink in this latest revelation.

"Captain, what was the name of the fisherman who was beaten and hospitalized at your direction?"

Joe Amalfi sprang to life. "I didn't direct anything."

"Really, Captain?" Bolton queried. "First, what was the name of the fisherman?"

"Peter Novello," responded Amalfi.

"Now Captain, Mr. Novello worked on your boat, isn't that right?"

"Yes."

Bolton sensed the anger just under the surface.

"You actually lived with him on the boat for ten day periods, twice a month for a couple of years. Isn't that right?"

"Yes," Amalfi retorted.

Speaking softly, Bolton continued. "And you knew this young man had a wife and children, didn't you?"

Amalfi nodded. "I did."

"In fact, Captain, you knew Peter Novello since he was a boy, didn't you?"

"Yes," Amalfi nodded. Hard eyes on the defense attorney. No twitch evident.

In the gallery Rosalie Amalfi dropped her eyes which were pooled with tears.

Katie Morrissey, sensing the sorrow and shame Rosalie felt, placed a supportive hand on Rosalie's shoulder. At the same time, Katie fully comprehended Marc's dislike and John's utter contempt for Joe Amalfi.

"So, Captain. You participated in the assault and hospitalization of Peter Novello, a man you knew, worked with, a man who had a family, because Mr. Novello chose to ignore your threats and come forward and tell the truth. Isn't that right?"

Bolton locked eyes with Amalfi, daring the Captain to challenge the statement. If he did, Bolton would again go piece by piece over the brutal assault.

Amalfi's eyes fired, but remembering the trial preparation, he bit back the anger and nodded. "Yes sir."

Bolton pointed his finger at the witness. In a powerful voice he proclaimed, "you obstructed justice. You committed perjury. You were an accessory to a felony assault." He paused for effect. "And you sank this boat to collect the insurance money."

John bellowed his objection with anger flashing in his eyes.

Calmly, Judge Adams sustained the objection and ordered Bolton's statement struck from the record. Then signaling John to his seat, he turned to the jury.

"Ladies and gentlemen, Mr. Bolton's comments and statements are not evidence and in this case they were totally inappropriate. I ask you to please recognize that they were stated for effect and as an experienced attorney he knows that he was playing fast and loose with the rules." The judge smiled. "I won't pretend you can simply forget it. I do ask that you ignore it."

The judge turned to Bolton, "Continue, Mr. Bolton."

Bolton looked up to the judge. "Please accept my apology for stepping over the line, Your Honor. I have nothing more for this witness."

Judge Adams ignored the apology and turned to John. "Mr. Palermo, is there any re-direct examination?"

John rose. "Yes, Your Honor." His eyes passed over the jury as John walked to the tripod. With his index finger tracing the line Bolton had drawn from George's Bank to Gloucester Harbor he nodded his head and turned to Amalfi. "Captain, after the *Mio Mondo* struck the submerged object causing you to fall and strike your head, did you know what course the boat was on while you were unconscious?"

Amalfi shrugged, "No."

"When you placed the May Day and checked your longitude and latitude readings, were you surprised that the boat was off course?"

"I didn't think about it."

"Really!" John exclaimed in a theatrical show of surprise. "The boat was sinking, three men were missing and you were bleeding profusely from a head wound. Do you really expect us to believe that you didn't think about the vessel's bearings under these circumstances?"

For the first time, Joe Amalfi smiled. John noted that none of the jurors smiled with him.

"Yes," Amalfi said. "I guess I do expect you to believe that."

John cast a hard look back at Bolton. "I guess that explains the red sticker, doesn't it Captain?"

Still smiling, Amalfi responded, "I guess so."

'Does it?' Thought juror, Len Harris. 'Just a coincidence that the boat sank at that point?' The problem was, Len Harris didn't believe in coincidence.

John walked to the far end of the jury box. He addressed Amalfi squarely. "Mr. Bolton asked you various questions concerning your testimony in the criminal case of the United States of America vs. Charles Dillon."

Amalfi nodded.

"In that trial you admitted to a number of actions that you knew were wrong, didn't you?"

Amalfi's eyes dropped. "Yes, very wrong."

"Did the government prosecute you for those wrongs?"

Eyes still down, Amalfi answered, "No."

"Is that because you cooperated with them in their case against Attorney Dillon?"

"Partly, yes."

John glanced at the jury whose attention was riveted on Joe Amalfi. "What was the other part, Captain?"

Amalfi hesitated, took a sip of water and looked up at John. "The government lawyers knew I was forced to do all those bad things."

"Who forced you, Captain?"

Amalfi's face flushed. "It was Mr. Dillon and his bosses that forced me."

"How did they force you, Captain?"

"They threatened me." He paused. "They told me if I didn't do what they said they would take away my insurance."

"What would the effect have been of you losing your insurance?"

"Without insurance the bank won't allow the boat to leave the dock."

"Couldn't you just get other insurance?"

Amalfi shook his head. "No, see that's what the case was about. Dillon and his bosses created a blacklist to stop boats from fishing and men from working if they didn't tell the insurance company's lies."

John nodded in recognition.

"So, it was Dillon's bosses who operated this illegal blacklist."

"Yes," Amalfi said. "And they hurt people."

"People like Peter Novello?" John asked.

"That's right."

"Who was Mr. Dillon's boss, Captain Amalfi?"

"It was the insurance company."

"Are you saying, Captain, that the insurance company ordered its lawyers to operate an illegal blacklist?"

Bolton jumped to his feet. "Objection, Your Honor."

"Sidebar, Gentlemen," Judge Adams ordered.

At sidebar and out of the hearing of the jury it was the judge who spoke, "Mr. Bolton, the entire issue of United States of America vs. Charles Dillon was your idea. Do you really expect me to limit Mr. Palermo on re-direct?"

"Your Honor, if I may."

The judge smiled. "I'll listen, Mr. Bolton."

"The credibility of a person is a different issue from the credibility of a multi-national insurance company. I believe . . ."

The judge cut him off. "I don't agree; objection overruled."

When the attorneys returned to their stations, the judge addressed the jury. "I overruled Mr. Bolton's objection." He turned to John. "Continue, Mr. Palermo."

"Thank you, Your Honor." Back at the podium at the far end of the jury box, John shuffled his papers and then focused on Amalfi.

"Captain, I asked you if it was the insurance company that ordered its lawyers to operate an illegal blacklist?"

"Yes, it was."

"And was it the insurance company that ordered you and others to commit perjury?"

Amalfi nodded. "That's right."

John shook his head in mock amazement. "And the insurance company ordered the felony assault on Peter Novello?"

Amalfi sat back. "That's right."

John stood stock-still. He looked from Amalfi to the jury who filled the silence by looking his way. When each juror was looking at him, John slowly passed his gaze to Jim Bolton. The jurors followed his eyes and studied Bolton who sat calmly.

John broke the silence. "Captain, do you know why this insurance company committed all these illegal acts?"

"Yes, I do."

"Do tell us Captain."

Amalfi shrugged. "Because they didn't want to pay boat owners and fishermen on legitimate claims."

"I see," John said.

"Captain Amalfi, what is the name of the insurance company that committed all these cruel and illegal acts just not to pay legitimate claims?"

Amalfi pointed at James Bolton. "It was the American Marine Insurance Company."

Every eye found Bolton as John asked. "Is that the same American Marine Insurance Company that is refusing to pay you and these widows, Captain?"

"Yes, it is."

"I have nothing further, Your Honor."

"Any re-cross Mr. Bolton?"

"No, Your Honor."

"Very well, we'll resume tomorrow at 9:00 a.m."

John stood and faced the gallery. His eyes met Katie's and he produced a smile.

* * *

In his office, John stood at the window overlooking Harbour Cove. He sipped at his bourbon rocks and turned over Amalfi's testimony in his head. He recalled the reactions of the jurors. The appraising glare of the pretty blond, the stern countenance of the black architect. 'Did I reach them?' He wondered. 'Do I want to?'

"Maybe you should go easy on the bourbon." Phil offered as he entered John's office. "Didn't you say that there's a party at your parents house tonight?"

John nodded, but said nothing.

"How did it go with Captain Amalfi today?" Phil asked.

John nodded as he sipped his drink. "It went about as well as could be expected," John replied.

"Larry thought you rehabilitated him well on re-direct." Phil responded.

John shook his head. "We're still in the game," he said softly. "I nursed the bastard through," John spit out.

Phil looked at the glass. "How many have you had?"

"I'm fine." There was an edge to his voice.

Decidedly unintimidated, Phil countered. "How many, John?"

John walked to his chair and plopped down. "This is my second."

"Okay," Phil responded. "Why don't you go see the kids, maybe take a nap before heading over to the Amicos."

John shrugged. "Good idea."

CHAPTER TWENTY-THREE

The Amico clan gathered to celebrate Benny's sixty-fifth birthday. John entered the home of his youth with Franco and Anna in tow. As always, they came through the back door into the disordered excitement of Maria's kitchen.

"Do you smell that?" John asked Franco and Anna as they enjoyed the aromas of baking bread, a rich tomato sauce bubbling on the stove and brascoili grilling. "That's the smell of love."

Excitedly, Franco and Anna ran into the arms of Nonna Amico. "I love your homemade bread, Nonna," Franco gushed. With big eyes he asked. "Are we having meatballs, too?"

Maria Amico laughed as she engulfed Franco and Anna in an enveloping hug. "Of course I made meatballs for my Franco." Maria assured. "And how is Little Anna?" Maria asked, as the children enthusiastically returned her warmth.

"I'm good, Nonna," Anna chirped.

John then scooted them off to the living room. "Go tell Nonno happy birthday." Excitedly, they ran into Benny's open arms.

John then embraced Maria. "How are you, Ma?"

After their hug, Maria placed her hands on John's face. She studied him closely. "I'm good, John. But how are you?"

John smiled down at the face of the only mother he had ever known. "I'm doing okay, Ma."

Her eyes misted. "When you were ten years old and you came here to live with us, you always smiled and said, 'I'm okay, Ma.' But are you okay?"

Emotion caught him as his eyes pooled with tears. "I miss her so much, sometimes I think I can't go on." He spoke softy for Maria's ears only. "Then I look at the kids and I see Connie in Anna's face and I know I will go on."

She forced a smile. "Like Franco did."

He smiled back through the tears. "Yeah, like my Papa, I guess."

John hugged Maria fiercely. "Thank you for taking me when Papa died. Thank you for letting me marry Connie." He paused. "And thank you for helping me with the children. I couldn't do this without you."

Maria held on. "No, John," she whispered into his ear. "Thank you for being the son I never had. And for loving Connie." There was a long silence. "And . . ." she choked. "I need to take care of my Connie's children."

Finally, he broke the embrace. He grinned. "This is a happy day. Dad is sixty-five. The whole family will be together. And," he laughed, "I get your handmade Gnocchi and bread. And Franco, your meatballs."

She met his laugh with a wet-eyed smile as she placed her hand on his cheek. "Go see dad and have some wine. Today is a happy day!"

The adults had the dining room and the seven grandchildren laughed, ate and bonded at the kitchen table. Maria scurried in repeatedly to help the younger ones cut their food and to guarantee all was well.

Filippa carefully checked the kitchen table from her seat, then turned to Anna. "It's nice to have dinner here. Ma does all the work and takes care of the kids."

Anna shook her head as she took in her younger sister. "Nothing new about that, Ma loves these dinners with the kids."

"Yeah, isn't it great?" Filippa laughed.

With a chuckle Anna agreed. "It is tough eating your meal hot and not bobbing up and down after the kids."

Feigning distress, Anna put the back of her wrist to her forehead. "Somehow, I'll manage."

The table joined the sisters in a hearty laugh as Anna's husband Dave Carrico put an arm around her shoulder. John smiled at his two adopted sisters from his chair at Benny's right hand. "Ma is something special, isn't she?"

Anna and Filippa exchanged a long amused look. Then Filippa angled flashing eyes at John.

"Ma is wonderful," Filippa agreed. With raised brows she continued, "And I hear you sorta see someone else as being special, John."

Benny looked across the table at Maria. Then looked at John. "I don't think I understand."

John's brothers-in-law, Dave Carrico and Mike Jeffries, sat back with quizzical looks as their eyes roamed from John to their respective wives and back to John.

Maria had grieved hard over the loss of her youngest child. Her pain was magnified as she watched John ache as he dealt with the loss of his wife and the fight to raise two young children alone. While she wanted no woman to replace Connie, she knew the children needed a mother and John needed a mate. For the sake of the living and to be faithful to the promises she made to Connie, she buried her private ache and wished for John to find the right woman.

John caught Benny's confusion and Maria's torn emotions as he realized Anna and Filippa would press for a response. He smiled at Filippa. "Ok, what do you think you know?"

Filippa put a hand to her chest in surprise as her eyes sparked mischief. "Well, I had a long chat with Eileen." She paused. "You know Eileen, don't you, John?"

John's smile held as he shook his head at his sister. "Eileen who?"

"Oh, Eileen Ferraco . . . But maybe you know her sister, Katie, better."

John sat back, amused. "Of course, she's a client."

Filippa and Anna grinned at each other. Anna then offered. "John, I hear there's more to your relationship than what's professional."

In a Groucho Marx type gesture, with leering eyes and suggestive tone, Filippa said, "I guess it depends on the profession in question."

That drew a general laugh. The laugh drew little Anna in from the kitchen. Reflexively, John pulled the three-year-old onto his lap and nuzzled her neck.

Benny had forced a smile while John saw a question in Maria's eyes. "Very well," he began. "This is not exactly the best time or place, but since my sisters have caused so much trouble . . . again." He smiled in their direction to soften his words. After a deep breath, he continued. "I sorta have been seeing Katie Morrissey."

Maria's mind flashed back to John as a teenager, romping through the house with Marc Morrissey and Peter Novello. The memory brought a smile.

"Marc's wife?" Maria asked.

"Yes, Ma . . . Marc's wife."

John saw a tumble of mixed emotions in Maria's eyes.

"I play with Kelly," little Anna blurted. "We went to her birthday party and we all went to Hungry Harrys." She smiled at her grandmother. "We have fun," She giggled. "And me and Katie have a secret."

John jostled Anna and kissed her neck. "Okay you, out with it. What's your secret?"

Anna laughed and Maria saw Connie in her granddaughter.

Anna glanced back at John and there was concern on the little girl's face. "Don't be mad, daddy," she hesitated. "But Katie fixes my hair."

John laughed and assured Anna that he wasn't angry.

Relieved, Anna smiled up at her daddy. "Katie brushed my hair and she told me about how I have pretty hair like my mother."

Maria felt a stab at her heart.

Then little Anna giggled. "She told me that Daddies don't know how to fix a little girl's hair."

Filippa smiled at little Anna. "Do you like Katie and Kelly?"

Anna nodded enthusiastically. "I do. Katie is so nice." Then hearing laughter from the kitchen she jumped off John's lap and ran out of the room.

The dining room fell silent. John saw Benny's raised eyebrows and realized that not filling in his family would be unfair, even cruel. He glanced at his sisters who smiled his way.

Mike shook his head at John's disquiet. "As your accountant and friend," he offered, "You may as well spill the whole story." He glanced at Filippa with love. "And don't be surprised if these ladies have more information on your life than you do."

John smiled on his sisters, delighted that they were happy and aware that they worried about him. Sitting back, John scanned the room. He lifted his glass of red wine and sipped as he contemplated his words. Benny and Maria had urged him to begin dating. Yet, John knew that the reality of his dating was vastly different from the theory. Connie had urged Maria, and John suspected, Phil and Mary Kaye as well, to encourage John to move on, to find a new wife and a mother for Franco and Anna. John knew Connie had spoken out of love for John and their children. And, he knew that Maria did as Connie asked. He also knew that there would be shock and a feeling of betrayal when he began seeing other women. Still, the subject was on the table, he was surrounded by his family and he knew they deserved the truth.

John smiled. "Ma, Dad, everyone, I guess some of you know I have been dating." He paused. Every eye was on him, the only sound emanated from the children in the kitchen.

"Over the past few months, I've seen two women." He grinned as he turned to Filippa. "You've heard that I've spent time with Katie." He sighed. "She's a great girl," John hesitated. "She's very fragile, so devastated and so lonely." There was a far away look in his eyes. In a soft voice, he continued. "I know what she's feeling." He sat, forced a smile. "We're like two car wrecks." He sought Maria's eyes. "Mom, I don't think Katie is anywhere near ready for a relationship."

"You care for her, John?" Maria asked.

"Yes, Ma, I do." He shifted in his seat. "But, I'm not sure what I feel is love rather than compassion for her situation." He shrugged. "Marc was my friend."

Anna reached across the table and took John's hand. "Marc is gone, John." She hesitated. "And, so is Connie."

Everyone lapsed into a respectful silence. Each lost in their thoughts.

Filippa broke the silence. "John, you said two women."

John nodded and grinned. "Phil and Mary Kaye introduced me to a nice woman. She's a teacher." He turned to Maria. "Ma, you remember that day when I went sailing with Phil and Mary Kaye?"

Maria nodded. "You didn't want to go," She said thoughtfully.

John nodded. "Ya, that's right. But, you and Mary Kaye double-teamed me." He grinned. "It was a fun day. Barbara was great."

Anna and Filippa glanced at each other. They noted how the mention of this woman seemed to lighten John's spirit and produce a smile.

"Have you seen this woman often?" Filippa asked.

John nodded. "A few times, our first date was a book discussion over dinner." He recalled with a smile. "The dinner was nice, the book was great."

"You're dating her then?" Maria inquired.

"No." John stated. "Not really." He paused. "Barbara's fun, we spend a lot of time laughing." He grew thoughtful. "She makes me feel good." He nodded. "It's been a long time since I've felt good."

"Is it serious?" Anna asked quietly.

John smiled. "No Anna, we've only had a few dates. She hasn't even met Franco and Anna." He frowned and grew serious. "No, not serious." He took a deep breath. "I'm not ready to be serious." He paused. "Besides, I'm not sure about Katie."

His family watched him wrestle with his conflicting emotions.

Finally, he admitted, "When I think of Katie . . ." He flushed. "I think of Connie and feel lousy . . . you know . . . like I'm cheating on her." He shrugged. "And I think Katie feels the same way."

The room was silent until Maria broke in. "Katie is a good girl." She swallowed and misted. "I know Connie liked her." Maria took a deep breath. "If she would be good for Franco and Anna, then you have to follow your heart, John."

Anna and Filippa nodded their agreement. Benny sat stonefaced.

"Hey," John grinned. "This is supposed to be a party." He put his hand on Benny's shoulder. "I want to celebrate a great man's birthday."

Benny smiled at John.

"I love you, Dad," John said.

Benny choked. "I love you, too, son."

*　　*　　*

As John would rise at 4:00 a.m. to prepare for the trial day ahead, he settled Franco and Anna in their beds at the Amicos.

"I wish we could sleep home, Daddy." Franco said sadly.

Little Anna nodded in agreement as she threw her arms around John. "I hate it when you're on trial." She stated with conviction.

John smiled. "I know, guys," he offered. "But, I have to leave the house so early tomorrow." He sighed and thought of the price his children continued to pay as a result of Connie's death. 'So unfair,' he thought.

"I promise, when this trial is over, I'll take a week off and we'll be together every day."

That won a smile from the children.

John tucked Franco in and kissed him. "Hang in there, Big Guy," he began. "When the trial's over we'll play catch. Okay?"

"Okay, Dad," Franco responded. "Good night."

Tucking in the dozing Anna, he kissed her. "Good night, sweetheart. Daddy loves you."

"I love you, too." She said with sleepy eyes.

John drove home with his children foremost in his thoughts. He knew it wasn't fair or right to deny them the security of their home, their beds, but he had little choice.

He went directly to his study to review Katie's deposition transcript and to study the outline of his direct examination of Katie Morrissey. He sat at his desk and noticed the red light of his answering machine was lit. He sighed and hit the playback button.

"Hi John," Barbara's voice filled the room. "I know you've been on trial on that terrible case where the men died at sea." There was a pause. "I don't know how you can do it. Anyway, I thought I'd call and wish you good luck." Another pause. Brightly, she added. "If you feel like taking a break from your work and want to talk, I'll be home." The line went dead.

John sat back and rubbed his eyes. Then he picked up the deposition transcript and the summary that Larry Smith had prepared and began to read. He worked for two hours, satisfied that all was set, sat back and checked his watch. Then he looked at the answering machine, wrestled with whether he should call Barbara or just go to bed, rose and walked to the bar. He poured himself a bourbon, checked his watch again, shrugged and reached for the phone.

Barbara was delighted to hear his voice.

"I hope it isn't too late." John offered. "I thought I'd call before turning in."

"I'm glad you did." She responded cheerily. "How's it going?"

"Not bad," John responded. "We still have a long way to go." He paused. "How have you been?"

"I've been good, busy correcting essays."

Her voice had a happy lilt. That brought a smile.

"What do you have the poor kids reading now?" He teased.

She laughed. "We're doing F. Scott Fitzgerald."

"Gatsby?" John asked.

"To start," she confirmed, still chuckling.

"Poor kids!" John offered, laughing.

"Hey, I'm the one who has to correct fifty essays." She rebutted, with a laugh. "How about sending a little sympathy this way?"

"Who are you kidding?" John pushed. "You love tormenting those kids."

"You sure figured me out." She laughed, enjoying the exchange.

"How are the kids, John?" She asked.

"They're good." He sighed. "They're not happy about having to spend so many nights at their grandparent's house. But . . ."

"Don't worry," she comforted. "You can only do so much."

"I guess." He paused. "I should say goodnight."

"Goodnight, John" she spoke softly. "Good luck with the trial."

"Thanks, Barbara, good night."

"Call me after the trial." She urged. "I'd like to know how it went."

John knew she was in contact with Mary Kaye. Still, it was nice she cared. "I'll call you." He promised.

"Okay," she responded. "I hope to see you soon."

"I'll call," he repeated. "Good night, Barbara."

"Good night, John."

The line went dead. John sat back, sipped his drink and sighed.

CHAPTER TWENTY-FOUR

Trial: Day Three

The first thing John noticed when entering the courtroom was that Joe Amalfi appeared calmer and more at ease than he had seen him in a very long time. While gaunt, he appeared rested, more comfortable in his skin. Also, there was no sign of the facial twitch. John's gaze passed over the Amalfis to meet Katie's.

He smiled. "Are you ready?"

She held Lorraine's hand, swallowed and forced a thin smile. "I'm ready."

"You'll be great," John assured.

All present rose as Judge Adams, with his clerk, entered the courtroom from his chambers behind the bench. The lawyers settled into their seats only after the jury was brought in and seated.

As the jury settled in, John studied their faces. Linda Noble flashed a smile. Len Harris shot a look of disdain at Joe Amalfi. In seat number eight, juror, Ruth Garron, a petite woman of seventy with bright eyes and an expressive face, studied the widows.

Judge Adams asked John if he planned on calling another witness.

John rose. "Yes, Your Honor. The Plaintiff calls Katarina Morrissey."

Katie rose and with a final squeeze released Helen's hand. Nervously, she passed through the rail and into the pit crossing to the witness stand.

Every eye was on the stunning blond, who seemed even more beautiful by her apparent indifference to the attention.

Taking a deep breath in hopes of steadying her emotions, she stood and raised her right hand, swearing to tell the whole truth.

John stood at plaintiff's counsel's table feeling a mix of emotions. He appreciated her beauty and taste. Katie wore a soft white sweater over a black skirt, with minimal make-up. Beside her gold wedding ring, she wore a gold locket on a simple gold necklace. The locket, a gift from Marc at their last Christmas together, held photos of Marc and Kelly. At her ears were gold earrings with a small diamond. These, as with the wedding band, locket and necklace were gifts from Marc. Absently, she ran the fingers of her right hand over the locket as she settled in the witness box and felt Marc with her as she raised her eyes to John.

While John knew Katie's testimony was necessary, he regretted having to take her through the emotional wringer of recounting her life with Marc, the shock of his sudden loss and the struggle, emotionally and financially to pick up the pieces of a shattered life.

He knew it was his task to impress upon the jury that Katie's struggle, as well as Helen's and Lorraine's, did not end with a jury verdict. It would go on and be re-lived at each special moment of Kelly's, and the other children's lives. A life without a father.

After much calculation and negotiation, the attorneys entered into two stipulations. The first was that Katie Morrissey would testify on behalf of all three widows. The second agreement or stipulation was that should the jury find in favor of the plaintiffs, the insurance company would pay the full policy amount with interest to each plaintiff.

Each side had their reasons for entering into the stipulations. Jim Bolton was concerned that the three widows, their grief and loss obvious, would generate an overwhelming sympathy factor, thereby tending to diminish the contradictory and questionable testimony of Captain Joe Amalfi. Bolton knew that his best hope was to keep the jury's attention on Captain Amalfi. Further, he considered it a stroke of luck that John would agree to limit the potential damage award to the policy limits.

The greatest concern of the insurance company, and of their attorney, was a judgment in excess of the policy of insurance. Bolton could easily see a jury, carried away by a wave of sympathy, finding that his client had acted in bad faith and trebling their award in punitive damages. By agreeing to the stipulations, the insurance company could still win outright, but in any event, never lose more than the policy limits.

John proposed the stipulations for a number of reasons. First, John believed Katie would be the most compelling witness. Katie showed a strength in her determination to push on, a quality, he believed, the jury would respect and a vulnerability and deep loneliness as she eloquently related her life with Marc and the grief she and Kelly lived with.

Second, Helen and Lorraine, while certainly intelligent, did not speak well. In John's years of litigating cases he had observed that jurors awarded less to those plaintiffs who had difficulty verbalizing their pain as well as their economic losses. John believed the misconception that eloquent speakers were more intelligent and more worthy was driven by the elite media to advance an agenda which was very different from their words. To his dismay, John had too often witnessed plain spoken honesty belittled in the written and electronic media, while politicians who deftly and eloquently danced around issues, parsed their words and opinions, based on the group they were addressing, were hailed as intelligent. In John's view, this exalting of form over substance was deliberate to advance an agenda that America would not support. In short, it was dishonest.

Still, his goal was to succeed for his clients, not change the world. As Katie was more eloquent and could deliver the message, he'd have her carry the torch for the three widows.

Third, Katie was beautiful, while Helen and Lorraine were beautiful people in a somewhat plain package. John knew that Katie's physical beauty, coupled with the tragic circumstances and painful losses, would move a jury.

Fourth, John worried that having all three women testify would diminish the power of the plaintiff's presentation. John knew that people moved from shock and horror to acceptance very quickly.

A student of human nature, John had seen jurors gasp at the sight of a burn victim or a child in a wheelchair, caused by the negligence of another. Then, as the days passed and the trial progressed, the jury would begin to lose their sense of shock as the child, crippled for life, or the burn victim, permanently disfigured, functioned under their circumstances, as well as possible. John had interviewed jurors who had said, "gee, at first I was so upset at that cute little girl in her wheelchair, but she seems to be doing okay."

John knew that the jury didn't see the little girls parents carrying her to the bathroom and drying her tears as each new limitation, from not being able to take ballet, run the bases or dance with her latest crush, became a reality.

John knew there were dangers, but he wanted to play his strongest hand. Katie Morrissey was his ace.

Finally, John wanted to shorten and simplify the trial. Acutely aware that his proposed stipulations may well cost his clients millions of dollars, he also knew that there were grave risks to a lengthy trial. He calculated, asking himself what were the chances of this jury finding that the defendant insurance company had acted in bad faith? On what evidence could they rely?

John felt certain that the jurors did not like Joe Amalfi, nor believe him to be sincere. His eyes missed little in a courtroom and the expressions of distaste on certain juror's faces when Amalfi testified told a story. John's gut told him that the jury did not buy Captain Guiseppe Amalfi! And, as the jury finding on Bad Faith would be advisory, John knew in his gut that Judge Adams would not enter Bad Faith damages, irrespective of the Jury's finding.

Having brooded over the potential benefits as against the risks, he reluctantly concluded that to shorten the trial was his best course. He had waited until the trial started to propose the stipulations to give Bolton as little time as possible to consider John's motivations. He could only pray he had calculated correctly.

As Katie took her seat in the witness box, John poured her a glass of water and brought it to her. His fingers grazed her hand as their eyes met. He offered a smile of encouragement before heading to the podium at the end of the jury box.

"Good morning, Mrs. Morrissey," he began. "For the record, could you give us your name and address?"

"Good morning," she responded. "My name is Katarina Morrissey. I live at 30 Periwinkle Drive in Gloucester, Massachusetts."

John felt his throat going dry. He sipped some water and fixed his eyes on Katie.

"Please tell us Mrs. Morrissey, when did you meet Marc Morrissey and how long did you know him?"

Katie cleared her throat. "I met Marc when I was a freshman at Gloucester High School." A smile hinted at the corners of her lips. "Marc was captain of the basketball team. He was tall and handsome." She paused. "I was just another freshman girl with a crush on a senior boy." She smiled at John. "My girlfriends and I went to all the home games and cheered along with the cheerleaders."

"Did you start dating?" John asked.

Katie shook her head. "No, I doubt he even knew I was alive." She paused. "I met him once at Friendly's after a game. One of my girlfriends introduced us."

"When did you begin to date Marc?" John asked.

"Marc went off to the University of Massachusetts to study oceanography." She paused. "He loved the ocean and wanted to understand fish stocks and help the industry prosper." Katie began. "I didn't really know him then." She continued. "I saw him occasionally in passing over the next few years, but we didn't date or anything." She smiled, reliving a pleasant memory. "Out of the blue, Marc called me in the spring of my senior year and asked if he could take me to my senior prom."

The jurors saw the light in Katie's eyes. "I was surprised and pleased." She paused. "My senior prom was our first date. We were a couple from that day forward." She hesitated, the smile faded. "Until . . ."

A silence fell on the room. Juror Linda Noble, felt Katie's sadness as the witness misted.

Softly, John asked, "Mrs. Morrissey, you told us how you came to meet Marc Morrissey."

Katie raised her moist eyes to meet John's. He read the pain that he has known so well and so completely. Still, he had to help her by winning this trial. He took a breath and continued.

"Please tell us how your relationship with Marc progressed from that first date?"

The pain was plain to see. The juror in seat two, Manuela Gonzales, wife and mother of two, swallowed and misted with Katie.

Katie held John's eyes. "We were a couple from that first date," she started. The memories flooded back. "Marc was so kind, so gentle." A small smile crossed her lips, "except on the basketball court." She shook her head. "On the court he was a tiger." Her voice became small. "He loved to run the floor, leap above the basket." She paused. "Fight for rebounds." Katie sipped her water. "I'll never forget the game at the Mullens Center at UMASS." Now pride infused her voice. "The Minutemen were fighting for the Atlantic 10 title. They had to have the game and Temple was tough." She nodded. "Marc scored a basket with ten seconds left to give UMASS the lead." She paused. "Marc sprinted back on defense." She took a deep breath. "I can still see him, running, yelling instructions, setting up the defense." Tears pooled in her eyes. "There was such a look of determination on his face." Now, she was lost in memory.

"John, you remember," she urged. "That great forward that Temple had, Marc was covering him. He put up a shot to win the game." Katie turned to the jury. "Marc was right on him," she explained. "Marc wanted that game so badly." Katie took a deep breath. "The ball hit the rim and bounced high. The seven footers went for it." Excitement lit her face. "There was time for a tap in." Her eyes on the jury. "All you could see was Marc jump above them all and grab the rebound with two hands." She smiled through her tears. "His face, a look of total happiness. His feet hit the floor and the buzzer sounded." Now Katie's tears flowed freely. "I was on my feet cheering with the crowd, my eyes on Marc." Katie closed her eyes, pain stabbed at a pleasant memory. Katie looked at the jurors.

"He looked right at me," She stated, her cheeks glistened with tears. "His eyes were gleaming, he was beaming. He held the ball above his head and he mouthed the words, 'I love you,' to me."

A sigh escaped juror, Linda Noble.

"At the moment of his biggest win, he told me he loved me for the first time." Katie wiped her eyes. "I knew I wanted to be with Marc for the rest of my life."

The courtroom was still, the only sound a soft sob.

John smiled at Katie, and knew that the jurors realized fully what Katie, Lorraine and Helen had lost.

Judge Adams's gavel fell. In a soft voice, "we'll take the recess here." He said.

"Oh my God!" was all that Linda Noble could say when the door closed them in the jury room.

"She loved him so . . ." Manuela Gonzales muttered, still too choked up to complete her thought. "What a shame."

Len Harris and the rest of the jurors nodded in silent agreement.

The courtroom was still. As Judge Adams and his clerk left, John walked slowly to Katie, tempted to take her hand, he put them instead in his pockets.

"You okay, Katie?" He asked.

Katie looked up, tears softly rolling down her face. Unable to speak, she merely nodded.

The Direct examination of Katie Morrissey renewed in a subdued courtroom. Jim Bolton was acutely aware of the witness's effect on the jury. He could feel her pain. 'How do I cross-examine this witness?' he thought.

Katie began to describe their wedding day. John remembered it well. He had been a groomsman. As Katie told the jury of the happy day, John let his mind wander back to that brilliant June day.

Marc and Katie were married by Father Capelli at St. Ann's Church. Katie had shone in her white gown. The veil did nothing to hide her joy.

John found himself smiling as he recalled the gathering at Marc's parents home the morning of the wedding. The groomsmen and best man, Marc's younger brother Arthur, did their best to agitate the already nervous groom.

Peter Novello, a groomsman, suggested that football players were superior lovers to basketball players.

John recalled the grin that creased Marc's face. "Really Peter, now why is that?"

"You see," Peter began, placing a hand on Marc's shoulder in a brotherly, concerned fashion.

"Football is a contact sport." A gleam sparked in Peter's eye. "And engaging your opponent with force and control is how you score."

Peter had the group's attention.

"Now, Marc, the trouble with basketball is that you avoid contact and try to score from a distance."

The group, including Marc, was rolling with laughter. Feigning a scholarly pose, Peter continued. "Marc, a jump shot just won't work."

The group dissolved with laughter as Marc listened to Peter's sage advice.

John pulled himself back as Katie, still engaging the jury, related Marc's pride on the day Kelly was born.

"He held her in his big hands." Katie recalled with a soft smile. "The love on his face for his little girl was overwhelming." Katie stopped, bowed her head. When Katie returned her gaze to the jury her eyes were filled. "Marc thanked me for Kelly." She hesitated. "He looked at me, told me he loved me and thanked me for giving him his little girl."

The tears flowed freely now.

"I miss him so much." Her eyes moved to John. "I loved him so much," she choked. "I could never love another man as I loved Marc."

Their eyes locked. John offered an understanding smile and a nod of agreement.

"I understand, Katie," he said.

There was a silence.

"I have no more questions, Your Honor."

Judge Adams turned to James Bolton. "Cross-examination Mr. Bolton?"

Jim Bolton rose, eyes on Katie who was dissolved in tears. "No, Your Honor. No cross-examination."

"Very well," the judge nodded, noting the jury's emotional exhaustion. "Tomorrow, we'll resume at nine."

CHAPTER TWENTY-FIVE

It was late autumn and the nights were cold. John had dinner at the Amicos with Franco, Anna and his parents. After spending time with his children, John helped Maria put them to bed. He kissed each good night and smiling, reminded them of the time they would spend together when the trial concluded. His promise was rewarded with smiles, hugs and kisses.

"I love you Guys," John told them.

"We love you, Daddy," they chimed in response.

John told Benny and Maria he needed to clear his head. He left the home of his youth, hands thrust deep in his jacket pockets against the cold, and began to walk the granite curbed streets. Deep in thought, he found himself on Commercial Street. The street lights threw shadows and he could hear the waves lapping at the hulls of the fishing draggers at dock. Against the gray/black sky, by the light of a three quarter moon, he saw the masts and spars on the draggers roll with the movement of the harbor. He walked in the direction of Fort Square, three decker homes to his right and to his left, beyond the covered carts and stands which would brim with fresh fruit, produce, fish, nuts and sweets in the morning, the working harbor. He could smell the salt in the air and feel the generations of immigrants who had made these apartments their homes. Irish, Norwegians, Nova Scotians, Portugese, Italians, all had come to Gloucester to fish or work the granite quarries. All had worked for a better life for their children. And, as fortune smiled and they left the cramped three deckers for one family homes with a yard for children, or a garden, a new wave of immigrants arrived. Even as the wind off the harbor cut across his face, he thought of how he loved this community and it's people, his people. And how he missed Connie.

The years with Connie seemed almost a dream. That first day in America, ten years old, alone and scared he had descended the gangplank of the ocean liner. His first step into the United States, a bag in each hand, amidst the joyous confusion of greetings, embraces and smiles of reunion, he had been lost in a sea of faces and swirling bodies.

'What if they're not here?' He had thought, the fear clutching at his gut. He had tried moving, but didn't know in which direction to turn. How he had wished to be back on the blue Mediterranean, in the ten meter skiff, with his Papa. 'Why is this happening to me?' he thought. 'Why?'

As his fears began to grow into panic, he heard his name and turning to the sound, battling back the tears, he had forced a smile in the direction of the family moving towards him.

And she was there.

Benny had handled the introductions. John had tried so hard to be polite and properly thankful. But his heart was breaking and he missed his Papa so much. And, humiliated, he couldn't hold back the tears.

Maria had embraced him, speaking softly, comforting him. Then he felt Connie's hand on his cheek. "It will be okay." She had assured, with those soulful, soft brown eyes, that angelic face. And somehow, he knew it would be.

As he walked Stacy Boulevard in the direction of Stage Fort Park, the wind freshened, bringing tears to his eyes, but still he looked at the harbor out to Eastern Point. The Eastern Point Light played on the rippled harbor. The night was clear and the sky brilliant with stars.

'How did I get here?' John thought. 'Things had been so simple.'

He had taken them all on. The powerful insurance companies with their blacklist that terrified his people into submission. The evil Judge, Arnold Bailey, determined to defeat justice.

Dillon, the lawyer who had mocked and humiliated Benny Amico all those years before.

He had fought them all for the Barnas. A wonderful, innocent family who had simply asked for justice.

And, his thoughts turned to Joe Amalfi. Captain Guiseppe Amalfi, the captain among captains, who was evil, personified. And now, John was Amalfi's tool!

He shook the thought away, as he remembered the day, amidst the battle, when John knew he was losing and he found, somehow discovered that the fear that gnawed at him was false. The fear that he had carried for a lifetime was simply dissolved in those beautiful brown eyes, those soft, yielding lips. He had discovered freedom in the arms of the great love of his life.

Those few, precious years of bliss. He had been hailed as the "People's Champion." The lawyer who had defeated the blacklist and in the process brought justice to the Barnas and to his people. And, he had Connie.

He stood at Stage Fort Park overlooking Cressy's Beach. The moon shone on tablet rock. The wind cut the waves, the harbor a sea of whitecaps, foaming and churning.

Alone, oblivious to the cold and the wind, he gazed at the clear sky, the blanket of stars. He felt so alone, so bitterly, so completely alone.

His thoughts turned to the trial. He closed his eyes and wished he was free of Joe Amalfi. Is this what the People's champion should be fighting for? A corrupt, utterly despicable and loathsome character.

Then he thought of Matt Alves. John took a deep breath. He knew that boy. He knew the pain of loss that he carried.

Again he thought of the risks he was taking. He needed to get the evidence closed and the case to the jury. Each day the trial continued the danger increased. Fortunately, Jim Bolton had accepted his proposed stipulations. Those agreements, John knew, cut days of testimony from his case. But, had he miscalculated? In his quest to speedily move the trial to the jury, had he erred in not having Helen and Lorraine tell their stories? Was it a mistake to go with stipulated damages and lose the effect of actuarial testimony of the staggering economic losses these three fatherless families faced?

Josh O'Rourke and his bank lurked, itching to foreclose and take the homes and the only security these families had left.

Had he miscalculated?

In his race to get his case in, had he made too many concessions?

He took a deep breath and watched as a fishing dragger, deck lights ablaze, made its quiet way across the outer harbor, around the Eastern Point Light, and on it's way past Halibut Point and out to the fishing grounds.

He assessed his evidence, such as it was.

Katie had done her job well. The jury had felt her pain. John had seen that in their eyes. The eyes, the windows of the soul.

Amalfi had stumbled, but not as badly as John had feared.

John took a deep breath of the cold, clear night air. The air was washed by the sea and smelled of salt.

Bolton had the burden of proof, he thought. It was his job to prove the fraud that was at the heart of his defense. Could he?

If the jury accepted Joe Amalfi's story, or at least were unconvinced of Bolton's theory, the widows and Amalfi would win.

John shook his head and swallowed. 'Amalfi would win.' The thought angered him.

CHAPTER TWENTY-SIX

Trial Day Four

It was a clear and cold autumn day when the jury was seated and the court readied to continue the testimony. The light from the windows behind the jury box was thin and harsh.

"Mr. Palermo," Judge Adams began, "please call your next witness."

Rising, John smiled at the jury who collectively had their eyes on Katie, Helen and Lorraine.

"Your Honor," John offered. "Based on the stipulations, the plaintiff has completed his presentation." He paused. "The Plaintiffs rest, Your Honor."

"Very well, Mr. Palermo," Judge Adams stated. John heard a question in his tone.

"Mr. Bolton," the judge continued. "You may call your first witness."

Jim Bolton began his evidence by calling Arthur Schmidt to the stand. Schmidt was tall and lanky with gray hair on the fringes and bald on top. At fifty-five years old, he had been a naval architect and marine engineer for twenty-five years.

Bolton began by detailing Arthur Schmidt's impressive education. Arthur Schmidt received his Bachelor of Science degree from Stanford University. He then served in the U.S. Navy for five years, rising from the rank of Ensign to Lieutenant Commander. He then studied Naval Architecture in Stockholm, Sweden and received his Doctorate degree in Marine Engineering from the University of Hawaii.

Arthur Schmidt testified to a long and illustrious career in the design and re-design of seagoing vessels. His company, of which he was president and chief engineer, had designed oil tankers, tug boats, even yachts in addition to its work in the design and construction of fishing boats.

"How many vessels similar in kind and purpose to the *F/V Mio Mondo* have you and your company designed?" Bolton asked.

Schmidt smiled at Bolton. "Hundreds for fishing out of New England, in the gulf and on the West Coast to Alaska."

"Dr. Schmidt," Bolton queried. "At my request did you examine the plans of the design of the *F/V Mio Mondo*?"

Schmidt nodded. "I did, sir."

"And Doctor, based on your review of the architectural plans of the *F/V Mio Mondo*, your education, training and work in designing fishing vessels, did you form an opinion as to the quality of design and construction of this boat?"

"Objection," John stated forcefully, as he rose.

Judge Adams turned to John. "Mr. Palermo?"

"Your Honor," John began. "Unless Mr. Schmidt oversaw the construction of this vessel," he glanced at the witness. "He is not qualified to reach an opinion on its construction."

Judge Adams nodded. "Interesting point." He looked at Bolton.

"If I may," Bolton responded. "Dr. Schmidt has studied the design plans of the vessel and Captain Amalfi has testified that the vessel was well constructed." He paused. "In fact," he continued, "Captain Amalfi stated that it was the best."

Judge Adams sat back and studied the lawyers.

John smiled and glanced at the jury. He won a return smile from Linda Noble. He then turned to face Judge Adams.

"Your Honor," John began. "I will concede that this witness may well be qualified to study the plans and discuss the intent of the designers." He paused. "But, he did not oversee its construction." He then spread his arms. "In fact, Your Honor, this witness has never even seen the vessel."

Judge Adams drummed his fingers as he studied John.

"As to Captain Amalfi," John continued. "We did not present him as an expert witness on vessel construction, but merely as the only eye witness to the tragic events." John shifted as he studied the Judge. "I request that the Court instruct the witness to limit his testimony to the sketches and blue-prints he reviewed."

Judge Adams leaned forward, eyes on John. "Objection overruled." He turned to the witness. "You may answer."

John shrugged and sat. His goal was to challenge the credibility of Dr. Schmidt's testimony. To give the jury another prism through which to view this testimony. He had little hope that Judge Adams would sustain his objection. He hoped he had brought the expert witness down a peg or two in the eyes of the jury.

The court stenographer read back the question as John sat back. The jurors exchanged glances.

The question before him, Arthur Schmidt responded with an edge.

"Yes, sir, I did." He paused and looked directly at the jury. "The design was impeccable. It was a solidly constructed boat."

Bolton glanced at the jury and then back at Amalfi before returning his gaze to the witness.

"Dr. Schmidt, at my request did you review a video tape of the vessel *Mio Mondo*, as taken by a submersible, on the ocean floor?"

"Yes sir, I did," he nodded, grimly. "I viewed the tape in whole, and in parts, numerous times."

Bolton then faced the bench. "Your Honor, with the court's permission I would like to play the video tape."

Judge Adams looked to John. "Any objection, Mr. Palermo?"

"None, Your Honor."

"Also, Your Honor, as the video is silent I may ask Dr. Schmidt questions as the film rolls."

"Very well, proceed," Judge Adams ordered. The lights were turned off and the shades were drawn as the monitors were set up, one for the judge, a larger one for the jury.

With the judge's permission John and Larry Smith took a seat at the far end of the jury box to follow the video.

From his place John watched the gallery who moved together to view the screen.

As the videotape began to roll all eyes focused on the murky scene. The darkness of the courtroom seemed to blend with the watery silence of the ocean depths.

The widows winced when the *Mio Mondo* materialized on the screen. John watched Katie close her eyes as tears spilled through her lashes onto her cheeks. Like a blow to the gut, Katie fixed on Marc's tomb.

Joe Amalfi watched with horror as the submersible slowly circled the boat, which set in the mud and muck of the ocean bottom on its keel, listing to the portside. It looked about to sail away.

When the light played on the stern, the words '*MIO MONDO*' 'GLOUCESTER, MA' filled the screen. The captain's eyes darted in terror. The facial twitch played as the boat beckoned.

When the camera moved about the starboard side the light played off of the painted hull in dull reflection. When the light hit the deck, the black deck tiles showed gray through the churned bottom. The rigging and steel blocks reflected brighter with the sharpest points being the brass fittings.

The empty deck was eerie as the light played off of the winch, rails, rigging and fo'c's'le. John watched the gallery closely as the widows sat and prayed, heads bowed until they were irresistibly pulled back to the monitor.

The camera moved around to the starboard forward quarter showing the raised bow and '*MIO MONDO*' emblazoned in bold black letters on the red hull. In the background was the pilothouse, barely visible through the murk. The brass fittings on the mast shone dully. Still, among the assorted shades of gray, they were the most prominent feature of the rust and barnacle-covered vessel.

When the submersible with camera and light had made a complete circumference of the boat, Jim Bolton hit the pause button. The courtroom was wrapped in silence.

"Dr. Schmidt," Bolton began. "In your professional opinion did the video we just viewed of the *F/V Mio Mondo* reveal hull damage or structural damage sufficient to cause the vessel to sink so quickly that three men would have no means of escape?"

"Objection, Your Honor. Mr. Bolton is mischaracterizing the evidence," John stated.

The judge turned to Bolton. "First of all, do you plan to show the balance of the video-tape Mr. Bolton?"

"Yes, Your Honor, I do."

The judge nodded. "Very well, we'll leave the shades drawn, but lets have the lights please." The court officer moved to and flipped the light switch. Then the Judge addressed Bolton. "Mr. Bolton are you asking this witness a hypothetical question?

Bolton shrugged. "I guess so, Your Honor."

Judge Adam's words hardened. "If so, then ask the question in that manner. Otherwise I will have to sustain Mr. Palermo's objection."

Bolton threw a hard look back at Amalfi, then turned back to the witness. "Dr. Schmidt, I'm going to ask you to assume certain facts as given." Schmidt nodded.

"I ask you to assume that the *F/V Mio Mondo* was steaming home from George's Bank to Gloucester Harbor." He walked over to the tripod.

He pointed at the chart and the red marker on the tripod. "And further assume that the vessel sank here."

Schmidt took in the chart with the black line drawn from George's Bank to Gloucester Harbor and the red marker so far off course.

"Now," Bolton continued. "Based on your review of the design specifications of the *F/V Mio Mondo* and the video tape you have seen, do you have an opinion to a reasonable degree of scientific certainty as to what caused the *F/V Mio Mondo* to sink on September 4th of last year?"

"I do," Schmidt answered.

"What is your opinion, Dr. Schmidt?"

The naval architect turned to the jury and struck a somber pose.

"I believe that the vessel was intentionally sunk."

The jurors leaned forward in their seats. Lorraine Alves worked her pocketbook strap. Helen Picardi dabbed at her eyes, while Katie sat stonefaced and angry.

"On what do you base your opinion, Dr. Schmidt?"

"To begin, I have studied the video tape very closely with magnification. I find no damage whatsoever to the exposed hull of the vessel. Second, the location in which it sank was the deepest area in the charted area. To believe that it sank there by coincidence is not reasonable. And finally, unless a large part of the hull had been ripped out, the boat just would not have sunk so fast." He sat back.

"Anything else, Dr. Schmidt?"

Schmidt set his jaw. "Actually, yes." John felt his gut clench, as the witness continued. "I cannot believe that while Captain Amalfi was unconscious, all three members of the crew were washed overboard or disabled." He shook his head. "Just too many coincidences."

"Thank you, Doctor." Bolton turned to the court officer. "Would you please turn off the lights?"

When the courtroom was again darkened, Bolton hit the play button. For the next thirty-five minutes the jury, judge and spectators studied the *F/V Mio Mondo* in its eternal resting place. And, in the quiet of the darkened room, considered Arthur Schmidt's testimony.

Finally, the lights came on and the shades were raised. John knew Bolton's witness had made a solid case. He also knew this cross-examination was crucial.

John rose and with jaw set went on the attack. "So, to summarize your testimony, Dr. Schmidt, you believe that the *F/V Mio Mondo* was intentionally sunk and the crew were murdered?"

The question caught Schmidt off balance. He hesitated as he deliberated his response.

John moved toward the witness. In a strong voice, as he pointed a finger at Amalfi, John repeated. "You say Captain Amalfi is a murderer, correct, sir?"

The naval architect sat back in his seat. Now John pointed the accusing finger at Schmidt. "Answer me, sir. Are you saying Captain Amalfi killed those men?"

Through narrowed eyes Schmidt responded in a small voice. "No, I'm not saying that."

John straightened and smiled.

"Excellent, we can agree Captain Amalfi did not kill those men."

Schmidt nodded with uncertainty as John walked to the tripod and took up a pointer. First, he ran the pointer over the chart from George's Bank to Gloucester Harbor along the black line. Then he placed the tip of the pointer on the red marker. "Dr. Schmidt, are you aware of Captain Amalfi's testimony?"

"Yes, sir."

"So then you're aware that Captain Amalfi was unconscious on the deck of the vessel for an unspecified time."

"That's what I understand." A certain haughtiness was back in his tone. John shot him a hard look.

"Do you have any facts to dispute that Captain Amalfi was in fact unconscious on the deck of the *F/V Mio Mondo* for an unspecified time?"

Arthur Schmidt was no shrinking violet. He set his eyes on John and shot back, "yes, I also reviewed Captain Amalfi's sworn statement to the Coast Guard on the day the vessel went down."

John stood tall. "Did you?"

Schmidt nodded. "I did."

"Then you read that Captain Amalfi told the Coast Guard investigating officer that he had been unconscious." John stated.

"Yes," Schmidt agreed. "But, he said for a short time."

John smiled and pointed his finger at Schmidt. "Well, Dr. Schmidt, could you tell us what it means to be unconscious for a short time?"

Schmidt's eyes narrowed. "I don't understand the question."

"It's pretty simple, actually." John began. "Captain Amalfi was unconscious, correct?"

Schmidt nodded. "That's what I read."

"And," John continued, "he was unconscious long enough for the vessel's deck to be awash with the ocean."

Schmidt glared hard at John. "Perhaps, but . . ."

"Wait a minute, sir," John ran over Schmidt. "We've heard your speculations and your theories. Now I'm asking for facts." He paused. "I'll ask you to please answer my questions." He smiled. "Is that reasonable, sir?"

Schmidt nodded.

"Do you have any facts to dispute that the vessel struck a submerged object and sank here?" He jabbed at the red mark.

"No, I don't."

"Ah," John smiled. "But you think it's too much of a coincidence, correct?"

"That's right."

John pointed at a different area of the chart. "If it had sunk here would you believe otherwise?"

Arthur Schmidt looked at the chart.

"I don't know."

"Indeed, you don't," John stated emphatically.

Judge Adams beat Bolton's objection.

"Ask questions," the judge ordered. "You'll have your chance for argument at the appropriate time."

John nodded to the bench. "Of course, Your Honor."

John poked the chart in four different locations. "Had the vessel sunk in three hundred feet or two hundred fifty feet or here," he jabbed the chart, "in four hundred feet of water, it still would have taken a submersible to film it, isn't that so?"

Schmidt nodded. "Yes, it is."

John walked over to the monitor where it set before the jury. He flashed a smile at the jury and Katie observed he received smiles in return. Placing his hand on the monitor, he asked, "Mr. Schmidt, in the video tape we saw the keel and approximately the bottom six feet of the boat buried in the ocean bottom, isn't that correct?"

Schmidt nodded grudgingly. "Yes."

John looked to the jury as he queried. "So it's fair to say that neither you nor anybody else can state with certainty what the condition of the keel and the vessel's bottom is? Isn't that true?"

The witness grimaced. "Yes, that is true."

John nodded at the jury, then turned to the witness. "So, Dr. Schmidt, it's fair to say that when the vessel struck the submerged object, the keel could have been damaged or the hull plates may well have been torn away, causing a force of water into the boat. Isn't that so?"

Arthur Schmidt's eyes narrowed, his jaw jutted as he said, "I don't believe that, sir."

John smiled. "But you cannot disprove it, can you?"

The witness hesitated, then conceded.

"Thank you, sir, no more questions."

"Any re-direct, Mr. Bolton?" The judge asked.

"No, Your Honor." Bolton responded. The judge turned to Schmidt. "You are excused, sir."

"Mr. Bolton, will you be calling another witness?" The judge asked.

Bolton rose slowly. While Schmidt had been effective, Bolton realized that he needed to focus the jury on Captain Amalfi. So, he decided to take a gamble.

"Yes, your Honor." He glanced about. "I issued a subpoena this morning, but my witness does not seem to be here."

As the words were spoken, Peter Novello burst into the courtroom, subpoena in hand and a scowl on his face.

He wore a two day beard and was dressed for unloading fish, in a flannel shirt, heavy wool pants, a hole at the knee, and heavy work boots. At his collar and knee, woolen underwear were visible to ward off the North Atlantic winds.

John could not help but grin at Peter, who clearly didn't see the humor in the situation.

"Your Honor," Bolton looked to the judge. "It appears my witness is here." Turning to Peter, Bolton gestured to the witness stand. "Would you take the witness stand, Mr. Novello?"

Peter glanced in the direction of the gallery. He nodded towards Katie, Helen and Lorraine, glared at Joe Amalfi as he moved through the rail to the witness box.

"I'm sorry for the inconvenience, Mr. Novello," Bolton began.

"I was taking out fish," Peter stated, an edge to his voice. "Your guy wouldn't even let me wash up and change."

Bolton raised his hands, palms out. "I'm sorry, but your fishing boat just arrived at the dock this morning."

Peter sat back, with a shrug. "Okay, if you can take it, I can." He conveyed the unmistakable image of power in his broad chest and shoulders. There was a challenge in his eyes.

John grinned at Peter's reference to the stench which slowly, but definitely, began to permeate the room.

Katie, along with Helen and Lorraine smiled as the jurors and judge's clerk who sat closest to the witness box, began to wrinkle their noses and lean away from the pungent smell of decaying fish, which clung to his work clothes.

In a strange way, the aroma, coupled with the solidness of body of Peter Novello, brought to the minds of these widows the image of their young, attractive, but aromatic husbands, returning from ten days at sea, with a gleam in their eye and a spring in their step at the thought of their wives waiting for them.

John knew that calling Peter was a calculated risk by Jim Bolton. Bolton had no idea what Peter would say and the trial lawyers' gospel made clear that a question is never asked unless the questioner already knew the answer that would be given. Here Bolton did not know. What was clear was that Bolton issued the subpoena after the trial day began, thus making it impossible for John to prepare Peter. Then, if necessary, Bolton could call Peter to the witness stand without the Plaintiffs' lawyers preparation. That Bolton had called Peter was an admission by Bolton that his case was in trouble. Still, that was known by John and by Bolton, not by the jury. John smiled at his lifelong friend and hoped for the best.

The examination began with Peter's life. He was a high school graduate who has been a full time fisherman for sixteen years.

"Mr. Novello, it's fair to say that you are familiar with Captain Amalfi and his attorney, John Palermo, isn't it?"

"Yes," Peter said without expression.

"In fact," Bolton said companionably, "John Palermo is and has been a good friend of yours for a long time, correct?"

"Absolutely."

"Is he honest?" Bolton asked directly.

Peter's temper flared. "You bet he is."

Bolton nodded, thoughtfully, as he studied Peter. "You know Captain Amalfi, don't you?"

"I told you I did."

Bolton offered an apologetic smile and shrug of the shoulders. "Yes, you did." He paused. "How do you know him?"

Peter sat back. "I was a crewmember on his boat for a few years."

Bolton leaned forward on the podium. "That means that you were at sea with Captain Amalfi for ten to twelve days, home for two days and then back at sea with Captain Amalfi for ten to twelve days, correct?"

"That's about right," Peter agreed warily.

"So you got to know the character of the man pretty well?"

"I guess so."

"Mr. Novello, what is your opinion of Captain Amalfi?"

John felt his gut tighten. Well aware of Peter's opinions on the subject of Joe Amalfi, he could do nothing but appear at ease and hope for the best.

"I don't like Joe Amalfi," Peter stated forthrightly.

Bolton nodded. Peter's response was not what he had hoped for.

"Mr. Novello, did you find Captain Amalfi cruel in his dealings with crew members?"

Peter studied Bolton momentarily, then nodded. "Yes."

"Did you find Captain Amalfi dishonest in his dealings with his crew?"

"Yes."

"In fact he was tyrannical, was he not?"

Peter sat back. "Yes, he was."

Now Bolton bore in. "In truth, Mr. Novello, Captain Amalfi always placed his best interests in front of his crews', isn't that true?"

Peter smiled. "Sure, but that's not unusual, is it?"

Bolton grinned in recognition of the point. "I agree, Mr. Novello." He paused and glanced at his notes.

"Do you know Benny Amico?"

Peter nodded slowly. "Yes, I do."

"What did Captain Amalfi do to Mr. Amico?"

John sat back and found himself still angry at the memory.

"Amalfi lied and cheated to get Benny Amico." Peter glanced at John. "Then he broke his promise and fired him."

Rosalie Amalfi lowered her eyes at Peter's words.

"Why did Captain Amalfi fire him?"

A scowl closed over Peter's face. "Benny was hurt and couldn't work as well as before his injury."

John noted how deftly Bolton skirted asking questions that would ultimately reflect on his client.

"Mr. Novello, do you know Busty Barna?"

"Yes sir, I do."

"When Mr. Barna was injured on the Fishing Vessel *Mio Mondo*, you were a member of the crew, correct?"

"I was," Peter agreed.

"And when he brought a claim against the boat, you were called to testify, weren't you?"

Eyes narrowed and focused, Peter nodded his head. "Yes, I was."

With a small smile Bolton asked, "Before trial you quit the *Mio Mondo* and Captain Amalfi, didn't you?"

"I did."

"And when you did, what reason did you give for leaving the boat and captain that earned more money per crewman than any in the fleet?"

Peter shrugged his shoulders, looked at Bolton.

"I was tired of being treated with no respect."

"In fact, Captain Amalfi belittled every member of his crew, didn't he?"

Peter took a deep breath. "Yes, he did."

"On the night Busty Barna was so badly injured, Captain Amalfi forced the entire crew to meet at the boat at midnight, on a windy and bitterly cold night, just to be told to go home, didn't he?"

Rosalie Amalfi flushed as she recalled the night and how she had pleaded with Joe to call the crew before they left their warm homes.

"Yes," Peter stated darkly.

"And because of that Busty Barna was badly hurt?"

Peter sighed. "Yes, that's right."

Bolton hesitated as he stood quietly. He glanced back at Amalfi who sat, eyes fixed angrily on the defense attorney. Then he took the plunge.

"Mr. Novello, based on your knowledge of the character of Captain Amalfi, do you have an opinion as to whether he would hesitate to risk his crews' safety to advance his self-interest?"

John thought about objecting to the question, but stayed in his seat, eyes on Peter.

In a soft voice, Peter responded, "Yes, I think he would."

Jim Bolton paused, studied Peter Novello and with a nod plunged forward.

"Mr. Novello, the defense in this case has advanced the theory that Captain Amalfi intentionally sank the *F/V MIO MONDO* in the deepest waters he could find for the purposes of fraudulently collecting on the vessel's insurance policy."

Peter nodded, but said nothing.

"In so doing," the defense attorney continued, "a terrible accident of some kind occurred, and the three man crew died."

Bolton took a breath, fixed his gaze on the witness, and in a strong tone laid it all out for the jury. "Mr. Novello, based on your intimate knowledge of the character of Captain Amalfi, do you believe him capable of committing fraud as described by intentionally and deliberately sinking the *F/V MIO MONDO* to collect the insurance policy?"

Peter sat back. His gaze passed over the widows and settled hard on Amalfi. Then, he looked back at Jim Bolton. "Yes, I believe he would."

The answer seemed to suck all the air out of the room.

Now in a softer voice, Bolton asked, "even at the risk of injury or death to his crew?"

Peter glanced at John, who offered a shrug and a thin smile.

Peter sat up, squared his shoulders. "Yes, I know he's capable of that."

Bolton saw his opening. "How do you know, Captain Novello?"

Peter's glare cut to Amalfi. Pointing his finger at the diminutive captain, Peter stated, "he had me attacked, beaten and hospitalized."

Bolton paused to allow the words to settle on the jury.

"Mr. Novello, I'm going to show you a short clip of a video tape taken by a submersible of the *F/V MIO MONDO* on the ocean floor."

The lights flashed out and the participants were plunged back to the ocean floor. The image seen was the deck of the *F/V MIO MONDO* from the stern and above the vessel, then the shot panned out to show the full circumference of the vessel's hull.

Bolton stopped the video and the court officer threw the switch to light the room.

Peter Novello's eyes were on John, who met his gaze evenly. Peter then sat back and looked toward the gallery, before eyeing Bolton.

"Mr. Novello, as an experienced fisherman and fishing captain, did you see any damage to the vessel that would result in its sinking?"

Peter looked at the jury, saw their eyes focused, intently, on him. He glanced, again, into the gallery at the three widows and then found Amalfi. His glare and the set of his jaw told a story in itself.

"No," he nodded. "Of what I can see, I see no damage." He paused. "But a good part of the hull is not visible." Peter looked from John back to Bolton. "It's impossible to say or to know what damage there is."

John sat back, eyes on Peter.

With a shake of the head, Bolton said, "thank you, Mr. Novello, I have no more questions." And he sat.

"Mr. Palermo, do you have any questions for the witness?" Judge Adams asked.

In John's mind, Bolton's gamble had failed. Certainly, Peter Novello had verified that Captain Joe Amalfi was the original Bastard. Still, as the insurance company had the burden of proving fraud, Peter's testimony had not advanced Bolton's case. Thus, John saw no benefit in cross-examining Peter. He rose, smiled at the witness before turning to the judge.

"No, your Honor."

"Very well." The judge turned to Peter. "You're excused."

Peter left the witness box and the courtroom.

The judge turned to Bolton. "Any further witnesses, Mr. Bolton?"

Bolton rose. "No, your Honor. The defense rests."

The judge then faced John. "Any rebuttal witnesses, Mr. Palermo?"

John rose and smiled. "No, Your Honor."

"Very well, tomorrow at 9:00 a.m. for argument and charge."

John stood as the jury departed. He watched them go, then turned and faced Bolton. The lawyers' eyes met for a moment before John shifted his gaze to the gallery. First, he focused on Amalfi, who sat and avoided his eyes. Then he saw Katie who smiled his way encouragingly, maybe even lovingly. He shrugged away the thought.

CHAPTER TWENTY-SEVEN

John spent the afternoon reviewing his trial notes and consulting with his associate, Larry Smith. It had been Larry's job to watch the jury closely during all phases of the trial, to study reactions and body language to determine just what evidence moved the jury and what evidence may prove difficult in swaying the jury.

Once satisfied, John closed himself in his office to outline his all-important final argument. Three hours later he emerged to work with Larry and Phil Harmon. Always a critical audience, Phil made comments and suggestions to tighten up John's presentation.

Phil sat back and smiled. "You're ready," he offered.

John nodded and glanced at his watch. "Why don't you guys head home, it's almost eight."

Alone, John paced his office deep in thought, glass of bourbon in hand. Finally, having called Maria and being assured the children were peacefully asleep; he locked the office and settled behind the wheel of his Jeep. He drove, operating on a kind of remote control, as he wrestled with random bits of his argument amid thoughts of Amalfi and the widows. His mind flashed to Matt Alves, bravely having faced the loss of his dad at eight years old. John knew the long and lonely road Matt would tread without a father's guiding hand. And how much more difficult that road would be without the money generated by winning this trial.

Josh O'Rourke came to mind. Should John fail tomorrow, Josh and his bank would swoop in like thieves in the night to steal the homes and the little security that remained to the desperate families.

He drove on aimlessly, lost in his thoughts, until he pulled up in front of Katie's house. Mentally, he shrugged, knowing she had been on his mind for months. A glance at his watch and he saw it was 9:30 p.m. It was getting late but he did want to see her. Oblivious to the cold on this November night, he walked to her door, took a deep breath and knocked.

She opened the door looking comfortably rumpled but beautiful in a long white robe. When she saw him a smile burst through.

"What a nice surprise, come in please."

John entered her living room at a loss to explain his presence. He looked at her. "I wanted to see you."

Her smile turned to concern. "Are you all right, John?"

He shrugged. "I was at the office."

"Yes," she replied, seeing that he was dressed as he had been in court. "Have you eaten?"

He managed a weak smile. "I hadn't thought about it."

Her eyes narrowed as she studied him. He was in turmoil. "What is it, John? Are Franco and Anna well?"

The question brought a trace of panic to her eyes. Her concern for his children brought Kelly to mind. Then he thought of the Alves and Picardi children. 'I can't let them down,' he thought.

"Anna and Franco are fine," he assured. "I was thinking about you today and . . ." he left the thought unfinished.

Katie's relief brought a smile. She put her hands on his face in a soft, loving gesture. "You scared me, John."

She studied him. "You've been working too hard. I know that you've been carrying the weight of all of us since the boat went down."

"Katie . . ."

"No, John, please," She sighed and held his eyes. "I was sitting here thinking. When you were a boy you had no mother and then your father, the only person that you had in the world, got sick."

John watched her closely and read the understanding in her blue eyes.

"The day he put you on that ship for America must have been awful." Her voice caught. "You were just a little boy." She shook her head. "Then when life seemed perfect for you, Connie became sick." Her voice became a whisper, "so unfair, so unfair." A single tear escaped to run down her cheek. "When she died you must have wanted to die yourself."

"You know," he responded in a husky voice.

"Yes, I know. But I didn't have to take on the pain of three others who lost their loves. I didn't have to fight for their futures while I was torn up inside. You did that, and now you face tomorrow alone before that jury with our homes and lives in the balance." She shook her head and found a smile. "I don't know how you can do it, and," she let out a deep breath, "I know I haven't been much of a help."

"Katie . . ."

She raised her hand to his lips. "I've been tying you up in knots. For that, I am sorry."

"Me, too," he offered wryly.

That produced a laugh. "Well, at least I can feed you. After all, I can't have my lawyer weak from hunger."

She led him into the kitchen. He sat at the table as she busied herself warming a pot of stew she had taken from the refrigerator. From the breadbox she took a freshly baked loaf of Italian bread and sliced two thick wedges.

When the stew was heated, she placed a heaping bowl before him, with the bread and a bottle of red wine.

John looked from the stew to Katie. "Thank you. Will you have a glass of wine?"

"Sure," she said. "I'll pour while you eat."

The beef stew was hearty and tasty. He smiled as he dipped a piece of bread into the gravy. "Excellent, Katie. You bake bread like an Italian girl."

She laughed. "A high compliment from an Italian boy."

John finished the bowl and used the bread to clean the last remnants of gravy. "That was great. Thank you again."

"You're welcome, John."

He rose. "I'm sorry I barged in so late." He paused.

Katie sat back and smiled. "Why did you come by?"

With a shrug of the shoulders, "I guess because today, putting together my argument . . ." He broke his thought and sighed. "It was tough thinking about Marc and you." He swallowed.

"And Peter?" she asked.

"Yes," he agreed, "and Peter."

Horror struck Katie's eyes. "Do you think Bolton is right?" she gasped. "Oh my God, you don't think . . . ?"

"No," he said firmly. "I don't."

"John," her eyes pleaded.

He moved to her and lifted her from her chair, held her at arm's length and engaged her eyes. "Katie," his voice was stern. "Amalfi has always been human garbage. But," he shook his head. "To Bolton this is just a way to save the insurance company money. Not even Joe Amalfi would do such a thing."

Her terror melted away in his grip and under his gaze. She fell against his chest, finding comfort.

He stroked her hair and gently kissed her cheek, now wet with tears. "It was a terrible accident Katie, just a terrible accident."

Sobbing, she nodded her head. "I know, I know."

She stayed in the circle of his arms, feeling safe. Katie could feel the beat of his heart and the strength of his arms. She recognized the stirring within her and wasn't afraid. Indeed, Katie sensed a re-awakening and cherished the feeling and the man who was its cause. She snuggled against him and looked up into his eyes. She felt his response and welcomed it. She smiled into his steady gaze.

"Thank you, I couldn't get through this without you." Her voice caught. "I know how difficult this case has been for you. After everything Amalfi did to your family and to Peter Novello . . ." She took a deep breath. "Then to help us you had to nurse him through all this. I know it has been tough."

"Katie . . ."

She shook her head. "I need to say this." She offered softly. "Lorraine, Helen and I talked on the ride home. You were wonderful, John. You kept Amalfi together, then took care of that naval architect." She looked deep into his eyes. "You're our savior, John. Where would we be without you?"

John closed his eyes and bowed his head.

Katie raised her hands to his face and then ran her hands through his hair, before wrapping her arms around him. "I haven't been fair with you," she whispered. "Get us through this, John. We need to close this and settle our lives." She choked. "Then we'll be able to think of you and me." She was crying now. "Please, get us through this."

John straightened and brushed the tears off her cheeks with his fingers. Then he found her eyes. Slowly he brought his lips to hers in a soft and reassuring kiss. "I will, Katie, I'll take care of everything."

She trembled at the kiss, but found her voice. "I have to give Marc justice. His death will take care of his daughter's future." She bit her lip. "I owe him that."

John nodded and smiled. "I'll see you tomorrow, Katie. We'll finish this tomorrow." He ran his fingertips over her lips. "I owe it to Marc, too." He turned and left, his decision made.

CHAPTER TWENTY-EIGHT

Trial: Day Five

John felt the surge that came with final argument. As he entered the courtroom he saw that all the actors were in place. Bolton and his associate at defense table. Rosalie and Joe Amalfi seated together in the gallery and the three widows side by side in the row behind the Amalfis.

Katie caught his eye and offered an encouraging smile. Amalfi appeared more at ease than at any time since that tragic day fourteen months before. The captain nodded in John's direction with a look of confidence in his eyes.

Judge Adams took the bench and the jury was brought in.

During the course of the judge's pre-argument instructions, John watched the jury glance to the gallery. He noted that Lorraine, Katie and Helen had joined hands.

When the judge concluded his comments he turned to Bolton. "Are you prepared for final argument, Mr. Bolton?"

Bolton nodded and rose. "I am, Your Honor." Then he strode to the jury box, adjusted his glasses, cleared his throat and looked to the jury.

He began by thanking them for serving. Then he pointed at Joe Amalfi. "That man intentionally sank the *Mio Mondo*."

It was a statement designed to shock and it succeeded.

"A wild statement?" he mused. "Not at all. Let us look at the facts."

"First, the boat sank at the deepest area on that entire chart." He shrugged. "A coincidence?" His head shook. "I don't think so. It's important to understand that when a vessel sinks in deep water, divers cannot dive on it. At six hundred feet, the best we could do was a submersible with a camera." He paused and turned to face the captain. "He knew the cost involved and fully expected that we would do nothing." Jim Bolton fixed his eyes on the jurors. "He was wrong!" Scanning their faces, he continued. "And, he is wrong to believe he can fool you."

Amalfi glowered at Bolton, while his breathing thickened and the twitch flared.

"You saw the video." Bolton's passion level rose. "The boat did not have a scratch." He paused and became thoughtful. "Ask yourself, how likely is it that the hull damage was so great that the pumps couldn't handle the flow of water but absolutely no damage would show on the exposed hull?" He shook his head, then glanced at the widows. "I'm sorry ladies," he turned back to the jury. "But the same man who could participate in the brutal beating of a man who crewed on his boat could just as easily sink that boat to collect the insurance!" Bolton shook his head with regret in his eyes. "And, inadvertently, cause the death of three young men." Bolton paused, as he fixed a glare at Amalfi.

"Yesterday you heard from Peter Novello. You will remember that Peter Novello was the key witness in the case of Barna versus the Boat Mio Mondo, Inc." He paused for effect. "Peter Novello was also the man pointed out by Captain Amalfi for a violent beating." Bolton glanced back at John. "You also heard from Peter Novello that John Palermo was a good friend and," Bolton shrugged in acquiescence, "a good man."

John sat, offering no re-action to the jury. Katie found herself nodding in agreement. 'Yes,' she thought. 'A very good man.'

The defense attorney paced the length of the jury box as he collected his thoughts. "As a good friend of Mr. Palermo, Peter Novello would have no reason to testify favorably to my client." Bolton's eyes sought out the jurors. "Still, that's exactly what he did."

John noted that two of the jurors nodded in agreement. One other juror, who had sat facing Bolton with his arms crossed and leaning back, away from his words, relaxed his face and uncrossed his arms. A sign that the defense attorney had hit a chord.

"Remember Mr. Novello's words. He described Captain Amalfi as cruel. He spoke of how Captain Amalfi belittled his crew as a means of control."

Two jurors, Len Harris and Manuela Gonzalez, told John through their eyes and tilt of the head that they recognized the pattern.

"Peter Novello told us that Busty Barna was severely injured because Captain Amalfi forced the crew to gather at the boat on a frigid midnight in February, for no other reason than to demonstrate his power." He paused and spoke softly but insistently. "How difficult is it to believe that the same man who placed his crew at risk on that February night and who caused the injury to Busty Barna through cruelty and a misguided sense of control," he pounded his fist into his open palm. "How difficult is it to believe that such a man could again risk his crew by intentionally sinking his boat and inadvertently killing three fine young men?" His voice rose an octave. "I submit that such a conclusion is not only conceivable but, based on his life, the likely scenario."

Bolton stopped and looked to the jury. "And please remember that Peter Novello, who worked and lived with Amalfi for ten to twelve days at a time for more than two years, stated that Amalfi would be fully capable and willing to do exactly that!"

"Just as he lied under oath to deny other just claims," he raged on. "Joe Amalfi would lie under oath to collect money he has no right to."

Bolton took a deep breath. John read the frustration in his eyes. "My client did not pay Captain Amalfi," Bolton declared. "Because to pay him would be to reward a cheat, a liar and the man who caused the deaths of three good men. When you begin to deliberate please consider just how many coincidences you have to accept to believe Mr. Amalfi." He studied the jurors. "First," he continued, "the *Mio Mondo* coincidentally sank at the deepest area on the chart. Second, the damage to the hull just coincidentally occurred on that part of the hull that settled into the ocean floor." He shook his head. "Third, nobody but Captain Amalfi survived, coincidentally, to tell us what occurred. And finally, this admitted perjurer is, coincidentally and for the first time, actually telling the truth."

Bolton considered the jury with a long look. "That is simply too many coincidences for me. I hope you see it the same way." Quietly, Jim Bolton sat.

John rose and turned a glance on Bolton. The frustration was there in the defense lawyer's eyes. As John moved to the jury box his gaze drifted to Katie where she sat with Lorraine and Helen. Katie's eyes shone with confidence and encouragement. The faces of Lorraine and Helen were set hard, eyes on John. He saw the desperation and the hope. The Amalfis sat in the first row behind the bar, directly before the widows. Rosalie smiled encouragingly while Joe's composure had dissolved into tortured eyes and a flaring twitch. The courtroom door then swung open and Josh O'Rourke entered. Instantly, O'Rourke's eyes locked with John's. A small smile played at the banker's lips and John saw menace in his eyes. John turned to face the jury.

"On behalf of Mr. and Mrs. Amalfi, the widows and the children of Marc Morrissey, Luke Alves and Joe Picardi, I thank you for your attention and your efforts as jurors in this trial." John focused on the jurors.

"Mr. Bolton's argument offered nothing to rebut the testimony you have heard in this trial." He paused. "The *Mio Mondo* struck a submerged object and ultimately sank." His voice lowered drawing the jurors to him. "And that evidence stands before you uncontested and unchallenged except for the paid opinions of Mr. Bolton's so-called expert witness."

John smiled and shook his head. "Coincidence . . . Yes that word was the heart and soul of Mr. Bolton's challenge. So, let's look at it." John walked to the chart and put his finger on the red marker. "The boat sank here." He took in Bolton with disbelief in his eyes. "Just how coincidental is that?" He turned back to the chart. "What if it sank here?" He placed his finger on the chart in an area with a depth of five hundred fifty feet. "Still too deep to dive." He stopped. "If it sank here, would that be too much of a coincidence for the insurance company?" Amused, he shook his head. "You know as well as I that the American Marine Insurance Company groped for any reason possible to deny Captain Amalfi and these women and children that which they were owed."

With an exasperated shake of the head, John continued. "The boat sank. Captain Amalfi was injured and three men died. Just what kind of lunacy is it to advance a theory that the boat was intentionally sunk and the men killed?" John's eyes shot daggers as he turned on Bolton. "It's more than lunacy, it's downright cruel." He raised his hand in a dramatic sweep. "And this lunacy is advanced in the name of insurance company greed." John's chiseled features became hard. "For the insurance company this is about money. You know the drill, take premiums for decades and never pay. For the American Marine Insurance Company this case isn't about three widows and six orphans. It is not about living up to a contract. It's not about honesty or decency or even justice. No, it's about money and the bottom line and nothing more."

John exhaled and shook his head. "Mr. Bolton made a good argument," he conceded. "That is, if the test of a final argument is the ability to deceive and convince decent jurors of a lie." He smiled. "My client, Captain Joe Amalfi, is not my friend." He shrugged. "In truth, I don't like him. I don't like what he did to Benny Amico. I don't like what he did to Busty Barna nor to Peter Novello." He searched out the jurors' eyes. "Still, in Mr. Bolton's rush to cloud the facts with hatred for Joe Amalfi, he neglected to mention the most important underlying fact. That fact is that everything that Captain Amalfi did, he did on orders of the American Marine Insurance Company."

John's jaw set hard and his eyes showed anger. "The American Marine Insurance Company directed a conspiracy to cheat fishermen." His voice rose. "And today they are trying to cheat widows and their children out of what is rightfully theirs." He paused as he moderated his tone. "Yes, Captain Amalfi was wrong to be intimidated by the threats of Mr. Bolton's clients." And now he played his ace. "Today Mr. Bolton's clients, this massive insurance company, seek to cheat the families of three fine men. Please don't let them do it."

John took a deep breath and sighed. "Finally, ladies and gentlemen, Mr. Bolton told you a story of the trial of United States vs. Charles Dillon. He slanted that story to embarrass Captain Amalfi." John's eyes embraced the jury as he moved on. "But he didn't tell you that it was Mr. Dillon, the lawyer for the American Marine Insurance Company, that was arrested, tried and convicted of obstruction of justice, suborning perjury and aggravated assault and battery." Slowly, he pointed to Amalfi. "Captain Amalfi was as much a victim of this massive insurance company, whose only thought was making money, as any of the others." He paused. "The criminals have been the American Marine Insurance Company and their lawyers."

Bolton's face reddened slightly, but noticeably.

"Ladies and gentlemen, please don't allow this insurance company and it's lawyers to cheat these innocent victims." His gaze passed to the gallery. Amalfi's head was down; the women's tears flowed as the anguish registered on their faces. The jurors' eyes followed John's; the widows' pain played out before them.

"When you retire to the jury room to decide the future of the Morrissey family, the Alves family, and the Picardi family, you will have one question to answer on the special verdict question form." He took the sheet and read. "Was the loss of the *F/V Mio Mondo* a covered loss under the policy of insurance?"

Softly he concluded, "there has been enough pain for my clients, they have suffered enough. Don't allow them to again be cheated."

He sat in a courtroom which was stunned into silence. The only sound, the sobs of Katie Morrissey, Lorraine Alves and Helen Picardi.

CHAPTER TWENTY-NINE

The jury began its deliberations following Judge Adams' instructions of law. James Bolton and his associate returned to their Boston offices leaving John and his entourage of lawyers and clients in possession of the courtroom.

John left the bar area to meet with his clients while Larry Smith packed the evidence box and briefcases. As he approached the gallery his eyes shot past Amalfi and the women. There was no trace of a smile as he approached O'Rourke with fire in his eyes. "What's up, Josh?"

All five of John's clients turned to view the scene.

O'Rourke flushed crimson as he rose to face John. He shrugged. "I just wanted to be here when the verdict came in." John's eyes bore into him. "Why, Josh? Are you concerned for these women and their children?"

O'Rourke's eyes hardened as he looked up at John. In a voice as hard as his gaze, he retorted, "I knew the men too. You're not the only one who cares."

"Really," John smirked. "You've been trying to put the mens' families on the street for months."

"I was doing my job," Josh protested.

John's anger flared. He put his finger in the banker's chest. "Your job stinks and so do you. Now get out of my sight before I throw you out."

Josh saw his eyes and knew to a certainty that John would do as he threatened. He also knew that to back down would appear cowardly. He glared back into John's eyes for a long moment.

Katie saw where this was heading. She gently put her hand on John's arm. In a soft voice she soothed, "John, you were wonderful, thank you."

Pulling his eyes from O'Rourke, John found Katie's face and read her concern.

"Don't do this, John," she urged. "He isn't worth it." Her timely intervention broke the mood.

John nodded. "Okay, I guess you're right." He turned his back on the banker.

Katie glanced at O'Rourke and in a kind voice she asked, "Josh, why don't you leave. We need to wait together, just us."

O'Rourke nodded and smiled in relief. "Okay, Katie, and good luck." He quickly exited through the doors, leaving an anxious group of plaintiffs to await their fate.

Waiting for a jury is an excruciating endeavor. Trial lawyers are by nature aggressive creatures and it is not unusual to find former athletes pursuing legal careers in the trial realm. Their hunger for competition, the one-on-one of batter v. pitcher, drives them to the adversarial struggle that is a jury trial. So, being on his feet presenting his case and arguing his cause fit John Palermo to his core, but waiting for a jury to decide his fate was pure agony.

Waiting in the quiet courtroom, Joe Amalfi stood silently at a window overlooking Post Office Square, his back to the group. The four women spoke quietly with each other. John noted that Rosalie Amalfi distracted the women by asking them questions about their children. John, nerves taut and tingling, found his gaze settling on Katie as he paced inside the bar. While he wanted to win for all of his clients, he desperately wanted to succeed for Katie. And, for Marc.

*   *   *

With remnants of their lunch still on the polished conference table, the jurors sat haphazardly around the room, sipping coffee. All, that is, except for Len Harris, who stood at the window, back to the room, studying the skyline and listening to the debate.

"How could you believe anything he said?" The question was directed by a powerfully built, thirty-year-old Bill Murdock, to the room in general, but to Manuela Gonzalez in particular. The plumber from Peabody spoke passionately, his big, rough hands waving for emphasis.

"Amalfi would say anything!" He paused. "Manuela, I know you feel for the women, but can we really accept Amalfi's story?"

"So we should believe the insurance company?" Asked Linda Noble. The young blond was dressed in a form fitting red dress that fell well above her knees. The light sash at her waist accentuated her shapely, toned body.

Bill Murdock's eyes passed to Linda. 'Why do women think being rail thin is attractive?' he thought as he appreciated the wonderful fullness of Linda's body.

Honest enough to acknowledge that she dressed for such appraisals, Linda only smiled at her co-juror. "So Bill, you think we should buy Bolton's pitch?" Her words came with a smile that lit her soft brown eyes.

Bill Murdock returned her smile and shrugged his shoulders.

Watching the exchange with approval, Ruth Garron smiled brightly with eyes that seemed to dance. The seventy-year-old had seen a lot of life and had dealt with more than her share of bad breaks. The light in her eyes made clear, however, that her ability to gauge truth and sift out garbage had not diminished her joy and positive spirit.

"I don't think Bolton was lying," She offered confidently. "Although, I'm pretty certain Amalfi wasn't giving us the truth."

Heads nodded and opinions shifted as the jury uncertainly sifted the testimony.

"What about Peter Novello?" a voice offered. "Did you see the way he looked at Amalfi?" Ruth Garron almost cackled with laughter. "I don't think those two will be exchanging Christmas cards."

Len Harris had listened for two hours. The architect saw that this deliberation was heading nowhere. He turned from the window and walked to the head of the table. The room fell silent as every eye was on him.

"Let's look at this," he began.

* * *

After three hours of deliberations, the jury reported that they had reached a verdict.

Mary Allen, Judge Adams' trial clerk, entered the courtroom from the judge's chambers to inform John of the jury's message.

John, seated in the gallery amongst his clients, asked if Bolton had been called.

The clerk nodded, then smiled. "Good luck, John."

She then disappeared into the judge's chambers.

John stood and felt an inner tremor. He forced a smile and wished his clients well. It seemed an eternity before Bolton arrived and the judge and jury entered the courtroom.

With the jury seated and the judge on the bench, the moment had arrived. John scanned the jurors. He read a mix of emotions. Steely eyed determination from Len Harris, a warm smile from Linda Noble.

In the gallery, the three widows joined hands. Rosalie Amalfi said a prayer as Joe sat stonefaced beside her.

At defense table, Jim Bolton sat with jaw set and eyes hard. John tortured himself with thoughts of what more he could have done or said. Had he given away too much with the stipulations? His mind raced to Matt Alves. How could he face that young man if he lost? Then he thought of Marc Morrissey and he felt a surge of anger.

Judge Adams broke into John's thoughts as he turned to the jury. "Mr. Foreman, has the jury reached its verdict?"

"We have," the jury foreman stated unemotionally.

John saw the hard set jaw and narrowed eyes of the juror, the plumber, he recalled, in seat one.

"Please hand the verdict slip to the court clerk."

The judge's clerk received the sheet of paper and walked directly to the judge.

John's eyes riveted on the verdict form. The fate of people he had come to care about deeply hung on the words contained on the simple document.

The clerk handed the verdict slip to Judge Adams. After a cursory glance and without emotion, he handed it back. "Publish the verdict," he ordered.

Mary Allen cleared her throat as she glanced at the jury. Then she read, "In the case of Boat Mio Mondo, Inc., et al vs. The American Marine Insurance Co."

The gallery was silent. 'This is the final act,' Katie thought. Somehow, the ordeal would end and she would be faced with picking up her life and building a future for Kelly. Lorraine Alves squeezed her hand with a fury. Tears rolled down Helen Picardi's face. One way or the other these women would leave the courtroom today with closure. Perhaps justice, but certainly closure.

The jury slip contained but one question. The clerk read the printed words.

"Was the loss of the *F/V Mio Mondo* a covered loss under the policy of insurance?" The clerk glanced at John.

Joe Amalfi sat straight as the color drained from his face. Katie thought of Marc.

In a strong voice Mary Allen said. "The jury answers, Yes."

A riot of emotion poured from the gallery. Smiles mixed with tears as the women embraced. As Larry Smith quietly congratulated him, John turned in his seat and saw the contrast of the resigned look of Jim Bolton and the jubilant gallery.

Judge Adams didn't try to stifle a smile as he thanked the jury for their efforts and service and dismissed them. He banged the gavel. "Judgment to enter accordingly." A quick glint of the eyes at John and he left the bench.

Jim Bolton moved to plaintiff's table. "Congratulations, John, good work."

They shook hands as John evenly said, "Thank you, you made it challenging."

Bolton shrugged. "That's my job."

John thought of how often wrongs were perpetrated with those very words as justification.

"Do you plan on appealing?" John asked.

Bolton shook his head. "I doubt it. I will recommend against it."

John nodded. "I need to see my clients."

Lorraine was the first to John, throwing her arms around him in joy. "Thank you for everything."

Katie hung back as Helen next embraced John.

Joe Amalfi offered his hand. "I knew you would win, John."

"Thank you," John responded evenly. "I'll be in touch."

Rosalie Amalfi filled the momentary silence. With a broad smile, which John thought looked good on her, Rosalie announced. "Please everybody, bring your children and we'll celebrate at our house." She eyed Joe. "Okay with you?"

The captain nodded. "Absolutely."

Rosalie turned back to the assembled group. "Six o'clock then."

* * *

Joe Amalfi played the gracious host to perfection. The dining room table was laden with Italian delicacies, which had been freshly prepared, that afternoon. The crusty Italian bread, still warm from the oven, was Katie's contribution. Other treats were prepared by Lorraine Alves and Helen Picardi.

While grief still played at the women's eyes, winning the case had lifted the financial pressure from their shoulders. John noted a bounce to their step and a softening of the worry lines that had become a feature on the faces of Lorraine and Helen. Even Katie appeared different. Where a year before Christmas was so difficult, she had arranged a day for a shopping expedition with Helen and Lorraine after the money was received. In what John saw as a typical Katie kindness, she had asked Rosalie Amalfi to join the group. With a mischievous grin she urged the older woman. "Come with us, we'll shop for the kids, have a fancy dinner we don't have to cook, and . . ." she laughed, "maybe, we'll have a facial and a manicure."

Rosalie smiled at the invitation. Having been the wife of Joe Amalfi had been difficult in so many ways. The tyrannical captain had left a wake of bruised egos and shattered friendships. Consequently, Rosalie had suffered socially as much as in her marriage.

Matt Alves led the younger children in games. Franco's eyes lit up when Matt designated him to be his assistant. John watched the children at play with special attention on Matt as well as Kelly's interaction with Franco and Anna. Earlier, when John first arrived with Franco and Anna, Matt had thanked John.

John studied the young face with concern. "I was glad to help, Matt."

Matt had shrugged. "Mom says we can keep our house."

John nodded. "You are happy about that, aren't you?"

Matt looked up at him with eyes dulled by a pain that no nine-year-old should know. "The house is okay, but . . ." He dropped his eyes.

John put his hand on Matt's shoulder. "But you miss your dad, right?"

Matt looked up with pooled eyes as a single tear escaped down his cheek. "Why did this have to happen? It's not fair."

As tears burst from Matt's grieving eyes, John led the youngster into Joe Amalfi's den, closing the door behind them.

They settled on the couch as Matt's tears flowed on a face crimson with embarrassment.

John held him to his chest. "Let it out," he counseled. "Don't be embarrassed to cry with me, Matt. When I lost my dad I was angry with the world."

For the first time since his father's death fifteen months before, Matt let go. John felt the sobs rack Matt's body as he gently stroked his raven black hair.

"Why did my dad have to die?" he choked. "That old guy didn't die. What happened to my dad?"

John held on tight, remembering that ten-year-old boy on the ship with the broken heart and inexhaustible supply of tears. He vividly recalled how alone he was with his grief and his anger.

"There's no way to explain it, Matt," he soothed. "And you're right, it's just not fair."

John held him until he cried himself out, whispering softly that he would be there for Matt and his family. Inwardly, John seethed at the injustice of it all.

When Matt's sobbing had ceased John wiped away his tears. He nodded toward the bathroom off of the den. "Use that bathroom and wash your face." He paused and studied Matt's face with a smile. "Take your time, then come back here."

Matt managed a grin and followed John's instructions. Fifteen minutes later, and with an embarrassed grin, Matt stood before John.

"How would you like a little job, Matt?"

"A job?"

John handed him twenty dollars and watched the boy's eyes pop.

"How about if you take charge of the kids. You know, play games with them, maybe tell them a story or two."

"Okay," Matt nodded enthusiastically.

John smiled. "I'll let you in on a secret. My son Franco really looks up to you."

"Really?" The thought brought a gleam to Matt's eyes and a smile to his lips.

"Great, let's go join the party," John cheered.

With smiles in place they merged into the group. John winked at Lorraine who brightened at their re-appearance.

John sauntered over to where Katie stood looking out at the harbor through an oversized bay window.

"Hello, lady," he teased. "What's weighing on your mind?"

Pulled out of deep thought, Katie eyed John with her sapphire blue eyes sparkling with intrigue.

John saw the query in her eyes, just as he had seen the fired golden hair and shapely body in the temptingly modest sky blue dress.

She glanced over to where Matt was busy organizing the children with Franco at his side. "That was nice what you did for Matt. Lorraine has been worried about him."

With a dismissive shrug, John noted. "Matt's a good boy who has been wronged. I know how he feels." He smiled. "So, are you planning on telling me what's on your mind?"

"You are," she stated forthrightly.

"Really?" he teased with a suggestive grin.

Katie shook her head, but couldn't suppress a smile. "I'm trying to figure you out."

John's eyes narrowed. "What's to figure out?"

She shrugged, eyes on John and smile in place. "I guess I wonder if you're healed enough to deal with me." Her eyes shone, sapphire warmth seeking his ice blues. "I worry that after all you've been through as a child, then losing Connie," she saw the flicker in his eyes. "If dumping my problems on you would be fair." She sipped at her glass of wine, noted John was drinking spring water. "Water?" She asked. "I thought this was a party."

John grinned. "I've tried to drown my pain in a bourbon haze." He paused, eyes on Katie. "It doesn't work, Katie." He took her hand. "I see what I want and I need to be clear headed." He looked into her eyes and smiled softly. "Katie, why don't we go out Saturday night and talk about how I can deal with you."

Then his eyes lit with amusement as he added, "And we can also talk about all you can do for me."

Katie laughed in surprise. Then angled amused eyes at John. "Dinner at the Point?" She teased as John shook his head and grinned.

"I do like the Point." He laughed.

"So, I've heard." She responded as she playfully punched his arm.

"So, Saturday?" John asked.

"I'd like that," Katie agreed, "but not Saturday." She turned thoughtful. "Kelly and I are going to my in-laws for dinner." She watched for his reaction.

` "Of course," he nodded and thought of Marc, then brightened. "Okay, Sunday morning we'll pick you and Kelly up for mass. Then the five of us will spend the day together. How does that sound?"

"Sounds wonderful," she agreed happily. "I'll take care of dinner and you can plan the remainder of the day."

John moved forward and gently kissed her cheek, sending a jolt through her.

"It's a deal."

CHAPTER THIRTY

Jim Bolton had explained his position to the insurance company. Reluctantly, the claims adjuster had accepted that an appeal was unlikely to succeed and as post-judgement interest grew daily, approved payment of the policy limits of one million dollars with interest to each of the estates of the men who died on the F/V *Mio Mondo* as well as five hundred thousand dollars with interest to Boat Mio Mondo, Inc.

Winter came in hard and early. The smell of snow was in the air as Jim Bolton drove the coast road to Gloucester to meet with John. The views as he passed through Salem, Beverly, and Manchester-by-the-Sea lifted his spirits. From the Magnolia section of Gloucester he saw a fishing trawler heading home. It's mast, pilothouse, and gallows frames glistened with ice and though the sky was clear and seas calm, at that moment, he could picture the harsh conditions the crew had worked under during the voyage.

Then he thought of the *Mio Mondo*. A chill shot through him as he imagined the men being swept from the deck into the churning sea. He wondered at their thoughts as they fought to stay afloat. Did they think of their wives and children? Did their lives flash before their eyes as people claimed? Or were the men so terrified as they faced death alone in the angry sea that rational thought was impossible?

A right turn off of Hesperus Avenue and he found himself facing Norman's Woe. He remembered the famous words of "The Wreck of the Hesperus." And he thought of the men who had left this port for almost four hundred years to challenge the Great Atlantic Ocean for it's bounty of cod, haddock and halibut only to die alone in the cruel, insatiable sea. Always they went to sea chasing a living for their families. And how many thousands left this beautiful port never to see land again?

He scanned the beauty of this harbor, dubbed 'Le Beau Port' by French expeditioner Champlain and considered how so very often death waited over the horizon.

Bolton arrived at the law offices of Palermo & Harmon and found Phil Harmon in John's office when he was ushered in. John rose to greet Bolton with a firm handshake. "Jim, you know Phil, of course." John smiled.

"Good to see you, Phil," Bolton said. "We should talk about the Cavanaugh case." Bolton added. "I'd like to review the trial exhibits and discuss scheduling."

"Sure thing, Jim," Phil agreed as the men shook hands. "I'll call you Monday."

Phil smiled warmly.

"John told me you gave him quite a run."

Bolton glanced John's way. 'Ever the gentleman,' he thought with professional approval. "Actually, I don't think it was that close a call," Bolton responded.

John moved to the bar as Phil and Jim Bolton settled in the casual area of his office.

"You shook me up pretty well when I saw Peter Novello in court," John laughed.

"Pure desperation," Bolton replied. "After you pulled my naval architect apart I had nothing to lose by trying."

"Can I offer you a drink?" John said as he poured drinks for Phil and himself. A scotch for Phil, soda water for himself.

"A short one," Bolton responded. "I'm driving back. Do you have bourbon?"

John smiled as he poured Bolton's drink. "Sure do," he confirmed. 'Now that I don't drink it.' He thought.

The three attorneys sat with drinks in hand. Bolton sipped his drink as he noticed two file boxes in the corner of John's office. On top of the two boxes was a videotape. The defense attorney nodded in the direction of the file. "I see you're ready to write your brief."

John shrugged. "I guess that's up to you." He paused and studied Bolton. "So, what's the decision?"

Bolton kept his eyes on the file boxes and videotape for a long moment before turning his gaze on John. "I feel as if I missed something."

Phil glanced at John who sat quietly. "What do you mean, Jim?"

Bolton shook his head and sighed. "I can't put my finger on it," he said, "but something just feels wrong." And then he looked hard at John.

John shrugged as he sipped his drink. Eyes locked with Bolton's, John agreed. "I know what you mean. What feels wrong is Amalfi. He's a hard guy to like." Then he grinned. "At least you didn't have to represent him." John added, smiling. "You should count your blessings."

Jim Bolton recognized the point with a nod, eyes still fixed on John.

John read the conflict in Bolton's eyes. Then he leaned forward and added pointedly. "However, the three widows and six children are easy to like and care about."

Bolton nodded. "Point taken."

"So, Jim," John pressed. "Are you going to pay or appeal?"

Bolton hesitated for a long moment as he considered the question. With a shrug, Bolton reached into his inside jacket pocket and pulled out an envelope. "Something tells me there's more to this." He passed the envelope over to John. "Still, I don't think an appeal would be successful." He shook his head. "So . . ."

John took the envelope to his desk. With a letter opener embossed with the Boston College seal, he slit the envelope open. It contained four checks and a simple cover letter. Each check appeared properly endorsed and matched John's calculation as to the interest owed. When he looked up, he found Bolton's eyes on him. John met his gaze evenly, until Bolton glanced away at the file boxes and video tape.

"I guess you won't be writing that brief after all," Bolton offered with a smile that didn't reach his eyes.

"I guess not," John agreed. Then their eyes met again. "Let it go Jim," John said. "You've helped make a good Christmas for three families that have been through enough."

Jim Bolton thought back to the ice covered fishing trawler he had seen. "I guess so. I'll be heading out now."

The men exchanged handshakes.

"Have a Merry Christmas, Jim," John said.

"Same to both of you," Jim replied. He studied John's eyes as they shook hands. Their eyes locked until Jim shrugged, folded his camel hair overcoat over his forearm and left.

John watched him leave quietly.

"What was that?" Phil queried with a shake of the head. "Since when does a lawyer of Bolton's credentials play delivery boy?"

"He doesn't trust Amalfi," John responded. "His gut tells him something is not right."

Phil glanced to John's desk and laughed. "Let's get those checks into the client account before he changes his mind."

"Sure," John said thoughtfully. Then laughed, "Relax, Phil, the checks will be good."

Phil grinned. "It will be good telling the women."

"Yes it will,' John agreed. "In fact, I should get to it."

CHAPTER THIRTY-ONE

"So he proposed a romantic evening, and now it's a family day?" Eileen asked incredulously.

Katie busied herself chopping vegetables for that evening's dinner, wearing a bib type apron over a loose fitting running suit. Her hair was pulled back in a ponytail.

"It's probably better if we take it slow," she said. "After all, we've all been through a tough time."

Eileen sat at the kitchen table studying her sister's face. Softly, she said, "Don't lose him, Katie."

Katie straightened from her task as Eileen's concern reached her. Inexplicably, Katie's eyes filled as she took in her sister.

"I'm afraid, Eileen. I don't want to hurt him."

Eileen considered Katie's words as she sipped her white wine. Finally she asked, "Do you love him, Katie? Is that what you're afraid of?"

Katie sank to a chair opposite Eileen, folded her hands before her and closed her eyes. Eileen read the turmoil within.

"I have strong feelings for him," Katie began haltingly. "Since Marc died he has done so much for all of us." She paused, then considered her sister. "Eileen, are my feelings for him gratitude or love?" She dabbed at her eyes. "He has had such a difficult life . . ." She closed her eyes. "He loved Connie so much." A tear escaped. "What if I don't measure up to Connie?"

Eileen poured a glass of wine for Katie.

"Thanks," she sipped it. Then wiped her eyes. "You know Eileen, John was Marc's friend. They were tight. What if John's feelings are sympathy rather than love?" She broke down and let the tears flow. Over her sobs she managed to say, "I couldn't take that. I just couldn't take it."

Eileen moved around the table to hug Katie, who let the river of tears flow.

When finally cried out, Katie washed her face and put on some makeup to diminish the appearance of red and puffy eyes. She returned to the kitchen and managed a shy smile. "I don't want to scare Kelly," she said, and resumed her dinner preparations.

Eileen nodded thoughtfully as she sipped from the tea she had prepared while Katie had left.

"Want some tea?" Eileen asked. "It'll replace the fluids you just lost."

Katie glanced at Eileen as they both burst into laughter. It was as if a pressure valve had released.

"When is Kelly due home?"

Katie glanced at the wall clock.

"Anytime now. Susan will drop her after play group."

"What does Kelly think of John?" Eileen asked.

Katie looked at her sister thoughtfully. "Kelly loves John, Franco, and Anna." She grinned. "Kelly says they're fun."

Eileen sat back and with a salacious grin commented, "I bet Kelly's right. John looks as if he would be a lot of fun."

Katie shook her head and met Eileen's eyes with an approving glance. "Yes, I imagine he could be amusing." The sisters shared a laugh.

Eileen allowed the laugh to settle, then engaged Katie's eyes. "You know, little sister, I loved Marc. He was funny and open and caring. He was a good father and a good husband." She paused to collect her thoughts, wanting to say this just right. "I know it is difficult to get over a man like Marc. And I agree you shouldn't rush it. But, if you need time, say that to John. Tell him you have doubts and fears and what they are." She swallowed and looked into Katie's big sapphire eyes. "Don't underrate him. John will help you through this. And the time you spend with him will ease the guilt and make the transition back to the world easier."

Eileen saw doubt in Katie's eyes.

"Katie, don't you think John has lived through the same feelings when he lost Connie?"

Katie nodded. "Sure, I guess he did."

"Of course," Eileen affirmed. "Give him a chance and he'll find a way to help you through all this." She smirked. "And you'll have a good time in the process."

The door flew open and Kelly rushed in and went directly to Katie, who moved across the room to the door to wave a thank you at Susan in the car.

"Hi, Auntie Eileen."

Eileen grinned. "Hello, Pumpkin. Are you ready for a big day tomorrow?"

Kelly smiled and went into Eileen's arms. "It's you and me kid, while your mother spends the day shopping and being pampered."

* * *

John had taken time off to spend with Franco and Anna. One day they visited the Children's Museum, another the Hands-On Exhibit at the

Museum of Science. There were movies and picnics on the living room floor.

"I've missed you guys," John told Franco and Anna over pizza. "I wish I could be home more often."

"Nonna says you have to work," Franco responded.

"Yes, I do. Do you like being at Nonna's house?"

Anna smiled. "We love Nonna and Nonno, but we love you best, daddy."

John grinned. "I love you, too." He choked as he thought of how unfair and disruptive Connie's death had been to Franco and Anna. Their grandparents had been wonderful, but Connie had been right; Franco and Anna deserved a mother. He had been thinking of Connie frequently of late. In truth, he was a bit upside down over his feelings for Katie and troubled by lingering feelings of guilt. Shaking the thought, he announced, "Sunday we'll be having dinner at Kelly's house. Then, do you know what we're all going to do?"

The children's eyes lit up. "What, Daddy?"

John raised his eyebrows and in a stage whisper announced, "We're going to Disney on Ice."

Franco and Anna clapped excitedly as Franco's drink was knocked across the table.

"Oops," he offered.

John laughed and wiped the table and his pants.

*   *   *

The end of the trial was not the end of Joe Amalfi's nightmares. On the night of the trial victory and party with his crew's family, Rosalie was ripped from a peaceful sleep by Joe's screaming. Rosalie shook him awake. The tee-shirt he wore was soaked through with sweat. The eyes showed the terror and desperation he felt.

"Calm down, Joe. You're awake now."

"I saw their faces," he anguished. "They were coming for me."

"Who, Joe? Who was coming for you?"

He turned to her. "The men, they blame me." He put his face in his hands. "They blame me."

"It was just a nightmare," Rosalie soothed. "Just a nightmare."

He rose and put on a robe against the chill. His anguished gaze passed over her as he left the bedroom and padded down to his den. "I can't take this anymore," he said over and over as he robed and left. "I can't take this anymore."

Rosalie Amalfi watched him go and knew he would not sleep this night. She thought how he needed help but refused to see a psychologist. Finally, she shrugged and settled back to sleep.

* * *

John had come to a decision. After the trial victory and the victory party at the Amalfis', he had called Barbara and invited her to dinner. She had been joyous at the news and happily accepted.

They met at the Point Restaurant and settled at a table overlooking the open ocean crashing against the breakwater. Barbara smiled at the fine beads of salt spray tossed into the air like pearls. She beamed a smile across the table at John. "I'm so happy the trial worked out so well." She paused. "Mary Kaye told me that you really saved those three families."

John shrugged. "I did my job." He said modestly. Then he engaged Barbara's eyes. "They were in trouble. I'm glad they will be okay." He paused and shook his head. "As okay as they can be after losing their husbands and fathers."

Barbara reached out and took John's hand. She offered a soft, understanding smile. "There's only so much you can do for them, John."

John looked into her eyes, saw the caring and the smile on her lips. He couldn't help but smile into that pretty face.

The waitress placed their drinks before them and took their dinner order, while flashing a bright smile at John.

"I was glad you called, John." Barbara began. "I wasn't sure that I would hear from you."

"Really?" John responded.

Eyes fixed on John, she angled a smile. "Mary Kaye told me that she thought something special was happening between you and Katie."

"Really?" he shook his head in wonder. "She doesn't miss much, does she?" John asked with a shake of the head.

Barbara's smile held. "Is something happening, John?"

John sat back, eyes on Barbara. He rolled the question around in his mind. Nodding, he leaned forward and engaged Barbara's eyes. "I think so, Barbara," he began. "See, Marc Morrissey was my friend." He paused collecting his thoughts. "I can't say that I'm sure that what I feel for Katie is love." He shook his head, uncertainty clouding his eyes. "Perhaps it's just a sense of loyalty." He paused. "I just don't know."

Barbara nodded, but said nothing.

"But, I need to find out." He stated. "I'm sorry if I've hurt you." He exhaled. "I've enjoyed our time together."

Barbara's eyes misted, but a soft, understanding smile held. "You're a great guy, John." She paused, sipped some water. "Be happy, John. You deserve it."

The waitress brought their soup to the table, recognized the quiet intensity and moved away quickly.

Barbara lifted her soup spoon. "I love the lobster bisque here." She said, as she brought the spoon to her mouth. She tasted nothing over the lump in her throat.

John simply smiled his thanks, recognizing that Barbara was making this easy on him. He tasted the soup and angled a sharp eye at Barbara. "So what are you torturing your students with now? Dante?"

That drew a laugh, as the conversation moved to a series of other topics. Barbara felt the ache in her heart but managed to converse lightly as they dined and managed a pleasant evening.

CHAPTER THIRTY TWO

It was with barely contained excitement that Rosalie dressed for her big day with Katie, Lorraine and Helen. It crossed her mind that she was old enough to be the mother of her shopping mates, but they had invited her to spend a day away from the hell her life had become. Was it pity that Katie had felt for her, living here with "The Captain" or "The Bastard?" Even so, Rosalie intended to enjoy the day. Pushing all negative thoughts aside she chose jewelry and applied her makeup.

Feeling fresh and vigorous she put up a pot of coffee for Joe and herself. His conversation was more grunts than dialogue.

"I'll be leaving. Are you okay?" she asked.

With a sour look and a nod he rose and left the kitchen.

'Fine,' she thought. 'But I'm not going to allow him to ruin my day.' She put on her winter coat and drove away from the house, eagerly anticipating a special day.

With their mortgages paid and bills current, the women looked to the future with hope, if not joy. And each vowed to give their children a wonderful Christmas.

From the end of the street John watched her leave. He stayed seated behind the wheel of his car for ten minutes. Once comfortable that she would not be back, he left the car, turned up his collar against the biting wind and walked to the front door of the Captain's house.

It seemed a long time after John rang the bell that Joe Amalfi opened the door. While he waited, John smelled snow in the air as he huddled in his warm fleece lined jacket.

When the door opened, Joe Amalfi's eyes registered surprise to see John before him. Especially so since John was not in suit and tie and wrapped in a camel hair coat. Today, corduroys and hiking boots were visible below the heavy oversized jacket. A wool hat was pulled low over his eyes and ears. On his hands he wore leather gloves.

"John, come in," Joe Amalfi said. A trace of a smile on his lips. "Don't stand here, come into my den."

John followed Amalfi across the foyer to his den.

"Please take off your jacket and sit down by the fire."

John removed his hat and jacket and laid them on the couch. He walked over to the fire and warmed himself before it.

Joe Amalfi sat down in an easy chair and spoke to John's back. "You did a great job, John," he laughed. "I knew when I hired you that we would win."

John turned from the fire and fixed his eyes on Amalfi.

The Captain saw John's face was set hard, his eyes blazed with anger.

"I know what you did," John said.

Amalfi gulped. His mouth went dry. Haltingly, he managed to say, "What do you mean?"

John took two steps toward Amalfi. "You murdered those men," he stated. "Before I leave here, I'll know why."

Amalfi studied John. "What are you talking about?" he protested.

John moved to the pocket of his jacket and pulled out a VHS tape. He walked to the television and put the tape in the VCR, turned on the T.V. and hit play on the VCR.

They were back in the murky world of the ocean floor. The camera and attached light moved slowly around the stern of the vessel to the starboard side. The light played off of the hull and rigging, dully reflecting the various surfaces. As the submersible cleared the elevated pilot house providing a full length shot of the deck to the raised fo'c's'le John hit the pause button and turned to Amalfi. The captain sat stunned, color drained from his face.

"Bolton sensed it," John began. "But he didn't know what to look for. Jim Bolton is a good lawyer, but he was never a fisherman."

Amalfi blanched behind frightened eyes.

"I don't know what you're talking about," he managed.

John glared hard, then walked to the television. He pointed at the fo'c's'le. "There, that reflection and these," he pointed at the four corners of the fo'c's'le entrance. "Hinges," he raged. "You could only see the hinges if the doors were closed." He turned back on Amalfi and walked toward the cowering Captain. "And that tiny glint in the middle of the two doors is a padlock." He stood over Amalfi. "Now why would the fo'c's'le doors be locked, Captain?" He spit the words.

Amalfi shrank back in the padded chair. With danger in his eyes, John grabbed and pulled him to his feet. "Why did you lock those men in the fo'c's'le?"

Terrified, he screamed, "I had to!" Then Amalfi broke down with sobs and tears.

John dumped him back into his seat, moved to the liquor cart, poured a stiff drink for Amalfi and gave it to him.

"Drink this," John ordered.

Amalfi gulped the liquor, felt the burn from his throat to his empty belly, then looked at John. John noticed that Amalfi's twitch was absent; a sign that John was about to hear the truth. With a hard bite to his words, John snapped, "Tell me all of it." He sat across from Amalfi and fixed angry eyes on the diminutive Captain.

"Can I get another drink?" Amalfi asked meekly, fear in his eyes.

John nodded.

With a double scotch in his hand, Amalfi sat back in his seat.

"There was an accident in the engine room," he began. "We were only four men, three really." He paused. "I didn't work the deck." He sipped the scotch and through his eyes John saw he was back on the boat again. "It was too much work for the crew. We should have had five or six men. But with all the restrictions and regulations," he shrugged. "The men had worked for thirty-six hours without sleep." He looked up at John. "We were on fish." Then softly, "I didn't let them rest. Set out, clean and ice fish, haul back, set out, clean and ice fish, over and over." He put his hand to his eyes, took a deep breath. "I heard something from the engine room, so I told Marc Morrissey to check it out." He took a deep pull on the scotch, choked a bit and wiped his troubled eyes. Pleadingly, he looked to John. "Marc must have fallen asleep or have been so groggy . . ." His voice fell off as he relived the moment. "Anyway, he fell into the gears." Amalfi closed his eyes. "We didn't hear him over the sound of the engine." He drank more scotch, his eyes streamed tears. "By the time we checked him he was so mangled." Eyes closed, he shook his head. "He was dead."

There was a long silence while Amalfi drank and wept. John thought of Marc, his boyhood friend, with regret. Then he thought of Katie and Kelly. It was when he thought of Matt Alves that his anger returned.

"Go on," John demanded as he rose and stood over Amalfi. The lawyer's eyes were set hard and his hands were clenched into fists.

Confused and half crazed, Amalfi looked into John's rage.

"They said it was my fault, that I had killed him. Joe Picardi attacked me. He hit me in the face. I fell and hit my head." Tears rolled down Amalfi's face. Luke pulled him off of me. But Joe said it was murder and he was going to go to the police."

Slowly, Amalfi rose and went to the liquor cart and refilled his glass as John sat on the edge of his seat.

"We put Marc on a bunk and then hauled back the gear so that we could come home." He paused and drank. "It was awful. We brought in the gear. There still were fish piled on the deck. I was scared, they kept whispering to each other and Joe would look at me with hate in his eyes." John read the terror in Amalfi's face. "When we got the gear on the boat, I told them to get some sleep while we headed home. They went down the fo'c's'le into the galley while I headed the boat for Gloucester." He paused, deep in memory, while he drank. "We had all been awake for so long. I was sure they were going to hurt me."

John saw the twitch flare and in one sudden motion bolted from his seat and smacked Amalfi across the face.

Stunned and bleeding from a gash on his lip, the Captain looked up at the tall, muscular and enraged lawyer hovering above him.

"One more lie and I'll kill you," John promised. "Do you understand me?"

Silently, Amalfi nodded and realized that John was angry enough to do it.

"Okay," was all he said.

"Go on," John ordered as he sat, eyes fixed on Amalfi.

"I was in the pilot house and I was thinking about what Joe Picardi had said." He looked at John. "I was scared. I was confused and I decided that I couldn't let anyone know what happened." His hands shook. "Can I get a drink?"

John nodded, his gaze even but Joe Amalfi knew how quickly he could explode.

The scotch stained the oriental rug on the highly polished hardwood floor where Amalfi had dropped his glass when struck by John.

Ignoring the stain, Amalfi picked up the glass with trembling fingers and filled it with scotch. He glanced at the den door, wishing fervently that Rosalie would return. It didn't occur to him that it had been at least a decade since he last yearned for Rosalie's presence.

"Sit down, Captain," John ordered.

Amalfi quickly complied and took a hit from the scotch.

"Go on," John commanded.

Amalfi took a deep breath but exhaled unevenly as emotion and the effect of the scotch began to cloud his mind.

"Please," he begged. "I can't."

John moved to the edge of his seat and snarled. "There is nothing I would like more than to beat you senseless. So just try clamming up on me."

Amalfi, with wide terrified eyes, nodded. "Okay," he gulped some scotch and wiped his eyes. "I waited about two hours until I was certain they were asleep. Then, I set the wheel on automatic pilot and left the pilothouse." He looked down at his drink, took a slug and kept his eyes down and away from the intense, ice-cold blue eyes that burned into him like hot ice.

"In that two hours you steamed to the deepest bottom on the chart," John stated. "Even though it was way off course." The rage flared. "You son of a bitch."

Fearing another blow, Amalfi cringed and spoke softly, "I went forward, unhooked the fo'c's'le doors, closed them and . . . ," he wiped his eyes and took a drink, "I locked the doors with the padlock."

"What about the emergency escape in the whaleback?" John asked.

"I bolted the whaleback door closed and dropped the steel starboard fishing door on the deck across it."

Anger rose in John. "So you trapped them to die," he raged.

Amalfi nodded, John saw the fear in his eyes.

"Then you opened the seacocks and let it sink." Amazement mixed with horror.

Amalfi took a deep drink then nodded and softly said, "Yes."

"You son of a bitch," John fumed. Then a thought struck him. "Did Joe and Luke wake up?"

Amalfi looked at him and gulped. Tears streaked his face. "Yeah," he choked. "They woke up."

John could picture the scene. "They must have banged at the door of the fo'c's'le." Consumed with rage and horror. "You listened to them beg, didn't you?"

"They cursed and vowed to get me," Amalfi responded. "And they are there every time I close my eyes." He buried his face in his hands.

"You never expected them to send a submersible down, did you?"

"No," Amalfi shrugged. "But it didn't matter."

John's eyes narrowed. "Why is that?"

Amalfi raised his eyes to face John. "Because I had you."

John glared but said nothing.

"I knew you would do anything for those women and children." He studied John's eyes, then he said, "I knew you hated me. Still, you won for me to help them." He paused and lowered his eyes. "I just didn't know the hell I would endure."

"You dirty, calculating bastard," John stormed.

The alcohol was getting to Amalfi. His guard came down and his speech slurred. John's shock emboldened him. Seemingly relaxed, he sat back and John saw some of the old Amalfi arrogance.

"Yeah, I'm a bastard. So what does that make you?" He paused and gave the answer. "The Bastard's Weapon."

John poised to strike. Only the slightest self control remained.

"And you can't say a word," Amalfi said, the smallest smile on his lips. "Because if you do, the insurance company will take back all that money that the widows used to pay their mortgages and put in their bank accounts for the future." He looked across at John. "Do you think that pretty blond that you're so sweet on will think you're so great if you do that? No . . ."

He never finished. The reference to Katie sent him over the edge. All his power and rage was behind the right cross he delivered to Amalfi's chin.

CHAPTER THIRTY THREE

The Morrissey family gathered to celebrate the trial victory, to remember Marc and to continue healing.

Katie and Kelly arrived at the Morrisseys with cheeks reddened from the cold and arms laden with gifts for Marc's parents, sister and brother and their spouses and children.

"What's this? An early Christmas?" Mike Morrissey asked, as he and Marc's brother, Arthur, relieved Katie and Kelly of the brightly wrapped boxes.

Gwen Morrissey scooped Kelly into her arms and won shrieks of laughter as she nuzzled Kelly's neck.

"Who loves Grandma?" Gwen asked Kelly as she kissed her.

Laughing and hugging Gwen, Kelly responded. "I love you Grandma. I love you the most."

Katie embraced Marc's sister, Lucille, then turned to her father-in-law smiling broadly. "Kelly and I want to share with all of you, who have been so supportive and helpful." She paused and misted. "I told myself that I wasn't going to do this." She smiled through the tears and went into the outstretched arms of Mike Morrissey.

"We're happy for you." Mike whispered in her ear. "Now, let's celebrate."

Katie's gift to Mike Morrissey, which an excited Kelly insisted be opened first, was Marc's warm-up suit from his University of Massachusetts basketball team

Mike held the maroon jacket with Marc's name and number stitched on the back. The material was still shiny and in perfect condition.

"This meant a lot to Marc." Katie said to her father-in-law. "Marc always told me how you worked with him on his game." She paused. "Dad, he loved that time with you. I thought you should have it."

Mike Morrissey looked at Katie through moist eyes. "Thank you Katie," he choked. Then, taking a deep breath, he gently, almost reverently, ran his fingers over Marc's name, then returned his gaze to Katie. "Thank you so much."

Katie met her father-in-laws eyes. She misted and nodded. "You're welcome, Dad."

"Okay Kelly," Katie grinned at her daughter. "Please give this to Uncle Arthur."

Arthur Morrissey pulled Kelly onto his lap. "Would you help me open this box, Kelly?" He asked.

Kelly eagerly tore away the paper and opened the box.

"Oh," was all Arthur said as he pulled out Marc's UMASS home game jersey.

"Arthur," Katie smiled, "Marc loved you so much. I know he would want you to have his game jersey."

In an emotion choked voice, Arthur thanked Katie and gave Kelly a hug.

Katie had gifts for each member of the family. Her eye for fashion had proved on the mark and Gwen, Lucille and Arthur's wife, Patty, loved the clothing she had chosen on her recent shopping expedition.

The family moved into dinner with the adults in the dining room and the five grandchildren seated happily at the kitchen table.

"So, how nervous were you at the trial?" Patty asked, leaning toward Katie.

Katie grinned and her eyes danced as she described her anxiety, but how at every crucial moment, John had found a way to prop up Joe Amalfi or score points against the insurance company's expert witness.

"I've heard that John is a very good trial lawyer." Gwen responded evenly.

"He's great," Katie beamed, then laughed. "I think one of the jurors had her eyes on John."

"Really?" Arthur grinned. "Was she pretty?"

Patty angled amused eyes at Arthur. "And, what would you care?"

Arthur laughed as he placed his arm around Patty's waist and pulled her close. "Not for me, beautiful," he kissed her neck. "For John, of course."

As always, Arthur caused smiles to bloom around the table, as he looked back at Katie. "A looker, I'll bet?"

Laughing at his teasing of Patty, Katie nodded. "Young, blond with a beautiful face and a killer body." She paused, smiling, "your basic nightmare."

Her descriptions drew laughs from the men and knowing nods from Lucille and Patty.

Arthur leaned toward Katie, grinning and in a stage whisper he asked. "You did get her number for me?" At that even Patty laughed.

"How is John?" Lucille asked, eyes on Katie, a smile playing at her lips.

Katie felt the weight of Gwen and Mike Morrissey's gaze on her.

"He's fine." She paused and smiled at her in-laws. Trying to speak casually, but feeling inner tremors, she continued. "I spoke to him Friday, when he called to confirm our plans for tomorrow."

Mike Morrissey straightened in his chair, but said nothing.

Gwen's eyes flickered to her husband and then back to Katie, where she read the anxiety in her daughter-in-law's eyes.

Lucille's husband, Greg, offered Katie a supportive smile, covered her hand with his and tried to sooth the bundle of nerves Katie had become. "It's okay, Katie. We all like John." He raised his brows to win a smile and succeeded. "So, what is it? Liquor, dancing and depravity?"

Laughs burst forth from Arthur, Patty and Lucille, lightening the mood. Gwen and Mike smiled but kept their eyes on Katie.

Katie laughed a bit nervously, and shook her head. "Something like that, Greg. John and his children Franco and Anna are taking Kelly and me to 10:30 Mass at St. Ann's and then we're having Sunday dinner at my house."

"Really?" With a look of shock, Arthur lamented, "that's all? What a disappointment."

Gwen thought she saw something in Katie's eyes that indicated Sunday Mass and dinner was not all.

The men retreated to the living room to watch one of the college football bowl games. The children took control of the den, while the women cleaned up and washed the dishes, pots and pans.

There was as much laughing as cleaning as Patty and Lucille teased Gwen over any number of decorating choices.

Gwen looked to Katie for help, laughing. "My only consolation is that all three of you have daughters. And, I'll have the opportunity to watch them torment you."

At that, the four women laughed heartily, as they realized how inevitable was Gwen's prediction.

Katie cherished her relationship with Marc's family. They had been strong when Katie needed their strength, protective of Katie and Kelly and always there when support was required. Katie was especially close and comfortable with her mother-in-law and two sisters-in-law. She smiled as she stood at the sink washing dishes, handing the wet plates to Patty who dried and stacked the plates, utensils and pots and pans to be stored in the proper cabinets and pantry by Gwen and Lucille, the two women who had shared this kitchen for twenty years.

As nobody knew Gwen like her daughter, Lucille asked the question on her mother's mind. "So, Katie," Lucille began with a smile. "Do you want to tell us about John?"

The moment and the opportunity had arrived. Katie had hoped to speak to Gwen about her feelings and plans and let Gwen fill in her husband. Cowardly? Perhaps, she admitted to herself. But, pouring out

THE BASTARD'S WEAPON

her heart to Marc's mother, sister and sister-in-law would be difficult enough.

As Katie took a moment to collect her thoughts, she felt the warm water cascading over her hands. Then she felt Gwen's hands gently massaging her shoulders. "It's okay, Katie." Gwen said softly. She took a deep breath, before asking, "do you love him?"

Katie turned to face her mother-in-law and met her eyes before falling into her arms.

The women cried together. "I understand, Katie," Gwen consoled. "You have to go on." Then a thought struck at Gwen's heart. "But please, don't let me lose my Kelly." She choked. "I couldn't take that."

CHAPTER THIRTY FOUR

Maria Amico knew in her heart that Franco and Anna needed a mother. John had tried valiantly to be both father and mother. Maria had welcomed the children into her house and her heart, in effect being their safety net. Still, father and grandmother were a pale substitute for a mother.

Alone with Benny and Maria, John had poured out his heart and stated his case. Dinner completed, Franco and Anna were bathed, in pajamas and tucked into their beds, John sat, over coffee, with the man and woman who had saved him and raised him.

"Ma and Dad, I know none of us are over the loss of Connie." John saw the now familiar pain in their eyes. The extinguished spark common to those who have lost a child. "I loved her with all my heart. I still miss her." Maria nodded in understanding and sympathy for John. "Still, I want to move on."

"With this woman that you've been seeing?" Benny asked with narrowed, disapproving eyes.

John studied Benny's defensive posture and the anger just below the surface. He smiled, understanding Benny's reluctance. "Dad, I didn't want to lose Connie. I loved her with my whole heart."

Benny wrestled with the need to immortalize his daughter and the reality that the very alive John, as well as Franco and Anna, lived in the present.

"I know." His eyes pooled. "I . . . I'm afraid everyone will forget Connie."

John reached across the table and covered Benny's hand with his own. He tapped his chest. "She will always live here, in my heart."

Maria knew John. "Why don't you tell us, John."

John shook his head and smiled. "You know me so well, Ma."

Maria smiled. "Of course, I'm your mother."

John took his mother's hand, while still holding onto Benny's. Maria Amico was the only mother John had ever known. She took him in at age ten with love and without condition. She was indeed the mother of his heart if not the mother of his blood. And he realized, once again, that her approval and Benny's was important to him.

"Ma, Dad, I loved Connie with my whole heart and soul." He shrugged. "You know that."

They watched his face closely.

"It has been a hard time for all of us. Franco and Anna need a mother." He paused. "I thought I would never feel again."

He squeezed Maria's hand. "With Katie I feel alive again," he choked. "I want to feel alive again."

"How does Katie feel?"

John's eyes clouded. "Ma, I don't know, but I need to find out." Benny took Maria's hand as he held John's.

"I can't do this without your support." John continued. "You two mean so much to the kids and to me." He paused. "If you can't handle it or don't approve, please tell me now." He took a deep breath. "I really need your support."

Maria exchanged a long glance with Benny. Then she turned to John. "It's time." She smiled at her son. "Thank you for sharing the children and this with us."

John turned to Benny. "Dad, are you okay with this?"

Benny's eyes brimmed with tears. He nodded his head, rose and embraced John.

*   *   *

Maria had Franco and Anna turned out splendidly for the big day. When the Palermos arrived to gather Katie and Kelly for mass, Katie grinned and looked at Anna. "Your hair looks so nice. I guess your dad didn't try to fix it," she teased.

Anna glanced at John, saw his smile, then agreed. "My Nonna fixed my hair." With a smile at Katie she said, "my Nonna says this is a special day."

"Really?" Katie queried. "And why is that?" she asked Anna.

"I don't know," Anna said.

"Is everybody ready for mass?" John said, pointedly changing the subject.

Mass had its usual calming effect. Father Capelli used his homily to speak of decency and justice in our daily lives. Afterward, John exchanged a warm embrace with Father Capelli.

Noting that John and Katie were together, Father Capelli said cheerily, "John, Katie, together you look like a nice family."

Katie flushed at the comment, though inwardly she felt a surge of joy as she glanced up at John.

John flashed a smile at the priest. "Who knows, Father, stranger things have happened."

Father Capelli winked in Katie's direction before turning to the next parishioner.

In the car on the way back to Katie's, she found herself stealing glances at John; the easy smile and handsome face, the jet black hair, the flashing blue eyes. Her check on the children found her thinking of raising Franco and Anna with Kelly. The thought cheered her.

While Katie prepared Sunday dinner she heard John on the floor of the living room rolling and wrestling with the children. Kelly's high pitch laugh and comfort with John, Franco and Anna brought her mind to Father Capelli's comment and John's airy comeback. Then she flashed to Anna's comment that today was a special day. As she considered the possibilities, while working her bread dough, she found herself excited and hopeful. 'A special day,' she thought. As she placed the raised loaves into the oven she found herself hoping for something which had seemed impossible to her just months ago.

"A special day," Anna had said. Katie hoped it would be so.

John seemed at ease, Katie thought. Was it simply the trial success or had he arrived at a decision?

At the sound of Franco's proclamation, "We won," Katie went through the kitchen door to the living room. She saw John on his back with Franco on his chest, arms raised in victory. Anna and Kelly each held a shoulder to the floor as they giggled in triumph.

John heard Katie enter. He raised himself to an elbow and smiled at Katie in the doorway, apron in place with a dusting of flour on her nose and cheek. He warmed at the thought of the body beneath the apron and modest violet dress. He noted the sparkle in her sapphire eyes. In a quick flash he imagined himself running his fingers through her golden, flamed hair.

She shook her head and eyed John. "You lost, I see."

He smiled back at her, ran his hand over the heads of the children, then turned his eyes on Katie. "Everything, including my heart."

Her smile turned from teasing to loving and John saw all he needed to see.

They sat for dinner as a family would. Katie placed John at the head of the table with Franco to his right. The girls sat to John's left and Katie settled across from him.

As they ate, Franco glanced up from his plate. "Dad, these ravioli are better than Nonna's."

John noticed the delight and acceptance in the five-year-old's eyes. Katie smiled warmly at Franco.

"Thank you," Katie said. "But you won't tell your Nonna that, will you?"

Franco shook his head. "No, I won't."

"Excellent," Katie grinned.

"He's right Katie," John agreed. "And this bread is wonderful." He paused and playfully said. "You know, you would make a great Italian wife."

"Really?" she responded as she flashed a smile. "Is that a proposal?"
John laughed. "Could be, could be."

Disney on Ice was a treat for all and a great surprise for Katie and Kelly. Katie noticed how Franco took both Anna and Kelly by the hand as they moved through the crowded arena. 'This really could work,' she thought.

The music, lights and performance enraptured the children.

"Pretty dazzling," Katie whispered to John.

John was pretty dazzled himself by the woman with the flamed golden hair, sparkling eyes and sensuous mouth. He particularly liked how she smiled when she looked his way.

When he leaned towards her, he captured her fragrance which honeyed the air about her.

After the afternoon show, it was Hungry Harrys for dinner. Anna and Kelly joined the wait staff on the floor as they danced to a collection of fifties music.

Burgers and ice-cream sodas were the perfect complement to a fun filled and very tiring day.

The ride from Rockport to Gloucester found three children asleep. A glance in the rear view mirror had John smiling. "They look like angels," he said.

A smile and knowing glance had Katie responding. "Yes, they do. However, my guess is their exhaustion was well planned by a man with less than angelic plans."

A sidewards glance at Katie showed John's gleaming blue eyes and encouraging smile.

"Do you mind my plans?"

She knew that protesting those plans would be the right thing to do. Yet, at this moment she couldn't think of why.

Her smile met his. "No, I don't."

Their eye contact was electric and she knew this was right.

John drove on to Magnolia. Once at his home, he carried the children. Kelly shared Anna's double bed. Katie pulled off their clothes, substituting nightclothes for the day's finery.

When Katie had completed tucking the children in and given each a goodnight kiss she descended the stairway to find John pouring champagne. On the coffee table were a dozen red roses with a card attached.

"Well, look at this," she offered with a smile.

John handed her a champagne flute bubbling with the sparkling wine.

John touched his flute to Katie's. "To happy days."

Touched by the sentiment and feeling caressed by his eyes, she nodded, her lips curving subtly. "To happy days," she repeated.

"Gee," John grinned. "What do you think the card says?" As he nodded in the direction of the flowers.

Her glance passed over the budding roses and back to him. "Shall I look?"

"Splendid idea," he laughed.

She pulled the envelope off of the card stand and removed the card from the envelope. John watched as the words struck her.

Her eyes widened in delight and her lips curved in joy. "Do you mean it?" She asked as tears began to flow.

John grinned. "Indeed, I do." He affirmed. "Please sit down."

They sat together on the couch. John held her hand and smiled. "We've both been through a lot over these past few years." He paused and engaged her eyes.

"The stress of me losing Connie, you losing Marc." He took a deep breath. "The lawsuit, with its traps and dangers." He paused. "The emotions of the trial and all you had to re-live." He shrugged and let out a sigh. "I don't think we are ready to do more than start. But, I want to start."

Katie's eyes filled with tears.

"Katie, I want you in my life. I want to help you heal." He smiled. "I want you to help me heal."

She nodded.

"It's going to take time," he continued. "We'll all deal with the loss, the guilt and the pain."

Gently, he wiped away her tears and moved his lips over hers. Placing his hand on her chin, he raised her eyes to his. "When Connie and Marc are pleasant memories and not stabs at our hearts, we'll be ready." He grinned and kissed her again. "You taste so good."

She grinned back through watery eyes.

"No pressure, Katie." He paused. "No decision out of fear."

She nodded.

"When we're ready to leave the past behind and look to the future, we'll be there for each other."

He pulled her close, resting her head on his shoulder.

"If either of us discover that we've confused our feelings of sympathy, gratitude or loyalty for love, we'll say so and part friends."

Her tears flowed freely.

"Katie, what I know, right now, is that I want you in my life. I want to heal with you." He grinned. "Katie Morrissey, may I court you?"

Tears ran freely down her cheek as she nodded yes, somehow finding a grin.

This time he didn't ask. He pulled her into his arms and thought how right she felt. "I love you," he whispered. And he put his lips on hers. She kissed him with an urgency and a passion he had only guessed at.

"Welcome home," he whispered.

Eyes sparkling, with moist cheeks she curved her lips in a saucy smile. "What took you so long?"

I hope you enjoyed *The Bastard's Weapon*, second novel in the Gloucester Trilogy. As I write One Man's Hero, the third novel in my trilogy, please feel free to consult my literary website:

www.JosephmOrlando.com

to learn more of the author, my other works including The Fisherman's Son, first novel in the Gloucester Trilogy.

On the following pages please read Chapter One of my novel *The Shortstop's Redemption*.

Please e-mail comments to *JosephmOrlando@MSN.com*